THE LUCK BRINGER

BY

NICK BROWN

New Generation **Publishing**

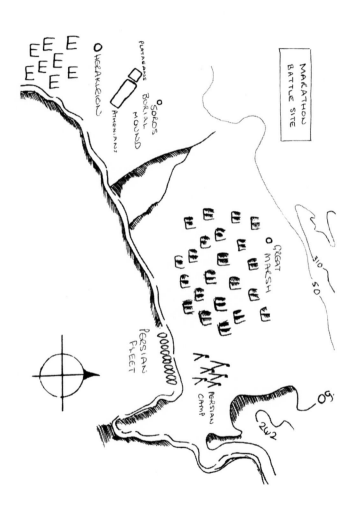

MAKATHON BATTLE SITE

PLATAEANS

ATHENIANS

SOROS BURIAL MOUND

HERAKLEION

GREAT MARSH

PERSIAN FLEET

PERSIAN CAMP

310
50

3

THESSALY

EUBOEA

PLATAEA

ATHENS
BRAURON MARATHON
BAY OF MARATHON

PELOPONNESE

SPARTA

GYTHIUM

MAINLAND GREECE

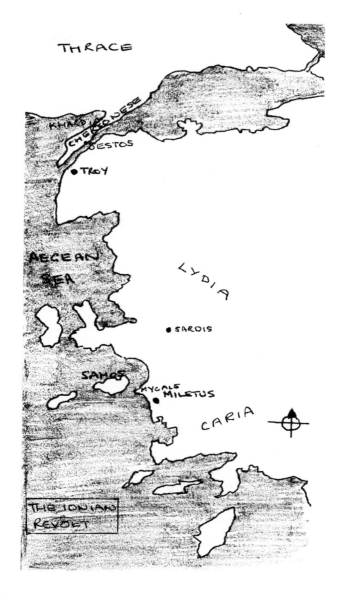

THRACE

KHARDONESE
CHERSONESE
SESTOS
● TROY

AEGEAN SEA

LYDIA

● SARDIS

SAMOS

MYCALE
● MILETUS

CARIA

THE IONIAN REVOLT

For Ron and June Brown

PROLOGUE

Soon after dark they brought home the body; I watched from my house above the great harbour as a wailing crowd gathered to escort the poor remains. The fire of torches reflected on the oil smooth water, the sound of flutes and drums hung in the still air as the funeral lights of the procession wound their way along the quayside up the road leading to the city. The same road he marched down as a young warrior to fight alongside the common people on our ships against the Persians. Now he is dead, General Miltiades' son, our last hope of peace, our last defence against ruin. Now I am too frail to follow the cortege so I sat on in my house staring out over our doomed war fleet and remembered the youth so full of strength and promise who Miltiades entrusted to my care.

I sat and remembered as the wine soured and the flaming wick floating in the oil of the lamp, guttered, flickered and died. It may have been those wisps of acrid smoke floating upwards that brought water to my eyes. But then often these days I find that tears well up at the simplest of things.

My friend the poet Aeschylus believed that every man is a compound of opposing elements, wise and foolish, gentle and murderous, moderate and excessive, and he was right. For as I sat weeping and blinded I saw, as if it were yesterday, the General that fateful morning, grim in his armour, standing on the mound in the bay of Marathon. The glint of sunlight flashing from the tip of his great spear as he held it aloft waving the men on to charge the massed ranks of the Persian immortals.

PART ONE

CHAPTER 1

I first saw the General's ships through a gap in the stable door where my father had locked me up while he decided my punishment. The sun was shining on sails far out in the bay towards Ikaria. Our home was the only house of any note on this wild side of the island, far from any town or decent road. This was where my father had been exiled as a consequence of displeasing the tyrant King Polycrates. It was where I and my brothers were born, far from Samos city where the tyrant held his court. My grandfather had been a wealthy noble at court and a friend of the philosopher Pythagoras, who had often been his house guest. My mother rarely spoke of those days, but from what she did say it seemed my father had not always been the harsh, bitter figure that I knew.

Our house was built on terraced land between the bay and the mountain surrounded by olive groves. Despite my father's pretensions it was more a farm than a house, with a threshing floor for the corn harvest and outbuildings for the slaves and animals. Below us was the cove that formed a small natural harbour for our boat, fringed by a strand of yellow sand. Above us the towering sheer grey rock slab of Mount Kerkis, where our nurse told us that storm demons played with thunder and lightning bolts. In summer the mountain baked in the heat and in winter, after the snows, water poured in torrents off it. The mountain shut us off from civilisation; there was no way over it to the city. Any contact we had with the world was by sea.

There were other people on our part of the Isle, strange, half human creatures left over from an ancient time. They lived in the woods, worshipped older gods and were descended from centaurs and lapiths, perhaps from the wood itself. We didn't see much of them; they kept to themselves. Occasionally, in the dead of night, they would worship some ancient wooden statues that stood in a clearing on a conical hill overlooking the next bay. Sometimes, if the wind was right, we could hear the sound of pipes and the noise of voices raised in ecstasy or maybe terror and then we checked the doors were fully locked and men slept with their weapons.

Once after such a night my brother and I crept up to the clearing. There was little evidence of demonic rites but each of the statues wore a crude wreath of myrtle leaves, and a flute made of bone had been left next to a roughly carved stone bowl, the inside of which was stained a brownish red with blood. My elder brother, Rhoikos, who was skilled at carving and whittling, went to pick up the flute but as he touched it there was a loud rustling deep in the dense foliage of the wood. We turned and ran for home. That night we huddled together in the cot we slept in for fear that something would come down from the wood to steal us away. Nothing did but the next day my father found that one of our oxen had had its forelegs broken. After that we left the hill alone.

Despite the isolation we lived well. We hunted game and boar in the woods, grew corn and vine. Our olive and fruit trees were rich and bountiful and below us the wine dark sea teemed with fish. We had plenty to see us through each winter and were able to maintain all the feast days of the year. So life went on, dancing to the same dull pattern dictated by the demands of the seasons. We grew up working alongside the slaves and bondsmen of our estate, dressing and eating like them. Father beat education into us but of what use it was we did not know. Occasionally, perhaps three or four times a year, a ship would pull into the bay, mainly merchants but sometimes visitors from father's past.

Then one day, shortly after my first growth of beard, the period between boyhood and manhood, I was returning with snares and dogs from hunting rabbits in the woods that fringed the mountain. The day was hot and I was weary so I halted in a grove by the source of one of the fresh clear springs that freshen the island. As I knelt to drink I felt, rather than saw, a presence and quickly turned. Standing behind me holding a pitcher for carrying water was a girl of my own age, perhaps slightly older. She wore the usual rough woollen tunic of the slaves or peasant farmers but wore it with a grace which made me too embarrassed to address her. She approached the stream and knelt to fill the jug and in crouching I could see the shape of the body beneath the tunic and her lithe sunburned legs naked to the knee. She was called Theopone, the daughter of a servant of my father and a slave girl he'd married. They lived in a rough farmstead nearby. I had not seen her for some time but the change in that time had been great and her close presence aroused me. We spoke little but she told me that she fetched water from the spring at the same time each day. Over the next months we came to know each other in the way that is forbidden. My brothers and I had watched animals rut and talked of girls and relieved ourselves as best we could.

Work on our lands was hard and free time was scarce, but when she could Theopone would slip away from her hut to meet me in the woods. She had a gentle way yet excited me greatly. Our last evening marked the great change in my life. Had the fates been kinder then perhaps she would have become my wife. We met in the grove of fruit trees between her hut and our land and after some talk and embraces we moved towards the act that bridges the gulf between men and women. In trying to delay the extreme moment I raised myself on my arms and was gazing down at her face below me, when I felt sharp pain across my shoulders and was hauled to my feet by my father. He threw me against the trunk of a tree and broke his stick across my back. When he stopped to pause for breath Theopone had gone. For the next week I was locked in the stables when I was not working. It was through the gaps in the planking that I first saw the sails of the ship that was to change my life.

Sometime later the door was unbolted. Light streamed in and my youngest brother, Minisarchus, named by my father in honour of the father of Pythagoras, told me to go to the house to wash and change into my best tunic. My mother greeted me at the door saying I was to take special care in my appearance and then to hurry down to the beach to join my father and brothers. By the time I left home for the shore the boat was landing. It was a warship, a trireme with a shining bronze ram at the front. My father and brothers were already on the beach; my father dressed in an ancient but finely patterned robe stood proud and dignified like the great noble he'd once been. This change in him distracted my attention from the ship which the sailors were now dragging up to the beach. The ship's commander was standing balanced at the stern with one hand raised in greeting. He was of average height with dark reddish hair and a neatly trimmed beard, sturdily built but graceful. Today there are many busts and statues of him, all showing a man with full beard in the old style but his beard and hair were always as neatly trimmed as they were that day. This was my first sight of the General, Miltiades, noble Athenian and tyrant of the Athenian territories in the Chersonese.

He climbed swiftly down the ladder lowered from the ship and clasped my father by his shoulders. My father returned the embrace and for a moment they stood like that, neither man speaking. My father indicated us as his sons and then dismissed us to the house with instructions to present ourselves smartly turned out at dinner in honour of our famous guest. I was surprised to be included and so from the outset had a favourable impression of our visitor. I also wondered how our humble dwelling would satisfy the tastes of such a great man. What I didn't know then, which is not surprising given his cheerful disposition, was the desperate adventure on which he had embarked.

For that night my mother had made the eating room fit for a king. The walls were garlanded, the finest lamps lit, the couches covered with hangings and on the tables were goblets and plates of gold of great age that I had never seen before. The kitchen slaves had roasted a kid and plates of meat, fish, nuts and fruit were liberally set at each table along with honey cakes and jugs of our finest Samian wine, something that our island does better than any other. In all my days I had never seen the like and never expected to in our house.

The greatest surprise though was my father. He wore a richly embroidered robe, his hair and beard were dressed and oiled and, like his guests, he wore a garland. It was the only time I had ever seen him like this and I am glad that I had had at least that one opportunity to see him as he wished to be seen. My mother and sisters of course did not eat with us; the old ways are best, despite what some in Athens now think. As boys we occupied the furthest table from my father, his guest and captains. Then the stage of the meal was reached when the men cut the wine with less water, talked of politics or played kotobos and other such drinking games. We boys were dismissed but as we were leaving my father called me back. The General beckoned me to approach.

"So, you are Mandrocles of whom your father has told me so much. Come nearer."

I did as I was ordered. He stared at me for a while then pinched my cheek between thumb and forefinger as a man would do to a young child. As I was wondering at this strange behaviour he slapped me hard across the face causing the blood to rush to my cheeks with shame and anger. Yet because this man was my father's guest, and also because I was no stranger to beating, I didn't react but stood looking at the floor in the modest manner in which I had been schooled. After what seemed a long period of silence he said to my father, not to me,

"He controls himself well, he'll do."

My father dismissed me and I left the room to the sound of sudden talk and laughter amongst the guests. Whether it was directed at me I don't know.

About an hour before dawn the door of the room where we slept opened and my father walked over to my sleeping place and whispered to me to get up and go with him. His breath smelt of wine and he was still dressed as he had been at dinner; even the garland was still on his head. He led me silently to his private chamber, where a lamp was burning. The first thing I noticed was that his hoplite armour was laid out and had been burnished. My senses were so awake that even now, if I close my eyes, I can see that room and hear my father's voice. It was the longest speech I ever heard him make.

"Mandrocles, your rutting with that girl was a serious matter that I will have to settle with her father even though he is my bondsman. It is a loss of honour and I fear that if you stay here there will be worse to come; you are too wild, boy. Miltiades is the companion of my youth. I sheltered his back in a skirmish long ago; I deflected a sword thrust, and then pierced the neck of its owner. Such memories run deep. So now the General, my friend, returns the favour because of his love of me and respect for our friendship. With him you will experience the world and see how it can both delight and torment. You are to go with him as his part of his household and if you are lucky, his squire.

He paused a moment before saying,

"You will, it seems, be the only one of our family to ever have need of this."

He pointed to the armour and paused for a while, perhaps overcome by some inner emotion, perhaps by drink. In the silence I could almost hear the lamps burning.

"The gods are not always kind but they are consistently surprising; dress quickly in the tunic and cloak I have laid out for you and put on those war sandals for we must hurry."

I was about to speak but he anticipated me.

"We will not have time to visit your mother; she would only become upset at something she cannot change. I will tell her later."

That was all. He lifted the armour. I dressed and picked up a pack he indicated and followed him through the door. So I left my home for the last time and followed him to the beach.

It is strange that some of the greatest events of a life can arrive so casually, almost as if nothing is happening. Perhaps the gods do have a hand in it. We walked out into the cool pre-dawn air towards the sea where the silhouettes of the ships came gradually into vision. I remember the sound of my sandals crunching on the shingle and the slap of the armour banging against my father's legs as he carried it before him. I can't remember if either of us spoke but I don't think we did. Then there was a rough hand helping me over the side of the boat, the smell of the boat, the sweat of the men, hot even in the pre-dawn chill. Then there was only sea. I think I only looked back once as we passed the headland and out of sight. I felt for a moment I saw movement – a slender, long haired figure waving at me from the headland picked out by the first rays of the sun. Was it Theopone or have I imagined it? Whatever it was it was the last glimpse I ever had of the bay that was my home.

CHAPTER 2

Life aboard a trireme's hard: I should know, I've spent half my life on one. But that day was my first experience and as I was pulled on deck I wondered how it was possible to pack so many men aboard so small a ship. Most of the space was taken by the rowers sitting either side of a central gangway in three tiers. The top tier had their heads and bodies in daylight but the bottom level tier of fifty-eight men, the Thalomoi, sat in the stinking dark of the hold, beneath the others, where they slept and ate. The smell of a trireme hits you, a mixture of sweat, urine, damp wood and salt. In rough weather this is augmented by vomit, and in battle by the effect of the looseness of bowels as fear grips the heart.

Once I was on board no one paid me any attention. My gear was stored in the hold except for my shield, which was hung on the outside of the outrigger that housed the top bank of oars. A line of shields was suspended there to provide a protective screen for the rowers. I was shown a place on the deck and told not to move unless instructed. The only places to sit were either near the prow with a small group of marines or in the stern where Miltiades sat in the trierarch's seat with the helmsman and behind him four Scythian archers. My place was in the prow, where I was ignored by the marines and archers. So I sat and stared at the sea and watched it change from dark to luminous grey to sparkling clear blue as the sun rose in the sky. I have always lived by the sea so I can stare at the patterns it makes and try to read the life and deaths it holds.

The heart of a trireme is a long gangway set between the banks of oarsmen. In the centre of this, midway between prow and stern, stands the rowing master, the man who controls our lives in battles. This man ensures that the rowers keep time and change their rhythms as each situation demands. The speed at which to ram and to disengage needs to be precise. A trireme can move quickly when it needs to but not for long, so a rowing master who exhausts the crew too quickly imperils the boat. Our rowing master called himself Theodorus, though I suspect that wasn't his real name. He was one of the best and would save our lives in the flight to Athens. He was helped by an assistant either side of him who relayed his calls to the rowers at the prow and stern, and by a piper keeping the stroke with shrill blasts of his flute. The triple band of oars made cacophonous noise and oarsmen need to hear when to pull and how hard. As our trireme pulled out of the bay the rowers followed the master's shouts with an almost musical chant of "O opop O opop opop opop" until the boat had found its rhythm, then they ceased and saved their energy for the effort of each stroke.

All this dislocated my senses. I can't remember how I felt but I must have watched with concentration because even now across the years I see it as clear as yesterday. The colour of the great mountain changed slowly from dark and brooding to glistening white as the sun rose above the sparkling sea. A pod of playful dolphins followed us, circling the boat, going under then emerging with a leap to greet the growing heat of the sun. The ship had become the heart of my universe with Theodorus, choosing its rhythms and driving us on. I was to sail with him for many years until a double barbed arrow head pierced his windpipe at the Eurymedon, changing his call mid shout to a hiss and gargle and stopping the rhythm forever.

We had been raised as children with tales of sea monsters, sprites and man killing storms raised by Poseidon, yet on that day I think I knew that my connection with the sea would be long and that it would not be the cause of my death. Still, I noted with relief, that we hugged the shoreline rather than sailed into the vastness of open sea. When we rounded the rocky headland the wind that blows from Ikaria each day in the late morning sprang up on our stern quarter and the helmsman ordered that the sails be spread. Theodorus told the oarsmen, by now rowing in shifts, to rest. To my surprise he left his position and walked, with surprising grace for a big man, across to where I sat cramped and uncomfortable.

"So, boy, what do you think of the 'Athene Nike'?"

I realised that this must be the name of the ship and asked him if I could stand and stretch my legs. He nodded but told me to move carefully.

"These are fighting boats, not good sea boats. They're rubbish in heavy weather. Where possible we keep close to shore and avoid sailing in the winter months. With too much movement she'll roll over and take us all with her; see how careful those lads are."

He pointed to the rowers on the top bank by the shields on the outrigger, who were passing round some goat skins of water and wine to wash down the salt fish and barley they were munching.

"Those lads are the strongest and best rowers, hard boys, rough and brutal when they need to be yet see how carefully they move. They understand what even a small movement can do to the boat."

He pulled an onion from his tunic, sliced it in half and offered part to me along with a swig from the wineskin he carried. I took a pull of the heavily watered wine and bit on the onion. I realised how hungry I was and as I ate I listened to Theodorus describe life on a trireme. I was filled with a feeling that my life had just begun and was now running on a tide of excitement, that I had been rescued from an existence of boredom and toil and beatings. Now I was part of an adventure like those in the tales of ancient heroes. I watched Theodorus as he talked and saw that despite the weather beaten features, lines around the corners of his eyes and the thickly muscled and scarred arms he couldn't be more than ten years older than me. Yet he seemed like a creature from a different and more exciting world where anything was possible. It's as well that the realities of life that age brings are not understood when we are young for then we would truly experience a life without hope. Still on that day, for that moment the world was young and the future filled with promise.

We sailed down the coast and each man found what shade he could under the sun awnings that the boat carried; some played knucklebones and dice, some slept whilst others talked or worked splicing rope, fixing oars or mending sails. In the stern, Miltiades and the Trierarch Lysias sat together holding an earnest conversation whilst the helmsman stood by the tiller, his eyes fixed on the horizon. In this period of space and rest Theodorus told me where we were bound and why.

"We're going to the great harbour and city, lad, but I doubt we'll stay long so you'd better make the most of what you see because the General will move fast."

He paused as if satisfied that he had explained everything, but it must have been obvious from my expression that I had no idea what he was talking about.

"Congratulations, lad, you've just joined the wrong side in a lost war, the great revolt is over, and the Persians have us beat. Our fleet from all the islands is gathering at the great harbour to attempt one last battle and win it all. We're beaten on land but our fleet's intact. The General thinks it's doomed, that there's treachery in the fleet and Samos Town. He wants them to see sense and disperse the fleet, move south to

Lemnos and the Chersonese. Rebuild there. He's come in person, he knows the commanders, he has influence but it must be desperate to draw him away from his stronghold because if there's one man King Darius would like to get his hands on it's Miltiades – they have history, see."

I must have looked as ignorant as I was for he continued,

"Way back over ten years and before our war, the great King launched an expedition to Scythia. He summoned the leaders and tyrants of all the Ionian Greek states including the General. The Persians built a large land bridge across the mouth of the Danube and marched over the sea and into the vast Scythian plains. He left the Greek allies defending the bridge to cover his rear if anything went wrong. Well, it did go wrong. The Scythians were tough and fought dirty; you know, attack at night then melt away, no real battles and the Persians ended in the middle of nowhere. Their supply lines cut, so they had to retreat. When the Greek allies heard about this, the General called a meeting of all the leaders. He suggested they destroy the bridge and leave the Great King and his army trapped on the other side. The weather had turned and Darius and his army would be left freezing on the wrong side of the Danube for the Scythians to massacre or enslave. Then we could all have liberated ourselves and the Persian Empire would have been too busy tearing itself apart in a civil war to see who would succeed Darius.

A good plan, nice and simple, but it's never simple to convince Greeks to co-operate. He almost persuaded them though but then they got cold feet. Almost all of them owed their positions as tyrants of their lands to Darius. Histiaeus, tyrant of Miletos, talked them out of it, pointed out how much they had to lose so it never happened. They were all there to welcome him back

23

when Darius returned cold and furious at his defeat. The General stood with the rest of them pretending to be overjoyed at the safe return. Darius knew what had gone on of course. He gave Histiaeus half of Thrace as a reward. He knew what the General had tried but having just escaped from Scythia it didn't suit to deal with him just yet, and the General knew he knew and was waiting for the reckoning. Then the revolt started and the funny thing is that most of those cowardly bastards at the bridgehead joined it; now most of them have lost their states and some their lives. The General's outlasted them all, and he's gained from the result, taken Lemnos and Imbros from the Persians and now he's come here to try and stop them making an even bigger mistake."

He got no further than this as there was a shout of command from Ariston the helmsman. Theodorus turned away and moved swiftly and surely onto his gang plank, shouting orders to the oarsmen. The wind had dropped and within seconds the rhythm was settled and to the shrill of the flute, the shouts of the rowing master and the chanted response of "O opop O opop", we rounded a cape and pulled into the bay of Hera.

It was near dark when we ran the trireme up onto a gently sloping beach. The crew knew exactly what was needed and as I stood uselessly by, some built fires to prepare food, some scouted the shoreline whilst others lowered the sails. In the hull of the boat oarsmen from the third and lowest bank of oars pulled out the bung holes to release the bilge water and prevent the hull planking becoming soggy and rotten. I watched in wonder and admiration as the area around the trireme was converted into a camp whilst the boat was secured on the beach and minor running repairs effected. Looking back I can't understand why I wasn't more frightened, away from home and sailing towards a war, having left my family, perhaps forever. But the truth is I wasn't, I was curious; well, curious and hungry.

But the curiosity and the hunger were soon to be appeased; one of the marines came over and told me to report to the General. He was sitting by one of the fires talking to the trierarchs of the five boats and ignored my presence until he had finished. He had an air of command that seemed absolute. He didn't raise his voice or try to impress the officers. It was just apparent that he was born to command and that it didn't occur to him that anyone would think of questioning what he said. By the time he had finished the sun had sunk like a red ball into the body of the sea and the horizon was streaked red. The captains stood and moved off to their boats and Miltiades turned as if he had just noticed me. In the glare of the firelight I saw that his hair was streaked with grey and that he seemed tired.

"You can start earning your keep now, boy, you're coming for a walk with me and if you can manage that without getting into any trouble I'll think about letting you have some barley, fruit and olives for your supper."

He stood up, covered his shoulders with an old salt damaged sailor's cloak, strapped on his sword, turned his back to the sea and, with a gesture to me to follow, set off. He didn't speak and I dared not question him so we walked in silence until the noise from the boats and the lights from the fires had faded into the distance behind us. Gradually I became aware of sounds ahead of us: shrill voices, the sound of flutes and a monotonous clanging sound like someone banging a great drum. Then I felt fear, remembering the rites of the ancient folk of the woods above our farm and for the first time that day I wished I was safe home with my mother and brothers. But Miltiades marched on, not breaking step until he had climbed a small rise where he stopped and waited for me to catch up. As I reached the top of the rise I was frightened enough to have decided to ask him where we were going but the sight in front of me drove the thought out of my mind.

"Look at that, boy, the great Heraion, birthplace of the goddess Hera, the biggest and most important temple in the world."

Before us, lit by torches and fires, was a series of huge buildings with great columns that seemed to reach the sky as if the gods truly had built them. These buildings seemed to cover the whole plain and reach towards the distant mountains. Yet as my eyes became accustomed to the light I realised that there was more. Hundreds of smaller buildings and tents, some no bigger than the outhouses at the farm at home, surrounded these great temples. In the light I could see that the paths and squares between the buildings were crowded with people. It seemed to me that the whole world was there and the noise they made seemed almost god like. Save for the noise of summer thunder I had never heard such a tumult. I turned to ask the General why we were there, but he had already set off striding towards the temple. I hurried after him.

Soon we reached the first buildings – rough shanties. People were drinking and eating as we walked among them heading towards the temples and the noise. In some of these hovels men and women made the beast with two backs and other shapes. Miltiades stopped by a booth selling food and bought some honey cakes, the biggest of which he gave to me and, following my gaze, said,

"They seem to interest you; do you want a turn with one of the temple prostitutes, Mandrocles?"

It was the first time that he had spoken my name and I knew then that I was his man for life. Perhaps he'd expected that this would be the effect and that's why he chose me to accompany him. My senses swam with the exotic excitement of the night. This was the greatest temple sacred to Hera yet in the small town of tents and booths that surrounded it, it seemed that any pleasure and excitement was for sale. There were more people and more noise outside the temple precinct than within it. In addition to wine stores, whores' booths, and eating places there were women peddling charms and love potions; members of different cults singing, chanting and dancing and above all the rhythmic beating of drums. The warm air was flavoured by the scent of spices, roasting meat, sweat, drink and sex. I noticed in one booth some men, naked save for loin cloths, in a state of trance inhaling fragrant smoke from a brazier. We were now at the entrance of the biggest and by far the tallest temple building. Miltiades looked quickly around him then passed me a few coins.

"I have business in there and may be some time. When you have spent this come back here and wait. You would be better advised sticking to some meat, cakes and wine as not all the girls will be clean."

With that he pulled the hood of his cloak over his head and entered the temple. I was left outside in the whirling mass of humanity, the air loud with cries, drums and pipes. I followed the smell of cooked meat to a sheep roasting on a spit and bought some slices served on a platter of coarse bread and carried them across to a rough tavern where I bought a small jug of wine and sat watching and listening. No one bothered me. I think I felt liberated at that moment more so than at any other time in my life. How long I sat there I can't remember but I noticed a girl who had been dancing to a flute. She was dark skinned and her face and shoulders were tattooed in a design of whirls and circles. She noticed my gaze and came to where I sat. The smell of her perfume and body excited me greatly but I had not enough coins left. She seemed genuinely sorry for this and said to me

"That's a shame, pretty one, I'd do it for free but I'd only get a beating. If you find some money come back here and I'll give you a time we'll both remember."

The men around me laughed and I rose hurriedly to leave trying to hide my shame. Outside the temple there was no sign of the General. After some time I began to wonder if I had missed him and I'd been left alone in this place to fend for myself. And that gnawed at me so, despite my orders, I decided to look inside. At the top of the steps by the entrance there were robed attendants of the goddess but they showed no interest in me and I was able to slip past them. The inside was disorientating; patches of complete dark contrasted with areas lit by lamps where ritual and other transactions I could not understand were taking place.

Then I saw him in a corner with a group of four or so men, dimly lit. From their dress they appeared foreign, wearing the tunics, trousers and headgear of the Persians. Their manner was animated but the conversation seemed friendly. I watched as a tall thin featured man with a sharp nose and beard cut in the Greek style grasped the General by his shoulders and kissed both his cheeks in the manner of one sealing a bargain. Then, sensing that the business was about to be concluded I moved away, making as little noise as I could, and returned to my place outside the door.

Shortly after, the General emerged and my curiosity overcame my reticence and I enquired if his business had been satisfactory. To my surprise he said that he'd met no one and that by business he had meant he needed to spend time alone in the temple in the presence of the goddess.

CHAPTER 3

You who have never seen the great harbour of Samos when the fleet is in have missed one of the great sights in the world. But to see it that day with the whole of the unconquered Ionian fleet riding at anchor was enough to make a man doubt the evidence of his eyes. The tyrant Polycrates had made his capital city one of the wonders of the world by building on so large a scale he committed the sin of hubris and that is why the gods ordered him to a death by slow torture at the hands of his enemies. It was this first sight of the town, dazzling white in the sun above the great fleet, that briefly touched my heart at what my father had missed through his banishment and for a second I understood his loss and bitterness. But there was no time for reflection on things past, I was young and this was for living.

The harbour was the biggest in the world, the breakwater two hundred and sixty metres long and a twenty fathoms deep. The mole protected a huge area, yet it was full. The Ionians had been beaten decisively on land and many of their cities sacked and razed to the ground. But the fleet was unbeaten and here it was in Samos almost spilling out of the harbour. There were almost as many ships again hauled up on the beaches for repair or to have their hulls scraped clean. Many of those in the harbour flew their captain's personal pennants, ships from Chios, Miletos, Samos and all the Ionian cities and islands riding next to each other crowding the harbour. The sight of this great fleet, the Greeks united in a patriotic war for the first time since the fight at Troy, made my heart leap at the thought that we were joining them, and I looked with pride at my father's shield hanging from the outrigger.

Our station was at the Mycale end of the harbour where there was space for the trierarchs to run their

29

ships up onto the shingle of the narrow sloping beach. While we were making camp the General sent Ariston to fetch me and I followed the grizzled helmsman as we picked our way among the ships and shelters to a leather tent where the General's pennant flew. On a trireme deck Ariston moved with ease and a precision that almost amounted to grace. On land he seemed to roll and stumble. Miltiades met us at the tent's entrance.

"Go and look out your good tunic, Mandrocles, tidy yourself up and scrape that bum fluff off your cheeks. Soon we go into town on business and then we dine with some Samian acquaintances. Tonight you must look your best. Some of those with whom we do business have an eye for a pretty boy."

I reddened with shame and anger and he noticed and softened his expression.

"I spoke in jest, lad, don't be so touchy, but do as I said all the same, we live in troubled times and for all its beauty this is a dangerous city. We may all be Greeks fighting together in this war but not everyone is as he seems. There is treachery and betrayal and we need all the advantages we hold."

Later that day, two hours before the sun set, we left the beach camp and made our way through the mass of sailors, marines and townspeople that packed the harbour towards the narrow streets of the town. The press of people was so thick that a party of our marines had to clear a path with shouts, pushes and blows from fists and cudgels. The streets around the harbour were narrow and stank of spices, burnt meats, spilled wine and human sweat. Above us, gleaming on the mountain was the acropolis of Polycrates encircled by the massive walls that seemed to stretch forever.

The noise in the street was deafening and I was relieved when we turned a corner and found ourselves in a small and almost deserted square hemmed in by blind walls with no windows, only strong doors. The General indicated a door in a wall painted white like all the others in the far corner of the square and Ariston hammered on it. It opened immediately and a tall and dignified slave ushered us in.

The contrast between the interior of the house and its unprepossessing exterior could not have been more marked. The door opened onto a large courtyard garden with a pool and a fountain whose centrepiece was a slim dryad for whom the artist's model must have been a very beautiful girl. The General ordered Ariston, Theodorus and the marines to wait outside while the rest of us crossed the courtyard through a door that led us to a finer courtyard with a larger fountain and a garden rich in bloom. In this courtyard slaves were serving guests with wine. There was a murmur of subdued conversations as if those present were overawed by some great event of which they were nervous. Miltiades was greeted by a richly dressed man with thinning grey hair and invited to follow him through a door at the far end of the courtyard.

"Come with me, boy, we are going to eat. Say nothing unless you're spoken to but keep your ears open, I'll want a report of all you hear."

I followed him into a large room with a fine marble floor that reflected the lamplight. There were couches arranged round the walls and tables with silver plates and delicate drinking cups. The General was escorted to a place of honour over by the far wall whilst I was directed to a couch in the corner near the door. My couch companion was a well built man with black hair and short beard wearing a robe of fine dyed wool. He introduced himself as Syloson, the son of a local landowner and one of the trierarchs of the Samian fleet. I was too timid to make conversation, not fully

31

understanding my role, but I need not have worried, my companion had been drinking and was accordingly voluble. I learnt much from him.

The room contained an odd mixture of Samiots, many from the fleet, but many to my surprise were aristocrats from the other side who had been close to the tyrant Aiakes before he was deposed for his brutality at the beginning of the revolt. I wondered what brought this group together and why such men should be apparently at ease dining with captains from the fleet who would soon be fighting the Persians with whom Aiakes had taken refuge.

But the food was choice as was the wine, although too lightly watered for my taste. For most of the meal Syloson talked across me to a merchant called Melissos on the next couch who owned several ships. Nothing was said directly but it seemed to me that none in the room had appetite for the revolt and that there was little bad feeling towards the Persians.

By the time that the slaves had brought round platters of spiced figs and seedcakes baked in honey the wine had done its work and the conversation was even less guarded. I had drunk little and was wondering how to deal with Syloson, who had taken to running his hand along my thigh, when suddenly his grasp tightened.

"Well, it seems you're greatly honoured, Mandrocles, look over there."

I followed the direction of his gaze to the table where the General was sitting and noticed he was sharing his couch with a man who had not been present during the meal. The light of the lamps was not bright enough for me to be sure but I could swear it was the sharp nosed man I had seen with the General in the temple.

"Things must be changing fast if he feels it's safe to attend dinner parties in the city."

Then seeing that I did not understand he pushed his head close to mine and said in a lower register.

"That's Aiakes, the deposed tyrant and ally of the Persians, you little fool. He's back but taking a hell of a risk."

I moved his hand off my thigh and sat up to look closer. The sharp nosed man was in earnest conversation with the General, who was listening intently to whatever he had to say, while interrupting from time to time. This was a conversation like no other in the room. It looked more like some kind of deal rather than just drinking party pleasantries. The final plates were being cleared away; there was some movement among the couches as a man with a lyre seated himself in the centre of the room to begin the night's entertainment. He began to chant a part of the song of the wandering hero Mopsus, a crowd pleaser for men well fed and still drinking. When I next looked towards the General, the thin nosed man had disappeared and Syloson had transferred his attention to a young serving boy. I was left to my own devices. Around the room there seemed to be perfect accord between the men from the fleet and the friends of the tyrant. This, even I, given my lack of political knowledge, felt strange. But I had little time to think before the General approached my couch; the wreath on his head was askew and his face was red with drink but his eyes were clear and hard.

"Come, Mandrocles, we need to be away."

I rose and followed him from the room where the poet sang his heroic tale listened to by some guests whilst others continued to drink and quarrel, or, like Syloson, grope and fondle the slaves of either sex. It was the first such gathering I had ever attended and it

33

set a tone for intrigue and dissonance I have seldom seen matched.

Perhaps someone will find this memoir so I ask you, reader, whoever you are, not too judge the youth I was too harshly. Looking back at that youth I was then, I too wonder how I questioned as little as I did or how I took so readily to that life. But to me then it was a new and exciting existence after the drudgery at home and, besides, if we possessed the knowledge that comes with age in our youth it is likely that we would never have done the things we did that let us acquire the knowledge in the first place. Anyway, age and memory play us false and it may be that there is much we choose not to remember and the rest we misremember.

The General seemed in some way troubled as we left the feast although he did his best to disguise it even as far as continuing to wear the wreath of friendship at a rakish angle and talk and joke with the trierarchs. The streets we threaded our way through were bright with the light of torches and loud with the noise of the revelling sailors and marines of the fleet as they debauched in the brothels, drank in the wine shops and rioted in the streets. So that as we approached the lanes behind the quay front he gave leave to our escort to join the fun saying that I was sufficient to accompany him to our camp on the beach. Theodorus and Ariston, I noticed, ignored this dispensation and shadowed us at a distance. I was feeling disappointed that I was not at liberty to join the crew in the evening's revels but also honoured that the General had chosen to keep me with him and must have been lost in thought as I never saw the start of what happened next.

As we neared the end of the quay, close to where our ships were beached, the noise from the town diminished with distance and the smell of food and humanity was replaced by the salt smell from the sea.

The narrow lane that we followed bent in an unlit dog's leg to join the main approach to the harbour. The harbour front was well lit but the abrupt bend of the lane took us through a patch of shadowed darkness. The General walked in silence whilst I was whistling softly to myself, a tune which all these years later still comes readily to my lips. Suddenly there came the sound of movement like the scurry of rats in a barn and the scrape of metal. I must have moved slightly but quickly as a heavy blow glanced off my shoulders followed by a shove that sent me reeling to the ground.

Then voices and the rasp and clang of blades clashing. Through the tangle of legs I caught a glimpse of the General moving backwards, sword in one hand, cloak wrapped round the other. He was fending off an indistinct group of three or four men who were pressing him into a blind alley in the dark cutting and stabbing. There was a noise between a grunt and an oath and one of them dropped to the ground and didn't move again. Then, loud and harsh the General's voice barked,

"Athene Nike to me."

I tried to rise but was unsteady when for a second time I was thrown to the ground as others rushed past me towards the General. There was the clash of weapons and then, apart from groans of pain, the noise of the skirmish ceased and I heard the General.

"No, leave this one alive, bring light and look to the boy. I think he took the thrust meant for me."

Almost at once more men arrived, carrying torches, sailors from our ship. I sat up and in the light saw a man lying on his back next to me, his throat a mess of blood and beyond him the General questioning another, clearly terrified, whom Theodorus was holding against a wall with a knife to his windpipe. The ground was dark with pools of blood and two other slumped shapes indistinct in darkness beyond the range of the torches' light.

"No, stay still, Mandrocles, let me look at your wound."

A voice, Ariston I think but I can't be sure. I felt rough but practised hands exploring my shoulder and neck. Strangely I don't remember feeling pain or fear. In the pool of light in the midst of a semi circle of sailors and marines the General was questioning the man Theodorus held against the wall. Then he stopped and spoke to Theodorus. I heard the words but could not make sense of the meaning.

"No, no point in further talk. You don't expect information from an attack dog. Ease his way, rowing master."

Theodorus removed the blade from the man's throat and with an almost graceful flick of the wrist thrust it between the ribs that cover the heart. He let the man sink to the floor and then bent to retrieve the knife, which he wiped casually on the man's tunic. To me it all seemed like a dream. I was helped to my feet and supported by Ariston, who told me I was lucky to have got off so lightly.

"You must have turned just in time. That was meant to be a death thrust but it scraped along your shoulder blade. Lucky for you that you're all skin and bone and sharp angles. Come lean on me, we'll get you cleaned up back at the boat."

Now I could feel pain and the sticky wetness that covered my back soaking my best tunic, my head started to spin as they raised me from the ground. I remember thinking, how could men die so quickly?

"Theodorus, help Ariston, get him to the camp and I think I'll require the rest of you lads to accompany us if you don't mind. The night hasn't turned out as quiet as I'd expected."

So we moved off together at a slow pace that accommodated my condition. The General had me taken to his tent and my wound dressed. It was only superficial and apart from some stiffness I never noticed it again, unlike some others I've worn. News of the event soon reached the rest of the fleet so we had many visitors to our camp that night. Yet the General found time to visit and enquire about the state of my hurt. He seemed more relaxed and at ease than he had at any stage since I had first seen him when he greeted my father. It was as if the events since the party had provided him with some sort of stimulant.

"You did your job well, Mandrocles, you took the blow. I am sorry for it especially after what I promised your father. But you have the makings of a useful man, a little courage but a lot of luck. From now on you'll stick close to me. I'm sure I'll find a use for you, but for now, drink that spiced wine and then sleep."

He turned to leave but then stopped and said half to himself and half to me,

"So one faction wants me dead, but which side it is only Hades knows."

With that he left the tent and as I slipped into the welcome oblivion of sleep I could hear him laughing and joking with the trierarchs and crews around the camp fires.

CHAPTER 4

Today there's no understanding of what we fought for.
In Athens everyone thinks that our Empire exists only
for their benefit and pleasure. I bet that's what you
think too, reader. That you just need to snap your
fingers and whatever you want, Nubian slave girls,
amphora of finest Samian wine, ivory, gold, will roll
off the ships queuing up to dock in the Piraeus. You
assume this is your right.

And you are encouraged in this by the new breed of
leaders, men of the polis, or politicians as we now style
them, who vie with each other for support and power
by offering everything for nothing. They offer you
everything we fought and suffered so hard to take from
the Persians. Or worse, they stand in the Agora and lie
and traduce each other. The best brought down by the
worst.

The worst; those buggers who never had to stand
firm in the heat of battle wearing full hoplite armour in
the shield wall against the elite guard of the Great King.
Stand firm and hold the line while their comrades
crashed to earth bleeding away their young lives into
the dust as their spirits fled wailing to Hades. Stand
firm shoulder to shoulder, arms weighed down by the
great shields, stand firm with sweat running down their
foreheads, piss running down their legs, yet standing.

Well we stood; I stood but now look where we are
headed. The General's son brought home dead. Killed
at an age when he should have looked for ease and
honour but was forced again to stand to defend the
polis against our external enemies, whilst Pericles, the
onion head, howled in the assembly about changing
times inciting the ignorant to think highly of
themselves. We have created a monster out of the
demos. Back then we felt it would all have been so

different. I fear I have begun to ramble as old men are prone; forgive me, reader.

I woke late next day. The drug they gave me for the pain helped me sleep through the early morning noise of the camp coming to life. In fact when I woke the camp had been struck and the fleet was ready to take to sea. Theodorus shook me awake, told me to grab my gear and board the Athene Nike as quick as I could for we sailed within the hour. Our station was to follow the Phocean contingent out of the great harbour.

The Phocean fleet was the smallest; only three ships so I needed to hurry. I didn't know it then but they were the last minutes I was to spend on my homeland. Short hours later as we sailed it would disappear over the horizon and I would never set foot on it again. But, such is the way that the gods trifle with us that I gave it no thought. In fact my clearest memory of that day is something which I feel is of no real account. Once I had boarded the ship and taken my place one of the marines, Lycas, a dark skinned man from the mainland, handed me a wineskin and husk of bread left out for me as I'd missed the morning meal. I was hungry and bit a chunk of the coarse bread and was grunting my thanks to him when a grit of stone in the badly ground flour cracked one of my side teeth in half. Even now though the stump is long rotted away it pains me still and when the ache returns at the touch of something cold I see for a moment the grizzled face of Lycas with the empty hole for his right eye socket where an arrow had struck and blinded him. But of the vanishing shoreline of Samos I have no memory. Such is life – what we should see we fail to recognise, whilst what doesn't count we cling to as if it were gold. I spat the tooth and blood into the sea and was soothing my mouth with the wine when Ariston's voice from the stern called me over to report to the General.

Moving from prow to stern on a trireme as the rowers are hitting their stroke is no easy matter, but I made my way between the rowers, being cursed by many as I lurched with the movement of the ship. Later, moving aboard a trireme would seem easier to me than walking on shore, but then it was like the earth shifting with each step. Lysias the trierarch helped me into the prow, the first sign he had shown that he realised I existed.

The General stood at the back, hands resting on the rail, looking at our other four ships and at the Chian contingent who followed us.

"You mend quick, lad, that'll serve you well. Those who don't recover quickly from a wound don't last long. This will be a short voyage; we are just crossing the straits to join the rest of the fleet at Mycale."

This surprised me as I thought the whole fleet had ridden at anchor in the great harbour of Samos. If there were more then this must certainly be the greatest fleet in the world. The significance of landing at Mycale I did understand. On the slopes of Mount Mycale stood the Panonium, the most sacred site of the Ionian Greeks, our communal shrine in days long before we were forced to abandon it by the empire of the Persians. A visit to the ancient Panonium was held to be one of the achievements in a man's life. Surely if such a large fleet was to be blessed by the gods at such a site then success would follow. As if he understood my thoughts the General continued,

"Don't look for any help from the gods in visiting that place; it did your father no good."

I had never heard that my father had had dealings with the shrine and was about to ask him but he swept on.

"Nothing good comes from that place. We go there to decide on our final throw of the dice. This fleet is all we have left. Without our help Miletos will fall, it cannot hold out much longer. The only hope is that we can defeat the Persian fleet and break the blockade."

"But with such a fleet surely no Persian force can stand against us."

"Don't talk balls, boy. Have you taken time to study the state this great fleet is in? Half of these ships are rotting in the water as we speak. Well perhaps the Samians, the Chians, the Lesbians and us are in reasonable shape but not the rest. They're the rotting homes of frightened fugitives."

He stopped and for a moment we stood listening to the creaking of the deck as the rowers strove to keep rhythm.

"But the real rot is in the hearts of the men and leaders. The fleet is beaten before it starts; the war is as good as over. These ships have Persian agents all over them. Many of the trierarchs and leaders have already been bought and others are considering their price. The agents of the expelled tyrants and of the Great King are almost as numerous here as honest Greeks who want to break the blockade."

I was shocked and asked,

"What? There are men in this fleet who would betray us for Persian gold?"

"Use your brains boy, who in hell do you think we went to talk to last night?"

Thus for the second time in forty-eight hours my understanding of the world was turned upside down. We stood looking back at the Chian ships as they attempted to keep pace and avoid tangling and fouling each other in the narrow strait. The silence continued, stretching it seemed to me into infinity. Should I stay? Had he forgotten my presence? The moments passed and the ache of my shattered tooth and the blood in my mouth combined with the rolling of the trireme made

41

me feel vomit surge up towards my gullet. I turned my head and heaved a mass of foul tasting, warm liquid into the sea, hearing the shouts of laughter from the sailors in the stern.

"You'll become used to it, boy, the sea; soon it'll seem easier to walk on deck to its rhythm than to stumble about on land. But now, to take your mind off your guts I'll answer the question you want to ask but daren't. Why are we sailing if the fleet is already betrayed and we're dead men?"

So, as the shadows lengthened towards evening and the sun ceased silvering the sea and began to bloody it, I learnt what it was that we were doing. Why he trusted me like this I have never fully understood, even today looking back, it still puzzles. Perhaps he needed to unburden himself of all the weight of the responsibility and I, a mere boy, was a safe audience. Perhaps it was because he trusted my father. Perhaps it was kindness, or gratitude for me taking the knife thrust meant for him. In fact over the years I have become more inclined to think it the latter. Despite his calculating and cynical nature he was as prone to acts of mercurial kindness as he was to acts of cruelty and savagery. No man I have met has been as capable of consistent self belief. His son came closest to it. So perhaps what he told me came as the result of a whim; he certainly never spoke to any other: of this I do know, it would have meant death and disgrace.

"You may be young and callow but you notice things like I do. I know you saw who I met in the Heraion and I know you recognised him last night. Do you know who he is, boy? No, I thought not. The man you saw is Aiakes, deposed tyrant of Samos and now close friend of the Great King. I can see by your face that the name means something even to you. If he feels it's safe to return to his old kingdom then he must be certain that the destruction of our revolt is at hand. So what is it that this great fleet is sailing towards and how must it be led?"

With that he cleared his throat and spat over the side, laid a rough hand gently on my shoulder and returned to his place by Ariston at the tiller, leaving me to watch the final rays of the sun illuminate the painted figureheads and pennants of the Chian ships sailing in our wake. Although scarcely more than a boy I had brains enough to realise from what I had seen that we were playing a double game, or at least he was playing a double game, for in truth I doubt whether the rest of our crew even knew there was a game to be played. But what was our purpose and which side were we on?

Miltiades had the greatest reputation as a strategos, or leader, in the fleet. He came from one of the greatest and oldest Athenian families, the Philiads. They had a reputation for ambiguity, or perhaps subtlety describes it better, in their diplomacy, loyalties and general dealings and these characteristics were prominent in the General. Had he been bought by the king through the agency of Aiakes? Perhaps, but then why had an attempt been made on his life so soon after the meeting at which I had noticed that the face of Aiakes was not that of a man well satisfied with the conversation? My young brain was reeling but then I was alerted by shouts to return to my station. We had rounded a point on the Mycale promontory and were making landfall.

The number of ships made landing that evening impossible so we rode at anchor through the calm night. I could not sleep; the proximity of so many ships, so many men. Their smells and sounds against the background noise of the water slapping the hulls. My mind reeled: I couldn't understand how the ordered safe drudgery of my childhood had been replaced by chaos, moving from one place to another in the

43

company of men I didn't know or understand. That night it was as if the great god Pan clutched my heart causing it to churn with terror and my eyes to weep. Each time I closed my eyes the fear caught me again and I sat up with a start. The men sleeping close cursed me but I couldn't lie still. I needed to piss but when I got to the heads I couldn't.

The night seemed to stretch forever, cloudy and black and only the thumping of my own heart persuaded me that I had not entered Hades. I couldn't think of any living being who could give me comfort. To think of my home, mother and brothers increased the anxiety. They were somewhere else, in a world where the next day brought no terrors. The next day was the same as the last day, and the one before that: peaceful and safe.

I must eventually have fallen into a fitful doze because the flute calling the men to their stations snapped me awake. The sun was rising behind Mount Mycale, the water shimmered, the triremes bobbed at anchor in the bay. I was passed bread, some cheese and a wineskin. I watched a seabird circle low over the water, passing from shade to be picked out by the sun, and felt a jolt of feeling I could not place, but I knew that I had left the child I had been behind in the night.

For the hours that it took for our contingent to beach at its appointed station I stood at the rail and watched. The General had been right, there were more ships, the whole bay and beach thick with men and triremes, swarming on the land and water like wasps, and as the day rose the noise grew with it. I was filled with excitement and expectation that some great thing was to happen. Once our squadron was beached, the hull bungs removed and the planking checked, we ate at our makeshift camp fires. The General brought all our crews together.

"From each contingent the strategos and one other will proceed to the Panonium and there we will decide the course of this war and elect one leader for the fleet. For us Athenians I decline to choose between our five trierarchs as all are men of equal valour and birth. Therefore for my sideman I take Mandrocles. His father was a good warrior and the gods have suggested that it was not chance that gave him to us. In fact it would appear that he brings us luck. Besides, he is from Samos and this shrine, our shrine, is on their ground."

There was much murmuring at this. I did not look at Lysias our trierarch but it seemed that the men accepted this as the type of fate that the gods decide and which is beyond our understanding. For myself I felt little surprise, so strange had life become.

Once the heat of the day had diminished we set off for the Panonium. The General didn't say a single word to me to explain his decision. As always he assumed that the company would accept his word without question. One strange thing I do remember clearly though was that as I followed him out of our camp towards the track that led to the shrine some of our men stepped forward and touched me as if for luck. In this way my presence was accepted and I ceased being the Samian brat and became Mandrocles the luck bringer.

CHAPTER 5

The Panonium may well have been the great shrine and prize of the Ionian gods but even in the dwindling light of sunset it was apparent that the recent years had not been kind to it. Weeds grew in the precinct, the roof had fallen in places, and timbers rotted. The sacred paintings which were the basis of our phrase "O sacred and bright Panonium shelter of the gods" were worn and faded. It looked small, shabby and diminished as though it had been deserted by whatever gods once lived here.

Eighteen men representing the nine Ionian cities who had brought their ships to join the great fleet and, in addition, the General and I representing the five Athenian ships that he had brought from his kingdom in the Chersonese met in this ruined place by torchlight. Some effort had been made to tidy the shrine and restore some sense of power and majesty but it was apparent from the faces of all the delegates that the atmosphere of the place lowered our spirits. To me it seemed ill omened and ill chosen.

The council of the Greeks was not able to start as it became apparent that we were awaiting the arrival of some delegates who should have been there to meet us. These were delegates from the besieged city of Miletos, the centre of the revolt when it had started long years ago. These delegates' journey was more hazardous than ours as they had to run the Persian blockade to escape from the city. So to pass the time the General walked with me to the outer limits of the precinct where we sat on the base of a column long since tumbled to the ground. He idly broke off a stem of dried grass growing between the masonry and chewed upon it deep in thought. So we sat as the light seeped from the day and dusk became evening. After some time he began to speak softly, perhaps for his own benefit, perhaps for mine. Whatever the purpose in those few sparse sentences I learnt the true nature of our position.

Reader, I know that you understand that sometimes the gods place us in circumstances in which there is no right course of action and no good or honourable outcome. Well, of all the difficult situations in my long and dangerous life, this one was the most unclear. But now looking back with the benefit of wisdom and experience I see that those who met at the shrine could truly account themselves cursed.

"If we fight with this fleet we lose and die and the rebellion ends. Maybe during the fight I can slip away, take Persian gold and cling on to my kingdom a little longer. But then my name will be cursed by all Greeks except for those aristocratic traitors whose families already enjoy that gold. Worse, the Great King and his agents like Aiakes know that I can't be trusted; already I am watched and spied on. My end will not be long in coming.

"If I urge the fleet to battle and then, along with others who have been bought like that Samian traitor Saurias, betray it and change sides in the heat of battle we may be killed anyway. Strange things happen in battle. If I urge withdrawal and the taking of the fleet to Athens to continue the fight from there I'll lose my kingdom and probably be betrayed by the traitors. Even if I get us back to the Chersonese and my kingdom I can't defend it. Once the Great King has reduced Miletos he'll send one of his satraps with an army. Or an assassin, who will probably be someone I know and trust. This, incidentally, Mandrocles, is why I have chosen you to accompany me tonight."

He saw my look of hurt and said,

"Surely you didn't believe all that balls about the gods giving you luck."

47

Then he stopped and we sat in silence. I understood that nothing was expected from me in terms of speech. That because I was of no importance and friendless he could talk this way in front of me and perhaps work out his thoughts. After a while he started again.

"Take the money now, probably the safest."

He got no further. There was shouting from the shrine. He spat out the straw, jumped to his feet and set off towards the noise with me dogging his heels.

We entered the shrine's inner sanctum and in that space lit by the flickering light from the pine resin torches understood the source of the noise. The delegates were shouting a paean in honour of the Miletos delegation. Three men had managed to scale the walls and make their way out of the city and through the Persian lines. Two of the men were highly placed in the democratic faction that currently governed Miletos but the third and most celebrated was now approaching the end of his life. He was the celebrated maker of maps, the legendary traveller Hecataeus. His age and celebrity accorded him respect across the world among both the Greeks and the barbarians and, as was fitting, now that the assembly was complete and silence was imposed, he gave the opening address.

The next few hours were to determine the future of both the Greeks and the barbarians, but not in a way any of us understood at the time. We stood in a semi circle as each delegation took it in turn to speak. Hecataeus spoke for Miletos. He reminded us how his city had led the revolt to defeat the Persians at sea and to sack the Persian city of Sardis. That Miletos had suffered more than any other city and fought the hardest. He could move men with his words and I noticed that many of the delegates wept as he spoke of the price of failure. His own voice cracked with emotion as he finished.

"If we fall, as without your help we will, the Great King will make real his promise to have our boys made eunuchs, to have our maidens transported to Bactria to grow up as slaves of the barbarians. To have our wives raped unto death by his troops and for any of our men who survive the last fight to be killed, and for our country to be delivered into the hands of foreigners."

He was then followed by his two companions, who urged that the fleet should sail to Miletos, defeat the Persian fleet and lift the siege. They told us we must do this to restore our honour and that of all the Greeks. They argued that once it was done we could again send for help to Athens and Sparta and perhaps from a position of strength negotiate an honourable settlement with the Great King. They spoke with the passion of desperate men and when they finished they had touched the hearts of many of the delegates. For a moment there was silence and the soft sounds of night filtered into the shrine.

Then each of the representatives of the cities spoke in turn, although when it was his turn to speak and state his opening position the General refused. By the end of the opening statements two courses of action had been proposed; the majority, led by the delegations from Miletos and Chios, proposed sailing to the aid of Miletos. The other argument was to keep the fleet together but for the present to avoid battle. As the debate progressed the momentum had swung towards the first proposition. Saurias, the senior Samian delegate, proposed a vote to be followed by the election of a commander in chief of the fleet so that our action could be co-ordinated. Before this could be agreed the General stepped forward.

"I, Miltiades, the Athenian, tyrant of the Chersonese, now wish to be heard."

Perhaps it was the torchlight but he looked both pale and ill at ease, his hands moving constantly as he spoke. I know now what a great orator he can be when he wants, but he appeared like a man being forced to do something against the run of common sense. His first argument was for the fleet to split up and evade the Persians to keep its separate parts free and wait for better times. This found no favour and was shouted down as cowardice and treachery by the Milesians. This accusation stung, I could see his face redden noticeably but he proceeded, keeping his emotions in check with some difficulty.

"My second reason why we must not break ourselves for the sake of Miletos concerns the will of the gods. You know well the reply of the oracle at Delphi to the Argives concerning the fate of Argos, and you will know that the reply concerned also the plight of Miletos:

Then shalt thou Miletos so oft the container of evil

Be thyself to many a feast and an excellent booty

Then shall thy matrons wash the feet of the longhaired Persians

Others shall then possess the loved temple."

This quote from the oracle was shouted down by the furious delegates from Miletos and others. It was not a strong argument anyway; we modern Greeks know that for every truth the oracle speaks there are many more mistakes and beyond that the oracle can be influenced by money, power or coercion. It seemed to me, young as I was, that the General had not tried to win his case. Rather that he had made the gesture in public so that he could use it in his defence later if things didn't turn out as he expected. It seemed to me Persian gold had won the day and that any talk of freedom or honour was just a cover to conceal the false hearts of men. But the gods' workings are beyond our understanding and matters did not quite turn out that way. I now understand that there were three factions in that shrine. One, the Miletos delegation, the men of honour, held the view that that they must fight and defeat the Persian navy. A second, held by men of sense was that this was folly and we must save the fleet.

But the third faction had been bought by Persian gold. For these men it was essential that the fleet must fight, be betrayed and destroyed. The General in his subtle way, it seemed, was of this faction but wanted to place his money on two runners at once; to run with the stag and hunt with the hounds. Knowing what I do of the men of the polis now I have learned that such dissembling treachery is considered clever. He could in the end in any event have claimed to have supported whichever side was ultimately successful and be believed by both. So it might have worked out if the leader of the Samians, between whom and the General there was bad blood had not chosen not to speak.

"I am surprised that the great Miltiades, who is always keen to boast of his great deeds and courage, should display such a lack of appetite for the fight. Perhaps it is because both his tyranny in the Chersonese and his home in Athens are far away and he considers them safe. Or perhaps it's because as a sociable man with many friends he does not wish to offend some of them. This would not be the first time that his sensitivity for the Great King and his fellow tyrants such as Aiakes has provoked such gentleness of feeling."

The implications were obvious even to me. The blood drained from the General's face and an ominous quiet bathed the room. For a moment it seemed as if his anger choked him, then he spoke.

"Yes, before I spoke with sensitivity but not for the Persians and certainly not for the renegades and traitors like Aiakes. So, now I will say direct what you wish to hear but what I will say will come as no surprise to some of you – you know it already. We cannot fight and win because we are betrayed. All of you know our camp crawls with agents, all of you, excepting you Hecataeus, have been offered a price. Some of you have taken it. You, Saurias, you double dealing, lying little bugger, you were bought long ago and needed no persuasion. You would run for a day to commit a foul deed rather than walk one step for good. We have all been offered. I, Miltiades, have been offered but I spat it back in their faces and that's why they tried to kill me. If you vote to relieve Miletos you will die there."

There was little reaction to this save from Saurias who strode towards the General with his hand on his sword hilt. For the rest it was clear, they understood the truth the General spoke. At this moment the fate of the fleet and the revolution hung in the balance but then the balance was tipped from a quarter from where it could not have been expected.

Dionysius, the captain of the Phocean contingent, strode to the centre of the floor. This was the smallest force in the fleet, only three ships and Dionysius was regarded as a man of no importance, a man that all other leaders felt they could look down on. He was regarded as little better than a pirate, which was prescient as that is what he later went on to become. Now, however, he was to enjoy his brief moment of greatness or maybe in that sacred place some greater force was acting through him.

"Our affairs hang on a razor's edge, men of Ionia, either to be free or to be slaves; and worse, slaves who have shown themselves runaways. Now you have to choose between some hardship and danger, but by doing so overcome your enemies and secure your own freedom or continue to jump this way and that like rabbits. But I tell you this, if you do not listen to what I council, you have no hope of escaping the Great King's vengeance. You have the power tonight to free the Greeks and win back what we have lost. Be persuaded by what I say and I promise that our foes will either decline a battle, or if they fight, suffer complete defeat."

He held a pose in the torchlight, chin thrust forwards, both arms held in a gesture like that of a supplicant and all the company looked to him. Then Hecataeus seized the moment.

"Fellow Greeks, we have at last found our true voice and our leader, the future course of action is agreed."

This was a clever move as for any of the leaders of the larger fleets to serve under one another would have involved a loss of status. Whereas all could say that they were prepared to serve under a man like Dionysius who could never in any way be regarded as their equal. He was acclaimed by general assent and issued his first order that the fleet would sail the next day for the island of Lade off the coast by Miletos.

As our procession wound its way by torchlight back down from the Panonium to the ships through the herb scented night, the General remarked quietly in my ear,

"So the rabbits jump straight into the snare just like in one of the satyr plays at the spring festival."

CHAPTER 6

So we missed the great betrayal that was the sea fight at Lade. We slipped away before dawn headed for the General's fastness in the Chersonese. There is no mention of any Athenian involvement or of Miltiades in the death throes of the Ionian revolt: just the understanding that we, like most other states, had our share of traitors. I still question myself as to what exactly happened that night in the Panonium on Mycale; was the General's performance all an act?

Perhaps, but it may be that at the end his passion and anger were genuine. Or then again was it just another example of his cunning? If the latter was the case it was badly misjudged for we now had no friends on either side and for the Persians he was now a man marked for death. Yet his advice had been good, the fleet was doomed. In spite of his diplomatic subtlety and the fact that he knew the position of both sides, it seemed to me that when he made his decision he was inspired by the moment. To speak the truth even at that late stage and then to slip away was more fitting and honourable than to sail with the fleet to Lade. There he would either have died with the Greeks or betrayed them and been rewarded by the Great King. In either event the history of the world would have been altered and Athens would have fallen.

So while we sailed north, the fleet, the last chance of the revolution, sailed for Lade to relieve the city of Miletos. They stayed on Lade for seven days while Dionysius drilled them in the tactic he intended to use against the Persians' allies, the Phoenician fleet. They say that his manner was arrogant and that he came to believe that he commanded the fleet as a consequence of his reputation for leadership rather than the fact that it was because of the lack of his authority or power. In any event the allies soon tired of his drill and they refused to turn out on the eighth and ninth days and lazed in their tents, grumbled, drank and quarrelled. During this time the Great King's agents went amongst them using threats or promises, whichever was most appropriate, to sow discord and weaken the spirit. On the tenth day the Persians appeared in line of battle having been advised by traitors in the Greek camp that this was the opportune moment.

The three Phocean ships led by Dionysius put to sea against them and gradually the other contingents followed. The enemy hung back until the whole Ionian fleet was in line of battle and too close to break off and run. Then they attacked. As the first ships engaged at ramming speed Saurias the Samian admiral ordered his ship to hoist its sails, turn and run. He was followed by all the Samian fleet except for eleven triremes that closed ranks and engaged the enemy. The Samians were followed by the ships from Lesbos and some others and in that moment the revolt and the honour of the Ionians and their freedom was lost.

The tragedy and bitter humour of it is that those who stayed fought well. Dionysius, the braggart, took the three Phocean ships, the Chians and the eleven Samian ships and fought with such courage and determination that for a long time it seemed that they might well fight their way out. But the odds were too heavy and one by one the ships were overcome. On the eleven Samian ships they fought to the death; some of the Chians and Dionysius managed to escape. Dionysius, the last, and perhaps bravest, of the Ionian leaders, set up as a pirate and quite a successful one too, preying on the Empire's coasts. Perhaps he had earned a little luck. He fought well. The citizens of Samos had the decency to erect a memorial to those who had fought to the death thereby saving a little of the island's honour.

But the fleet was no more and soon after Miletos was taken and its citizens suffered the fate that the General had predicted in the debate on Mycale.

I heard the news of the defeat as I was drinking wine and trying to fend off the unwelcome attentions of Metiochus, the General's oldest son by his first wife. We were in Miltiades' palace in the Thracian Chersonese, regarded by Athenians as beyond the civilised world. A gateway to the barbarian wilderness, inhabited by wild tribes who lived in the wastelands of the interior and fit only as a staging post for ancient heroes such as Jason on his adventures. It was this use as a staging post that had led to the General's uncle being dispatched from Athens to take it for a kingdom almost thirty years before.

The Chersonese was a peninsula that stood across the water from ancient Troy and controlled the Hellespont. It guarded the entry to the Black Sea and the Euxine region, wild, but rich in grain and gold that lay on its shores. Although in name independent, it was in reality a fief that the General held for Athens.

But to add to his troubles the Athens he had left was now a very different place. The tyrant Hippias had been overthrown and had fled to the court of the Great King. The General's first wife, and Metiochus' mother, was the daughter of Hippias so Miltiades was tainted by links to both tyranny and the Persians.

The aristocrats who now ran Athens drew their influence from a new and unpredictable monster: democracy. These aristocrats were not men aligned to the General's family and were in many cases openly hostile to him. So, with the end of the revolt he found that his position was neither sustainable in the Great King's empire which bordered on his territory or in the new Athens governed by the Demos, who were as good as his enemies.

The General's main residence in the Chersonese was Sestos, a port on the northern side of the isthmus. Across the narrow strait it faced Abydos and Dardanos, the ancient home of Prince Aeneas, the ancient Trojan hero. Miltiades' Chersonese colony was as wealthy as it was strategic and thus important to Athens. This position Miltiades had jeopardised and this had been the theme of my couch companion Metiochus throughout the meal. Metiochus was my host in the absence of his father, who was conducting a rapid inspection of the defences of his kingdom. He was currently at Agora, a town his uncle had founded on the eastern border. Here he had built a defensive rampart across the neck of the isthmus to provide a barrier to any attacks from beyond. He was now making repairs to this defensive wall, which had, over the years, fallen into a state of decay. This effort of his father's was regarded with derision by Metiochus.

"Just like the old boy to lock the gate after the slaves have bolted but depressingly typical of his conduct throughout the whole sorry affair of this infantile revolt."

During this speech he poured from a bowl two cups of freshly mixed wine. The cups were fine pieces of work of great age that had been in the family for over a hundred years. Today, as a cultured Athenian, I would instantly recognise them as rare examples of lip cups fashioned by the potter Exekias for the little master to paint. But even then as an ignorant youth I was aware of the beauty and fragility of these cups decorated with the black figures of heroes. So I took my cup in both hands lest it should drop and break. Metiochus moved closer to me on the couch and placed his hand lightly on my thigh before continuing.

"Consider my father's kingdom, rich in trade, rich in land and in a position on the straits through which all

57

shipping must pass and pay a toll. With good harbours we lack for nothing except perhaps the benefits of the peculiar new custom of consulting the unwashed and ignorant on their opinion, which it seems has become the fashion in Athens."

He made an exaggerated grimace as he said this, turning his head to spit.

"I think we manage well enough without the squabbles that this produces and I do not feel that I lack anything by not having to heed the opinion of any ignorant yokel with a pot to piss in. Apart from the winds even the weather is better here than in Athens. There is only one thing that our prosperity depends on. Can you guess what that is, Mandrocles? Of course you can. Even you who, despite your good birth, has the cultural experience of a goat boy.

"It is the good will of the Great King and his satrap across the water Artaphernes. We hold a little strip of strategically important and rich land miles from Athens but within spitting distance of the Great King."

His hand had moved further up my thigh as he talked. I shifted away but he was too involved in his subject to notice.

"The Persian navy patrol these straits and if we were to climb to the roof of this comfortable but provincial palace then look across the waters we would see the Great King's lands. So, when this revolt starts my father has an opportunity to put behind him his earlier act of foolish treachery towards the Great King, which was of course noted despite what my father thinks, and act as a loyal friend."

He refilled his cup, replaced his hand on my leg and continued, his voice sarcastic and angry.

"But that would have been too easy for the great and cunning Miltiades, who seems to see himself as a modern day Odysseus. He decides to enrich himself at the Great King's expense and at the same time ingratiate himself with the new breed at Athens. So while the island pirates make war on the empire he enriches himself by taking for himself in the name of Athens the islands of Lemnos and Imbros, boasting all the while about his political acumen. Whereas any fool could predict that the Great King would win this war like he has all the others. Then when Miletos was taken and the fleet destroyed he would look to reward his friends and punish his enemies. Which even my father has at last realised, hence his ridiculous and inconclusive trip to Mycale, and he even got that wrong in the end. Still, I suppose it did bring you to visit us, Mandrocles the beautiful."

During this speech his demeanour of aristocratic disdain gradually slipped and the red colour of anger began to flush his cheeks. I could feel his hand grow sweaty against my flesh.

"His strategy with Athens, that's all balls as well. The families that have espoused the Demos are our traditional enemies whilst the true ruler of Athens, my grandfather Hippias, is in exile at the court of the Great King pending his restoration at the head of a Persian army. So, my father's decision to put my mother, Hippias' daughter, to one side so that he could marry that scarcely civilised Thracian bitch was hardly the act of a new Odysseus. So here we are, waiting to be driven from our kingdom by the Great King with nowhere to run to. But that's my father all over; grab any short term gain with no thought for the future. The gods must wonder how he gets men to follow him."

He paused. The room had grown dim with the onset of evening, and he clapped for the servants to light the evening lamps. While they took lighted tapers to the wicks floating in the bowls of oil he whispered more instructions to the steward, leaving me to reflect on the

59

complexity of the world I had entered. Looking back to the callow and ignorant youth that I was I often wonder how I have survived as long as I have. It seemed at the time inconceivable that a son should speak so of his father, particularly one who held so much respect and influence. In fact back then it seemed curious to me that a son should be so unlike his father. Whereas the General was red haired and strongly built, in many ways resembling the poets' heroic Achaeans, his son was tall, languid and dark haired. His dress was more Persian than Greek, his beard was styled Persian fashion. He had a wife but I had never seen her and it was clear from his preferences that he had taken her from duty rather than inclination.

Whereas it is respectable that a woman should be modestly kept from the company of men, despite the scandalous behaviour of some of our modern Athenian young women, the gods place a solemn responsibility on the duties of a husband. The obligations of these responsibilities it seemed were not practised by Metiochus. It is true that there is also an honourable tradition of love and learning between an experienced man and a youth and that this is part of the heroic condition. But this forms a stage of one's education and at the onset of marriage and the assumption of full responsibility it is put aside by those who live a full span and do not die young or unwed like Achilles and Patroculus, or live unnatural lives like those buggers in Thebes today. Metiochus didn't strike me as being in any way part of a heroic tradition.

Once the lamps were fully lit he dismissed the servants. The steward had placed on the low table a new bowl of mixed wine and next to it a deep drinking cup of great antiquity and beauty. During this Metiochus had calmed down.

"I am aware of my responsibilities as my father's eldest son to show his guests honour. The men on his ship the Athene Nike, I understand, refer to you as Mandrocles luck bringer because of the way the knife intended for my father failed to kill you. I think, however, that my own epithet, Mandrocles the beautiful, is more fitting so in that spirit I present you this as a friendship gift. Take this as a token of lasting friendship and perhaps more."

He handed me the cup. It was in the old style. On the rim of the cup was a lengthy inscription that read:

"I am Nestor's cup, good to drink with, but whoever drinks from this cup at once the desire of fair crowned Aphrodite will seize him!"

I may have been an inexperienced youth but my father had schooled me well. I knew my Homer by heart and the meaning of the joke that the cup made was obvious to me. Still it was a thing of great worth and beauty. I have it still. It sits at my elbow as I write these words, one of the few things I have retained in my long life.

Metiochus poured from the mixing bowl to the cup.

"Come, let us together share this cup of love in this time of war."

There was the noise of shouting from the corridor and the barking of dogs. Metiochus sat upright and a look of rage suffused his face. The door burst open and an excited hunting dog burst into the room followed by a laughing boy of about eight or nine. The boy was well built with a head of reddish gold hair that fell in curls over his shoulders. He grabbed the dog and pulled it to him calling,

"Come, Pleistonax. I think that neither of us will be welcome here by my half brother and his..."

He paused for a moment as if thinking then said the word,

61

"Guest."

He turned and left the room with the hound and the sound of his laughter could be heard retreating down the corridor.

His presence had an exaggerated effect on Metiochus, who rose to his feet and shouted for his brother's tutor to be sent to discipline the boy.

"That, Mandrocles, is the by-blow of my father's second marriage to the Thracian bitch. Cimon: the apple of his eye, that booby who it is impossible to teach, who runs wild with his tomboy of a sister, Elpinice. That is what my great father would like to see as his heir, to grow up rich, drunk, gambling and short sighted just like him, whilst the pure aristocratic blood that runs in my veins is relegated, replaced by that, that golden turd."

With that he strode from the room and I heard his voice again shouting for the tutor as it receded up the corridor.

It was in this way that I first met Cimon, whom I would serve all my life. Fitting then that his first act should be to save me from a situation which I dreaded and didn't know how to handle.

CHAPTER 7

In the early hours of the morning the noise of Miltiades and his entourage returning woke the palace. There much excitement as his senior men and Metiochus were roused from their beds and fetched to the council chamber. I remember that it was still dark enough for lamps to be lit and there was the first hint of early morning chill that betokened the end of late summer. I still had no understanding of my place in this society but followed the sound of the noise. At the door Lysias stopped me entering but as I turned to go the General called my name.

"Mandrocles, we have urgent matters to discuss which will take the best part of the day. Go see my son Cimon, he will want to ride and hunt, you accompany him, it will give you a chance to get acquainted."

The door was shut so I made my way to the wing of the house near to the domestic slaves' quarters where Cimon slept near to the room of his tutor. However, before I could reach the room I could hear a boy's voice speaking with a curious, for one so young, mixture of authority and reasonableness.

"Something is happening, I should be there not here wasting my time with the wisdom of the ancients. You can say what you like but I will not take up the wax board and stylus today – that is my final word."

Standing in a bare room furnished by two stools and a table with a lamp, Cimon, his hands on his hips, lectured his tutor, a tall and slightly stooped greybeard who, I was to learn later, had a minor reputation as a philosopher of the Pythagorean breed. These days despite my grandfather's friendship with Pythagoras I tend to think of him as a potentially decent military engineer gone astray. His notions of the soul and eating beans, his long windedness and lack of understanding of the affairs of men may have won him a reputation for wisdom among rich young men with time on their hands but to me he was a potentially good craftsman who became crazed.

The tutor acknowledged my presence with a thin smile, as if relieved that there was now a diversion from the battle of wills that he was condemned to wage daily with his young pupil.

"I come from Lord Miltiades with his command that I accompany the young master on horseback for the morning."

The tutor gave assent with a slight bow of the head, adding with some asperity as an afterthought,

"That would be wise, I may be needed. There are, it seems, great affairs of state to be decided in this house today – no place for a child."

Metiochus considered Cimon a booby but he was bright enough to have recognised the slight and had begun to bridle when I took him by the arm and led him from the room. In the corridor that led to the yard and the stables his mood quickly changed.

"So, Mandrocles, they consider you to be also too young or unimportant to stay in this house while affairs of state are being discussed. That will make it not so bad for me. I'll show you my dogs and horses."

Before he reached the gate to the yard a girl's voice called,

"Brother, where are you going?"

I turned and saw a girl of an age somewhere between maiden and woman. She bore a resemblance to Cimon but where he was fair she was dark with long wavy hair falling loose over her shoulders. She possessed even at that age a striking beauty with high cheek bones and a chin narrowing almost to a point. Her eyes were large and sharp blue shaded by long black lashes, a contrast to the normal run of beauty. Her demeanour was not the modesty expected of a young noble Greek girl approaching womanhood, it was obvious she was accustomed to an unusual degree of freedom; my sisters would have been scolded or more probably beaten for such looseness of behaviour.

"It seems, sister, that my father wishes me to be kept out of the house and watched by Mandrocles."

"Ah, so this is who you go with."

She treated me to a half smile and a direct but teasing gaze.

"You'd better take care that our elder brother does not grow jealous, Mandrocles the beautiful."

And with a clear ringing laughter she turned on her heels and stalked back towards the women's quarters. From that first sight of her until now, when she is an old but still beautiful woman, I have never been able to predict or feel in any way secure in the company of Elpinice. She behaves with a freedom no other woman in Greece, save perhaps for Pericles' courtesan Aspasia, is allowed, and like Aspasia, she has constantly been the target of spite and malice, particularly from the comic poets. Even young Aristophanes, whose understanding of politics is more sensible than most, cannot resist a jibe. So, I will set down here in plain speech that she has always behaved with loyalty to those she loves the most and her courage is equal to that of any brave man. I will also nail the cruel slander spread by his enemies, that she and Cimon practised unnatural acts and lived as man and wife. In the hard times, before her marriage, he took her into his household else she would have been destitute. I was there, no one knows better than I, or was closer to both.

Cimon chose the horses we were to ride. His was a fine white mare bred across the waters in the Troad and mine a more docile bay. We rode through the day with his pack of dogs and he showed me his favourite trails

65

for the hunt. We caught little but roamed freely. The day was fine but not too hot. At midday we ate a simple meal in the shade of an olive grove where a stream flowed out from the forest that covered this part of the peninsula. Beneath a small waterfall was a pool, cool and pleasant to bathe in. Cimon swam as well as he rode and although he may have had little interest in his studies he was quick and thoughtful and already possessed the natural charm for which he became famed. That day has remained locked in memory like a bubble of sun drenched ease amidst the storms of life. We returned as the sun was dipping into the sea, our limbs aching slightly from the chase, covered in dust from the trail but relaxed in mind.

Back in the palace I was sought out by the steward and told to be ready to dine with the General. I sluiced the dirt from my limbs and face, dressed in my best, though still shabby, robe and hurried to the great hall. All the tables were occupied; the General's full staff sat down to eat that night. I was pleased to be assigned a place some distance away from Metiochus by a table with two of the trierarchs and a grizzled looking veteran with heavily scarred arms and face. This man, Metopes, was the commander of the garrison which maintained the wall across the isthmus. He had spent the last fifteen years repelling the attempted incursions of the Scythians who roamed the wilderness of the interior. He kept us entertained with his tales of these raids and the savage fate that awaited any of his troops who were taken prisoner. He was explaining how it was possible to strip almost all the skin from a man's body before he died, when a latecomer entered the room. He moved hurriedly between the tables to Miltiades. Even by lamplight it was obvious that this man had travelled hard and quickly. His dress, which was Persian in style rather than Greek, was travel stained and in places was stuck to his body by sweat. The dirt on his face was streaked with runnels of perspiration and he walked with a limp that favoured a damaged right leg. Miltiades rose from his place and after having placed a cup of wine in the man's hand, which he drained in one go, he walked with him to a corner of the room and listened earnestly to the news he brought. A silence descended on the company and each man sat with his eyes on the conversation, straining to hear what was said.

Metiochus left his place and moved to join them but his father waved him away leaving him to stand in embarrassment between the tables of silent attentive men and the two talking figures, whose shadows the lamps elongated, making them seem scarcely human. Then, dismissing the messenger, Miltiades turned to the assembled company and made a gesture demanding our attention. Metopes whispered in my ear.

"Whatever news that bugger brought it can't have been good, mark my words."

Then he spat onto his platter and sat back to listen with the rest of us.

"Gentlemen, the news I have just received from one of our friends on the mainland is not of great comfort. It seems that the Great King is moving with a speed with which we did not think him capable. We need to prepare the defences of our kingdom. There is an army on the march which will within days reach the opposite shore. You are now all dismissed to return to your posts with the exception of my son and the ships' captains who I will see shortly in the council chamber."

With that he walked from the room. Metopes grabbed my arm.

"He must be mad, there is no way we can defend our borders against the Persians, they'll overrun my men in minutes."

67

Then he, like the rest, had gone, undecided what to do. I followed Metiochus and the captains to the chamber. No one protested at my presence so I sat alone on a stool near the wall. The captains sat in a group whilst Metiochus nervously paced the floor; no one talked. After some minutes the General entered and took his place on his chair on the dais.

"This land is no longer safe for us. The Persian army is only days away but we have no idea where the fleet is. You know as well as I that we can't fight. Also I have just learned that the last leader of the revolt, Histiaeus, has been taken and killed. Artaphernes had him impaled as a traitor and has sent his head, pickled in brine, to the Great King as a gift. Now there's only me and I don't intend to go the same way. Therefore gentlemen get your ships ready to sail tomorrow. My steward will show you what to carry with you; we will take what wealth we can. He will allocate each captain what he must carry. You will sail round the Isthmus to the port of Khardia, where you will wait for me to join you. Go quickly and quietly but tell your sailors and anyone else you speak to that you are scouting the seas for the Persian fleet. Load your ships secretly, we don't want panic. We need the people to think that we intend to stay and fight. Metiochus, stay, the rest of you go."

The captains filed out to prepare their ships. Metiochus moved closer to his father. For the first time, the General acknowledged my presence and beckoned me to sit.

"There is even a role for you, Mandrocles; we may all need some of your luck."

Metiochus seized his father's hand.

"Father, this is madness, we have nowhere to go. Even if we make it to Imbros or Lemnos the Great King will follow us and take the islands. Go to him, make your peace. My grandfather Hippias is with him. He will make sure you are spared for my sake. We have friends at the court. We have no choice: you have enemies in Athens – you cannot hope to survive there. It seems to me that you can either live the life of a pirate like that Phocean braggart Dionysius, until you are hunted down, impaled and beheaded, or you must throw yourself on the mercy of the Great King."

The General stared silently at his son whilst he spoke, as if in deep thought, until Metiochus finished. Then he stretched out his hand as if to stroke his son's face. Metiochus seemed to relax at this gesture but the General drew his hand back and then slapped him hard across the cheek.

"Don't think that I don't understand the reason for your advice. You would be safe with that traitor Hippias but not me. Soon there would be an accident and you would have my place and be a faithful vassal to the king. I would rather die than crawl and beg for mercy so we will take what wealth we can and sail for Imbros as soon as we may."

Metiochus controlled his anger, just stood rubbing his reddening cheek and meeting his father's gaze.

"Tomorrow, Metiochus, we will ride to review the defences. Be ready at dawn."

Metiochus turned and, controlling his fury, walked out of the room. Miltiades sat down and for what seemed an age, silence filled the room. Then he looked at me and spoke.

"Mandrocles, just before dawn you take my son Cimon and his sister Elpinice down to the harbour and board the Athene Nike. Do it quietly so that no one sees you. Tell them that I will see them at Khardia and that the voyage is a treat, a reward for good behaviour."

I stood to leave but he called me back.

"And, just to be on the safe side, for tonight you will sleep outside my son's door. No one is to have access to him."

"What, even his brother?"

"Especially his brother. You have been here long enough to realise that there's no love between them. Oh, and Mandrocles, you will not be coming back so if there is anything you have of value take it to the ship. I charge you with my son and daughter being safely delivered to the Athene Nike. I have sent for Ariston and Theodorus to fetch you before dawn; be ready."

He turned away and sat on his chair deep in thought. I realised I'd been dismissed and moved to return to my cell. The passages and corridors, usually quiet at this hour, were filled with the bustle of slaves, soldiers and officers hurrying to dismantle and pack that which was to be taken. All the lamps were lit so this scene of near frenzy was amplified by each person and chest throwing several shadows. I crossed this outer courtyard to the range of buildings where my small cell was situated. The night air had cooled and the stars seemed to flash with a particular brightness. As I reached the crowded passage that led to my quarters I noticed a figure move from the shadows in the corner of the courtyard and walk towards the house. As it passed one of the wall sconces that held flaming torches I recognised him as the man in the Persian garb who had brought the news to Miltiades. Then the voice of Metiochus from the darkness of the courtyard called to me.

"Mandrocles, there is more to our position here than you understand, you would be well advised to be a good friend to me, these times are dangerous for those alone and without influence."

Then he was gone, leaving me to wonder if this had happened or if I imagined it. I returned to my cell and put my few possessions in a travelling sack. Most of my gear was stored on the Athene Nike. As I left the room I noticed the drinking cup that Metiochus had given me and on an impulse took it as well. I made my way to Cimon's quarters. The boy was in bed and there was no sign of his tutor. I spread my bedroll on the floor outside his door and sat with my back against the wall and my sword across my knees. My head spun with the confusion of the world I now lived in but I determined to watch through the night then wake Cimon an hour before dawn. But I must have dozed off for sometime later I jerked awake and sensed someone approaching the door. At my movement the figure turned and moved away, at least that is how it seemed to me, but then again it was dark and I was confused. After that I didn't sleep until I heard footsteps on the corridor; two burly figures with a lamp approached me.

"Here's our new shipmate in a cushy billet, Ariston, sleeping on watch. The General will have his balls for this."

Ariston laughed softly.

"Come on, Mandrocles, help us to get the young master up, his sister's waiting round the corner."

Minutes later we left the palace for the last time to make our furtive way to the harbour.

CHAPTER 8

The harbour was a scene of great activity but ordered and well disciplined. Cimon was tired but calm. Elpinice was almost unable to control her excitement and when she saw the Athene Nike ready to set out shrilled out a peal of laughter. Before the time the first rays of the sun were softly beginning to streak the horizon we cast off from the harbour at Sestos. There's always a feeling of anticipation at the start of a sea voyage but there was something particular about this one. Maybe as I look back at youth I see it as a time of promise and wonder that distorts the memory, but I can still recall the feeling of thrill and excitement as the ship passed out of the harbour mouth. A great adventure was beginning and I was part of it. Theodorus called the rowers to their stroke. I stood in the prow with Cimon as Ariston steered the ship round the harbour wall and out into the channel. The early sunlight shone on the pennant illuminating the gold painting on the figurehead and the marble eye on the prow as we turned towards the open sea. To the shrill of the flute and the beat of the drum the other triremes followed.

The day was calm and for the first time on board I didn't heave my breakfast up over the side. Cimon seemed unaffected by the roll and pitch of the ship and of Elpinice there was no sign; the crew had fashioned a small tent of rough leather for her near the storage. Women were not welcomed on board unless as prizes. We followed the coastline towards the open sea through the morning. At the heat of day the rowers ceased and tried to find what shelter they could whilst the ship moved slowly driven only by the gentle wind in its large square sail. I was sitting cross legged in the stern, polishing my father's sword, when I noticed that

Lysias had left his captain's seat and stood by the stern rail looking at our squadron. Suddenly he shouted for Theodorus.

"Bosun, prepare your rowers, it looks like we've got company."

Ariston replied calmly.

"They've been trailing us most of the day. I saw one ship put out from Abydos as soon as we left. I doubt if I'll need to disturb the boys yet, their men will be as tired as ours."

I got to my feet carefully, wary of disturbing the ship's balance, and went to join them. Just behind us and hugging the opposite shore I could see three ships, triremes like ours, following a parallel course.

Lysias favoured me with the first friendly acknowledgement in our brief acquaintanceship, and smiled,

"You won't need the sword just yet, Mandrocles; there are only three of them, no match for us. We just need to hope that there aren't any more waiting for us where the straits open."

We were trailed by the three ships all the way down the straits. They kept to their side and made no attempt to close on us staying well out of the range of our archers. Each of our ships carried four archers stationed in the stern, where in battle they had to provide protection for the helmsman in his exposed position. All of them were Scythians in their barbarian costume of trousers, long sleeved top and soft leather cap, talking in their barbarian tongue.

The dress seems effeminate to us, men shouldn't wear trousers, but they were tough. Although I knew these men by now it did cross my mind that it was their relatives that Metopes and his men were defending the wall across the peninsula against. Long before we reached Elaeus and open sea, the crew had stopped

73

shouting insults at the Persian ships and the archers had unstrung their bows and were lounging on the deck. One of them was even showing Cimon how to fire a full sized bow, to the amusement of the crew. I noticed that despite frustration at not being big or strong enough to master the weapon he maintained a calm type of dignity despite the laughter of the archers and sailors. It seemed that even as a boy he had the rare quality that some men have of inspiring loyalty and affection even from a position of weakness.

We reached the point at dusk and Lysias gave orders for the ships to be beached for the night. As usual at the end of the day there was a steady breeze blowing across the point from the sea. Rounding it in triremes isn't easy and not to be attempted at night unless in desperation. We saw our Persian shadows across the water begin to move towards the far shore to camp for the night. We beached the ships, knocked out the bung holes to let them drain and set up camp, including a private shelter for Elpinice. I slept in my bedroll next to Cimon and, as I always do after a day at sea, fell straight asleep. Sometime later, not long I think, I was woken by Cimon shaking my shoulder.

"Mandrocles, come down to the water's edge with me, something's happening."

Then he was gone, so I followed. By the sea a group of men stood talking and looking out across the straits. By the time we reached them my eyes had become used to the dark. I recognised Lysias, Theodorus and Ariston with officers from the other boats. Cimon stood at the edge of this circle listening and I silently joined him. I remember a luminous quality to that night, something about the starlight and phosphorescence of the water seemed to sharpen our senses. The murmured conversation of the officers and the gentle lap of the sea against the beach; it was if we were in a new and vivid world of our own specially created by the gods. The scents too were particularly strong. Sage, and thyme from the rocky slopes above the bay mingled with the fresh salt tang from the sea. But there was another smell too, one that I was to come later to recognise only too well, one that could not be disguised by the stale oil and sweat smell of our unwashed bodies: fear.

Across the water and stretching down the coast into the far and almost imperceptible distance there were lights. The light of camp fires, some in little groups, some so numerous it seemed as if there was a thin line of flame covering miles of beach. Cimon tugged at my arm.

"Look, Mandrocles, the far shore's on fire."

His excited whisper drew attention to us and Lysias turned his gaze from the sea.

"Those, young master, are the camp fires of the Persian navy; it looks like the whole fleet's here."

The boy looked back at him.

"They've come for us, come for my father, haven't they? We need to go back and warn him."

"He'll know already, and he's made his plans to move, he's to meet us at the port of Khardia by the end of the wall. It was going to be in some days time but I think now it will be earlier. You need to go back to sleep, we're going to be up earlier than expected."

"I understand my responsibilities, trierarch," the boy replied and made his way back towards our own fires.

"The rest of you follow him, I want the camp roused early. We need to be at sea in time to round the point by dawn to get the advantage of the early breeze. Bank up the fires so that they'll still burn when we're gone, make them think we're still asleep."

The group moved off in silence after taking a last glance at the watch fires of the great fleet, dispersed for miles along a series of beaches, unlike ours with our pitifully few fires and five triremes. Lysias walked back with me.

"It's not as bad as it looks, Mandrocles, there's a good few hours between them and us and with a fleet that big strung out over that length of coast it'll take them ages to organise their order of sailing. With us we just run our five into the water and we're off round the point, and it would take a very special boat to overhaul the Athene Nike."

We had reached the fires and my bedroll; he took a few steps then turned back,

"Unless of course they're thinking the same, in which case they'll send out some of their fastest ships early and then we'll all need some of your luck. Oh, and Mandrocles, once you've got the boy stored safe with his sister on board check your gear. Tomorrow those of us who fight will be wearing full hoplite armour so have yours ready and a good edge to your father's sword. Sleep well."

With that he stalked off to his bedroll leaving me to what was left of the night. I didn't sleep.

Perhaps I may have dozed in snatches because I suddenly became aware of the rowers moving towards the boats. Each man had with him his oar, a cushion of some kind of animal hide and the rope oar loops that attached the oar to the thole pin. For such rowdy and rough men they moved with an orderliness that must have developed from years of training, and once the boats had been run down the beach, they boarded in fixed order. First, the Thalomoi, who sat at the bottom of the hold: they'd spend the day in the dark and heat of the hold with their faces close up to the arses of the Zugioi on the row above. During the day, particularly in action, they'd row in the heat as the sweat and worse dripped down from the rowers above. If the ship was holed and went down they would drown down there, and if the ship was taken they'd be captured or killed. A rower on the lowest bench truly knew Hades. After the Zugioi of the middle tier, the last of the rowers aboard, the upper rows, were the Thranitai, so called because of the little stools they sat on to row and who rowed through the outrigger that extended the width of the deck. These men were the rowing elite, hard as nails and aware of their superiority. They led the strokes, followed the shouts and commands of the Bosun, Theodorus. They were the difference between life and death in battle and received a bonus with their wages. Being Athenians they were free men, not captives or slaves, and if a boat could be said to truly have a heart they were it.

Cimon, complaining, and Elpinice, still sleepy, were stored safely with their gear. There was a morning haze so we couldn't see across the straits and had no idea if there was a swift and deadly flotilla already heading for us. I struggled into my gear then sat with the other nine armoured men in the centre of the prow, keeping as still as possible so as not to disturb the balance of the ship, the stroke of the rowers or worse. Sitting in heavy bronze and leather armour on a flimsy deck in hostile sea is not a comfortable experience. To be out of the boat and in the water is to die, pulled down by the weight of metal into the deep as the lungs fill and the chest bursts. I've never overcome the fear of this; familiarity with something like this doesn't improve it. Strangely, unlike Athenians, most Persian oarsmen and marines can't swim, never bother to learn. When I asked Theodorus about this one night in a tavern he shrugged his shoulders and said,

"Why bother, it just puts off the inevitable."

He, though, I noticed, could swim, and very well at that.

We stayed close to the shore, scarcely moving until, faintly at first, it became imperceptibly lighter, then a pale glimpse of the sun, still low over the water, then at once as if by magic light flashing and sparkling. At a great shout from Theodorus the rowers' chant started, slow and deep at first, then moving to full speed with the chant of "O opop O opop" rasping from one hundred and seventy pairs of straining lungs. We gathered speed towards the point with the other four ships keeping pace.

The dark blue of the sky paled as the sunlight dazzled from the sea. Across the straits the coast was now clearly visible. I didn't need the shouts from the archers in the stern to warn me of what I and every man on board could now see plainly. Astern of us, in the open sea spreading for what seemed miles, there were flashes of light twinkling as if the stars had descended from the heavens to rest and splash on the waters.

There, in the distance was the great Persian fleet at sea. The sun was glistening on prows, rams and weapons. Not just a flotilla, the full fleet. The General had been right the Great King wanted his revenge.

For an instant I was gripped by the terror the god Pan curses us with when he makes us mad. Despite the fact that we were in the open sea I felt trapped and helpless, unable to move, cased in heavy armour, doomed. My bladder felt itself bursting but my mouth was so dry I could hardly get my tongue to move, sweat seemed suddenly to run from every crease and crack in my body although the day was hardly yet warm. Now I'm older I know this is how we all feel as we wait, and that it's only when it begins that we begin to move as normal. But that day was my first experience of the panic. I turned to Kleitus, the grizzled marine next to me.

"Why don't we increase speed? They'll catch us."

"Not today, young'un, however quick they come it won't be today and we'll be in port tonight. Put that sword away, you'll cut somebody if the ship rolls."

He turned away, spat over the side and settled back into the decking, trying to find a comfortable position. He was right, they came no nearer that day; in fact I think we increased the distance. Our small squadron was quick and well handled; the other ships not quite as swift as the Athene Nike but fast enough.

When we reached the port of Khardia they were over the horizon but the day after they would arrive and we'd be trapped. There are days of fear and indecision in every life but this was one of the worst in mine. I've been in much more dangerous situations, like later at Marathon, but have never felt as helpless. Still sometimes that day returns to me in dreams: the same dream, a rising panic, dry mouth, full bladder. Now I'm an old man it can still make me piss my bed. But when you're young you soon come round and by the time we came into the harbour I was pretty much recovered. Cimon had come up on deck and was looking for signs of his father on the quayside. The quay looked suspiciously empty and for such a well built and modern harbour there were very few ships.

We dragged the triremes up the slipway by the boat sheds. Lysias ordered the crews to stay in the port and for the boats to be kept in a state of readiness to leave. The oarsmen were given permission to go in relays to the few open taverns that fringed the quayside but not to get drunk. Theodorus relayed this to our crew.

"Any of you buggers who even look drunk will be flogged senseless. Believe me, lads, there'll be work to do soon. Keep the boats in sight, be ready to get back at the sound of my whistle and leave the whores alone."

I followed Lysias and the other trierarchs up into the town to the General's residence. Elpinice talked excitedly, delighted at the change of routine. Cimon was quiet. I noted that the town too was strangely quiet, doors shut, little sign of lights or life, as if the people had left. Khardia was usually a noisy bustling town. The General's uncle had built it when he constructed the wall across the isthmus.

There couldn't have been a greater contrast between the palace and the deserted streets. The corridors were packed with slaves, servants and soldiers shifting furniture, boxes and the like and getting in each other's way. It had the appearance of a place just about in control of itself but gripped with a feverish excitement.

Lysias led us up to a large chamber across the courtyard towards the back of the building. In this room amidst soldiers humping boxes of scrolls Miltiades stood at a table looking at a chart, giving directions to a knot of officers, among whom I was pleased to see Metopes. Cimon ran to his father, dignity and responsibility temporarily forgotten. Elpinice looked at me, rolled her eyes and fluttered her long lashes. The General ruffled his son's hair and then turned to us.

"Just in time, gentlemen, things have moved more quickly than I expected."

There was a newly stitched gash above his right eyebrow and a dressing on his right arm.

"They landed a raiding party just after you left. I'm not sure if it's the start of a full scale invasion but we had to move out quickly. Lucky we did. As it was we had to fight off a group that surprised us not far from the palace. Seems that the Great King is not in quite the forgiving mood that Metiochus thought he would be."

Metiochus, who was unscathed, ignored this as he had more pointedly ignored his brother. He did, however, exchange a brief smile with his sister and managed a leer for me.

"So our own plans have changed. Cimon I'm sorry but we can't wait for your mother to reach us; I've sent messengers to meet her en route and escort her to her father's. She'll be safe there till things settle down. The Persians have no quarrel with King Olorus of Thrace. I'm sending most of our troops to her along with whatever they can carry from here."

I noticed a look of satisfaction cross Metiochus' face at the mention of Hegesipyle, Cimon's mother, being sent back to her father. Miltiades had divorced his mother, whose father, Hippias, was the disposed Athenian tyrant. Hippias had wasted no time and had her married to Aciatides, King of Lampacsus, the rival in trade and politics of the Chersonese, and I wondered, not for the last time, if Metiochus' loyalties were truly with his father and not his mother. His father continued,

"It just remains for us to get away from here and establish another base for ourselves, perhaps on Imbros, where we can sit things out."

"Father, that's madness, you either make peace with the king or you run forever. If he's followed you here there'll be no peace anywhere. For all we know his fleet could be on Imbros and Lemnos now. Send him Cimon as a guarantee of good behaviour – I'll take him for you. My grandfather will intercede on your behalf and by giving him your precious little son you establish good will. Darius is a practical man; you have skills he can use."

Miltiades seemed not to react to this but to stoop as if deep in thought. This was not characteristic. Before Metiochus could further press his case, Lysias broke the silence.

"Lord Metiochus is right about the speed of the fleet, they are less than a day behind us. Unless we move at first light we'll be boxed in. If there are strong Persian raiding parties heading overland we must either sail now or push overland into Thrace and join King Olorus."

Metiochus cut across him:

"If you try to link up with that barbarian, father, the Great King will follow you. Take my advice; let me take Cimon to my grandfather. He can bring Mandrocles with him as a wet nurse if he likes, the boy's obviously attached to him."

A spasm of anger, one I'd seen before, briefly contorted the General's face.

"Yes, and you'd like that too, Metiochus. But no, Cimon won't be going to visit your grandfather and his master."

At the word master, and its implications, it was Metiochus' face that coloured but Miltiades continued,

"No, we sail before first light. I'll not stay here to be hunted down. Lysias, Metiochus and I will join you on the Athene Nike. Metopes, have your men ready to march for Thrace by dawn. By noon this place will be crawling with Persians. Anything we can't take, we burn. There's much to do. Mandrocles, see that Cimon and Elpinice are fed and kept safe tonight. You've already done it once, shouldn't be too difficult. Metiochus, stay and help me. Lysias, get back to the harbour and make sure the ships are provisioned for a long voyage. Go all of you."

As I left with Cimon and a reluctant Elpinice, Metopes touched my arm.

"Go, with luck, Mandrocles, I doubt we will meet again. It seems that we both travel dangerous paths by ways we do not know."

CHAPTER 9

Metopes was right on both counts. It's the nature of the gods that their humour is satisfied by our misfortune. Tired as I was I had little sleep in the corridor outside the room in which the children slept. For one thing, I had for the first time worn hoplite armour for a full day. The straps and plate edges chafed the skin of my neck, shoulders and hips. Although my father was close to the same build as I, he had more weight and muscle and the armour had been made to fit him. So despite adjusting the strapping, the plates shifted, leaving me raw. But even if it had fitted like the armour of Achilles I wouldn't have slept as the night was soon disturbed.

The noise started faintly like the rumble of distant thunder but gradually grew in intensity as it came nearer. It was the sound of the lost, the sound of panic, the noise of fear. The mainland Greeks who had followed the General's uncle to his new kingdom of the Chersonese as colonists were converging on Khardia hoping to escape on one of the ships in the harbour. They'd brought their families out from Athens, a large number of them were ex-soldiers who had fought for the General or his uncle. The obligation was clear: if the General was to flee the island to escape the revenge of King Darius, he should take them.

The first of them arrived from nearby farms, with families and belongings on carts, shortly after midnight. Those with personal connections to the General, or who had rendered private service to him or his uncle, surrounded the palace. Others clogged up the streets leading to the port, or made for the harbour to find space on the ships. Soon there were hundreds pleading and begging for refuge. Who could blame them? They'd heard the tales brought from the islands of the Great King's revenge. On my own home, Samos, it was said that the Persians formed a human chain that stretched from side to side of the island and walked its length to flush out any rebels. I feared for my own family, my father had been exiled so he should have been safe, but then again he had been no friend of Aiakes and the oligarch. Our island is mountainous so whether the Persians actually did this I am not sure, but there had been savage killing and reprisal in all the territories where the revolt had taken hold. The destruction of Miletos was not the only atrocity.

From the cries of those outside it was clear that they expected the same fate, and the hammering at the doors and shutters increased in volume. So, sleep was not possible and when Lysias, looking haggard and weary, came to wake me I was already up and armed. Neither was I alone as Elpinice appeared out of the shadows dressed for a journey.

"Mandrocles, today please watch me as carefully as you do my brother; don't let Metiochus take me with him on his boat."

"There is no fear of that, lady, for we all go aboard the Athene Nike together."

Such conversations were difficult, not only because of her teasing ways, it was difficult to know if one was talking to a young woman or a girl and, besides, I had no experience of talking to either women or girls of rank. But this one was difficult for a different reason, as she was afflicted by fear, but not the fear that threatened the rest of us. Her eyes were red and her cheeks slightly swollen as if she had been wracked by some violent emotion.

"Whatever might happen at the harbour, Mandrocles, swear that you will see me safe on the Athene Nike alongside Cimon and my father."

I had no time to give her further reassurance: Lysias was upon us.

"It is good you are ready, lady, the General wishes you to know that we leave soon. We will face some difficulty reaching the harbour. Mandrocles, arm yourself, then wake Master Cimon and report to the General with the children."

Cimon as usual slept soundly and took some waking but treated the event as a game, showing no fear at all as we pushed our way through the confused and crowded corridors towards the General's private room. The children moved quickly but my limbs were stiff with tension. My bowels felt loose and the leather and plate of the armour rubbed my skin through the linen tunic I wore under it.

Miltiades stood in the centre of the room calmly giving orders to his staff. He was wearing a heavy cloak over full armour and ready to move.

"There may be problems on the way to the harbour, Mandrocles; the soldiers will clear a path. Make sure you keep the children with you in the centre. Stay close to Lysias and when we reach the harbour follow him to the Athene Nike and get them on board. We will form a perimeter to keep the crowds back while we get you and our gear on the boats. Metiochus and I will follow. Move out."

But, before he could lead off, Metiochus stopped him.

"Father, let me command my own ship. I am your eldest son, I deserve that honour. You left me behind last time. Give me the command my birth demands."

Miltiades seemed to hesitate, torn between the need to move and doubts about his son.

"Let me take the Kouphotate, it's as fast as its name suggests. Alexius is a skilled trierarch."

"All right take it; but now draw your blade; we move."

Using their shields and the flat of their swords the soldiers forced the crowd back from the door and we set off. Outside it was cold. The weather had changed and a fine rain was falling. From my position in the centre of a moving diamond of armed men I saw a mass of anxious faces, arms and shoulders of people being driven back, heard the cries, shrieks and odd, clear words shouted at the General. By the time we reached the narrow lane that sloped down towards the docks, the going was slower. The press of the crowd thickened and the space at the centre of the diamond was squeezed. At times when we were suddenly forced to stop the children and I were pushed against the men in front.

I noticed during one pause there was blood on the street. The soldiers were no longer using just the flat of their swords. By now Miltiades, Metiochus and I had all drawn our swords. Cimon and Elpinice stayed calm, walking on either side of me each clutching a small bundle of belongings. I don't know how long it took to reach the harbour but by the time we had pushed our way there the night was less dark so it must have been close to dawn. I was soaked and my head rang from the noise of howls of pain, curses and the clash of weapons. We forced our way to the harbour's edge. By the slipway, beneath the boat sheds a circle of soldiers and oarsmen held back a pushing and baying mob. The other side of the harbour was thick with people trying to board the few merchant ships, whose crews were struggling to cast off while keeping the boats from being overloaded. One heavily laden ship, low in the water, had got away and was wallowing towards the harbour mouth and the open sea. As I watched in horror one of the others, an ancient looking pentecontor, with people clinging to the side, began to list and then turned over. The screaming of those falling into the water or clinging to the ship as it began to capsize cut through to us, and the pressure on our thin line of shields increased. Miltiades pushed his way to the front, seized a shield off an injured soldier and bellowed to the troops.

"No time for delicacy, use the points, kill if you have to, it's live or die with us now."

He then began to chant his war cry, which was taken up by our troops and echoed by those at the boats. It must have been slaughter; the quayside was slippery with blood. Elpinice went down and I only just managed to pull her to her feet saving her being crushed beneath the trampling hobnailed war sandals of the soldiers and ripped apart by the mob beyond. We covered the distance between the quayside and the boats quickly, carried there by the impetus of our charge. Then we were behind the wall of soldiers and sailors guarding the boats. The Scythian archers were firing directly from the prow of the boats into the crowd. I saw a young, well dressed man trying to pull an old man, perhaps his father, back out of danger. An arrow took him in the cheek, smashed through his teeth and the head came out from his throat in a gush of blood. He and his father went down and disappeared from sight. Strange, I only ever saw him or knew he existed for those few seconds yet, as I write, I can clearly recall his face these fifty years later.

By the Athene Nike I saw Ariston calmly ordering our putting to sea and made my way towards him. Suddenly Metiochus was beside me, long hair matted to his face and shoulders by the rain. His sword blade was bloody and there was blood on his face. He made a grab for Elpinice.

"She comes with me."

Elpinice screamed and pulled back as Metiochus lunged towards her. I forced my way between them.

For an instance we stood face to face breathing heavily and I saw from his eyes that he would kill me, a blood rage had taken him. Then with all the pushing and shoving we were jostled apart. I saw Theodorus lift Elpinice above his head and pass her up to a much scarred oarsman with the build of a heavy wrestler, who set her down gently on the deck. I was relieved to see Cimon by her side for in the last moments I'd forgotten him. Then Miltiades' voice in my ear,

"They're on board, now get on yourself, Mandrocles, we need to go."

I followed him through the water to the boat side and was helped up by rough hands. From the deck I could see the hell we were leaving. Miltiades' troops holding back the crowd to cover our flight. Our five black hulled ships began to pull towards the harbour mouth. On the quayside all attention now focused on the few merchant ships struggling to pull away from the dock. They were low in the water, the decks filled with fighting people. I saw that one of the harbour towers was burning. The rain beat down and worsened visibility so our eyes didn't have to endure these dreadful images for too long. But even beyond the harbour wall the wails of despair and cries of pain and anger followed us across the sea.

One last detail stands clear. A man stood on the wall at the harbour mouth; he must have scrambled along the breakwater to get there. He made no attempt to reach our boat but stood quite still with one hand on the metal bracket that held the torch lighting the harbour edge at night. Weirdly lit, with his tall frame draped with a long dark cloak, standing still, contrasting with the noise and panic from the harbour. We passed close enough for him to jump on board but he made no move, just stared fixedly at the General standing in the prow. I saw their eyes meet then the man spoke, his words carried clearly.

"Traitor Miltiades, betrayer of friend and foe alike, think not that you escape. There's nowhere to hide. The king's vengeance follows you as surely as my curse."

Then he turned and walked slowly back along the breakwater, towards the nightmare which was the quayside. Miltiades wrapped his cloak around himself and sat brooding in the trierarch's chair. None dared approach him, none spoke, but the curse moved among us as real as any of the crew.

Our small flotilla soon swept past the heavily laden merchant ship we'd seen leave port before us. If anything, it was now lower in the water, its deck a swarming mass of confusion. I watched from the deck rail next to Lysias, who had been displaced from his chair by the General.

"These seas will have them over if they don't head for land soon. I'd rather take my chances on land with the Great King's men than sail with that ship of fools."

"Where will we make landfall tonight, Captain?"

"I don't know. Where's safe now? We don't have any real position for their fleet. If this mist doesn't clear we'll have to stop rowing or founder. The swell's too heavy and we're at the end of the season when triremes should sail at all, particularly the distance and amount of water we have to cross. Lucky we decided to strap the ships with six sets of under belts instead of four."

Being used to the ship now I understood the significance of these six heavy twisted ropes fitted low in the ship and stretched from stem to stern to help protect the hull from the murderous force of rough seas. I also noticed that the holes for the lower oars, which were now only half a metre above the water line, had been sealed by leather bags attached to the oars to keep the water out. Lysias said nothing more, just gazed over the side as the General brooded, and Ariston skilfully kept course with minor adjustments to the twin rudders, one on each side of the stern. But as I stared into the mist and rain I remembered what Theodorus had told me on my first day on the Athene Nike: these were fighting boats designed for short trips at speed, good at withstanding impact but vulnerable in open sea. Good fighting platforms but poor bad weather ships.

Soon we cut our speed, not wanting to lose our course, and the boat bobbed on the swell as we sat drenched on the deck. The sun awnings of the upper deck were soon sodden and the ships began to take on water, which we could hear sloshing about in the bilges. Even the hardiest of the oarsmen stopped cursing and lapsed into sullen, miserable silence. Only Cimon and Elpinice in their makeshift leather tent by the storage were unaffected; they slept. The pitching of the boat made some of us, myself first, vomit up what little our empty stomachs contained. I think there is probably only one thing worse than being stuck on a pitching vessel, soaked and sick, unable to see more than a hundred metres, with the cold grey waters rolling all around. Yet that thing was also with us that rough, early morning.

Because somewhere out there, beyond sight but perhaps very near was the Persian fleet. A fleet manned by Phoenician sailors, experienced crews with centuries of seafaring in their blood. Hundreds of ships covering a large area and us unable to move at speed or even know which direction was safe to set a course. But beyond this, and eating away at the back of each man's mind, not the least Miltiades', a remembrance of the curse. A curse made stronger by the method of our leaving. In our haste to get away we had neglected to pour a libation to the gods into water and speak the necessary prayers to invoke their protection. There are no men on earth as superstitious as seamen and to sail without observing the correct rites of propitiation was to invite disaster and death in the deeps of the sea. The Persians would not have failed to make offerings to their savage and merciless gods.

So we drifted on; forever so it seemed, but luckily the gods are fickle and soon grow bored and the weather front passed over. To our relief when the skies cleared we found ourselves alone on the sea and Theodorus set the rowers to work. Sometime after midday the sun appeared and we raised the sail and stopped to dine on some hard bread, olives and onions washed down by watered wine. The strength returned to our limbs and courage to our hearts as we dried out.

After we'd eaten, Ariston checked the course, Theodorus called the stroke and the Athene Nike moved on. We followed the coast, retracing our journey of the day before. A risky decision, but Ariston, Miltiades and Lysias decided that as long as visibility was good and there was no sign of the Persians, we should put off heading out to open sea for as long as possible. If our luck held we'd cross the straits, follow the coast the other side past ancient, broken Troy until we could see the island of Tenedos. Then we would head west out to sea towards Lemnos hoping to make landfall at the city of Poliochni, where Miltiades had a house. On Lemnos he could decide where next while we provisioned and repaired the ships.

That night we dared not beach the ships or light fires but spent an anxious night moored in a bay near where the river Scammander empties itself into the sea. The day dawned fine and we were away early. Again, the horizon was clear, we made good progress and our spirits lifted. Around midday I was standing in the stern showing the island of Tenedos to Cimon and Elpinice, who had insisted to her father that she be allowed on deck.

My father had schooled me keenly and beaten into me the ancient poets and their tales of the age of heroes. I was explaining to the children how in the last year of the Trojan War the cunning Odysseus had travelled with the son of Achilles to Tenedos to persuade the diseased and marooned hero Philoctetes to return to the war with them, the gods having foretold that without his aid Troy would not fall. I was explaining to Cimon that the Greeks had earlier left Philoctetes alone on the island because he had been bitten by a poisonous snake and they could no longer bear his cries of pain or the smell of his rotting snake bitten leg. So they had left him with only his great bow to help him keep alive. That bow was now needed to end the siege. Cimon listened politely but Elpinice was the more interested. She was asking me why if the Greek heroes were so clever they'd left the bow there in the first place.

Then there was a shout from the trireme sailing next in line. All heads turned towards the stern to try to understand the shouted message. Elpinice screamed,

"There, look there."

I turned and saw her beautiful face, eyes wide, framed by dark hair, then followed the direction she was pointing. Sailing out from behind the far promontory on Tenedos and following a course to intercept us were warships.

CHAPTER 10

Poets say that at the instant of his death, the first man you kill up close is more intimately linked to you than any lover in the act of congress. That may be true for some, not for me. For me there was no time for sensual reflections. Perhaps the poets never actually killed with their own hands; although the Athenian poet who was later to be my friend certainly would have known what he was writing about. Later I was to stand next to him in the shield line, shoulder to shoulder as we both dealt the blows that send a man's soul wailing to Hades, as ancient poets would put it. To me the experience lives fresh in my memory but at the time the sensation was more like the feeling you get when trying to correct the course of a horse at full gallop; excitement and instinct, no thought. When later I did have time to reflect on killing, to my surprise it seemed to me to have been easier than I thought; perhaps I was good at it.

Fighting at sea takes some getting used to, mainly I think because it takes so long to begin; the waiting is the worst part of it. We watched the warships emerge in line from behind the promontory. Not the whole fleet but enough, about thirty of them, too many to fight anyway. At least we didn't have to waste much time on what our best course of action might be. We couldn't change course and run, it would slow us down, and besides that way would most probably lead us to the main part of the Persian fleet. So before the General even roared out the orders we knew what they would be.

"Open sea, set course for Lemnos. Rowing master, fast stroke."

This way if we were quick they wouldn't intercept and we'd outrun them. Even if some of their quicker ships tried to cut us off then perhaps we could ram them and still get away.

"Ariston, course straight to Lemnos, and rowing master you make sure your rowers keep the pace. Marines, to your positions and keep still and hold steady. We hit anything that gets in our way."

Apart from acknowledgement there was no reply. The rate of the oar stroke steadily intensified as the men worked to keep the increasing pace set by Theodorus. The speed smoothly accelerated to a measured rhythm with no missed strokes, no oars skimming above the surface or clashing with each other. The top level oarsmen, the Thranitai, looking almost relaxed and rowing within themselves, set the example, letting the chant control their motion, breathing in on the "O" and exhaling with "opop". It sounded like some great fire-breathing serpent approaching, the O opop O opop getting faster by degrees.

I chivvied Cimon and Elpinice into the hold, both protesting. Then as I turned to go back on deck I heard Cimon say as much to himself as to his sister or me,

"If we are boarded I will fight alongside my father."

I remember I turned back to look and saw that he had a hunting knife in his hand. He caught my eye.

"Be lucky, Mandrocles."

On deck I took my shield from the outrigger and clasping my spear with the other hand gingerly made my way round Theodorus and between the banks of oars to the stern. As I passed I heard some call to me,

"Bring us luck Mandrocles."

In the stern I took my place next to Lysias on my right side and the veteran Kleitus on my left and we waited, keeping as still as we could. Behind us our small squadron moved in line, the great bronze ram of each ship gleaming as it cut its path through the water, leaving a wake of foam on either side, marking our track as we headed out into the open sea. Our line of battle was: Athene Nike, then behind us Thetis, then Hera's Grace and Amphitrite. Last in line, although in our original sailing order it should have been third, came Kouphotate, commanded by Metiochus. Despite its name, meaning lightness, it looked as if it was unable to keep the pace.

Away towards the island of Tenedos were the Persians also in line and steering a course to intercept, and looking as if they would succeed. Two straight lines converging on a point, it reminded me of the metaphysics of triangles that my father had drawn for me in the sand when I was little. Something he had got from his father's friend the thinker and oddball Pythagoras. To pass the time I tried to remember what the point of this had been. All this talk of angles and celestial measurement hadn't done Pythagoras any good, whatever the point had been. I remembered enough though to recognise that the pattern that the ships made seemed to correspond to what my father had said was the great right angle. This apparently had some great significance for the bean hater that I could never understand; now suddenly it seemed to make sense.

So, through the morning we sailed on towards our point of impact. The weather was fine now, the year being old enough for the sun to be not too hot at this time in the morning. There was also I think a breeze. But so slow, so much time to kill, as my guts tied themselves in knots, my palms sweated and my bladder seemed to refill immediately each time I emptied it.

I turned to Lysias, who seemed to feel none of this, just stood, face immobile, and asked him,

"What if they do manage to cut across our path?"

He shrugged his shoulders.

"Then we kill them."

"We can't kill all of them."

Kleitus looked across me at Lysias, winked and said,

"Then we kill as many as we can, eh Captain?"

"That's right, we kill as many as we can."

They both grinned and went back to staring out to sea. Behind us I noticed the Kouphotate was falling further behind and wondered if I should tell the General but I didn't. Perhaps the mood of the rest of the crew infected me because I suddenly realised it didn't matter what I said or did, it wouldn't change anything. So I stood at the rail and watched, watched the Persian ships getting bigger, saw detail more clearly, saw the sunlight flash off individual weapons, picked out the detail of armour and bearded faces. Then suddenly the world seemed to speed up. I noticed that our archers were testing their bow strings and checking the flights of their arrows. Noticed Ariston make a signal to Theodorus, noticed the rhythm of the stroke change.

Soon there were only a few field lengths separating the Athene Nike from the leading Persian ships. Six of them in a group had moved out ahead of the pack and it was clear that the leading two of these would beat us in our race. They would cross our path and block the way to freedom.

Miltiades stood up from the Captain's chair and shouted,

"Diekplous."

Just one word yet whether we would live or die was decided. Back then I didn't understand the consequences of that word despite having heard it in the conversations of the oarsmen. It was a manoeuvre that only a skilled and veteran trireme crew could execute and even then fraught with danger as it involved sailing in between two ships in an opposing fleet and at the last moment swinging either left or right to ram one of them in the stern. Lysias said in a low tone, almost under his breath, to no one in particular,

"Dangerous that, but then there's no other choice."

I asked him what would happen.

"Our only chance is to sink or at least cripple those bastards in front. If the Diekplous works we can ram one quickly, then back oars and leave it to sink or flounder."

"What about the other one?"

"Be plenty of time to think about that if we manage to get the first."

He turned away, the conversation finished, and shouted an order for the marines to keep still as we approached the enemy. We sat and watched as the scene slowly but inexorably unfolded before our eyes. Yes, waiting's the hard part; you watch something you can't change like in a nightmare. Ahead of us the two fastest Persian ships began to cut us off. It seemed now that four of them were well ahead of the others, sailing in a line with about the length of two ships between each. Our line of sail was different: to our left and half a length behind was the Thetis. I could clearly see the strokes of her oars and the marines crowded in the prow. Behind us in similar formation was the Amphitrite with the Hera's Grace on her left flank. So, if we kept our current course it would be four against four. The fast Kouphotate had lost more ground, it seemed almost as if it wasn't even trying, and was now several lengths behind and in danger of being intercepted by the second group of five Persian ships. The captains of these ships seemed to have realised they couldn't catch us so had altered course to take a shorter route that would cut off the Kouphotate. If the General had any idea that his son's ship had fallen behind or if he wondered why it had slowed down he

97

showed no sign of it. He sat in the trierarchs' chair, upright, still and terrible, seeming like the rams to be cast in bronze.

So, we waited as the sun climbed and the ships maintained their courses at a consistent pace so as to conserve the strength of the rowers for the final burst to impact. No point in anything else. We couldn't outrun them, nor they us. The dice were cast, the gods had decided. Our fate lay in the skills of the helmsman, Ariston, who would order our turn when he decided the moment to ram.

To my left I could see the prow of the Thetis, its ram partly submerged. The murderous bronze ram with its three chisel like blades, stretching seven feet from the forward tip of the deck. The combination of the ram and the talismanic eye of the goddess painted above it on the prow made the ship seem like some grim living incarnation of approaching death.

So we moved towards each other as if to the rhythm of the harvest-time dance in the satyr plays. But such a grim dance. My mouth was so dry that my tongue seemed to stick to its roof whilst sweat soaked the linen corselet beneath my leather and bronze armour. I couldn't stop my hands fiddling with my breast plate, trying to adjust its position. I felt a hard shove on my shoulders.

"Stop that fucking twitching, it's driving me mad."

Kleitus had never before spoken to me so roughly. I felt shame and tried to remain still. I wondered if my father had also stood or sat in this same armour and felt his bones turn to water as he waited. I could not imagine he had; surely he would have stood tall and grim ready to deal death. I prayed to Poseidon, ocean shaker, to give me courage.

But time did pass. By the time the sun stood directly overhead cooking us in our leather and bronze we closed with the Persians. Now they were near we could see them as individual men like us, waiting to kill. Then about three lengths from the gap between their leading two ships, Lysias shouted,

"Marines, arm and brace."

He pulled the Corinthian helmet down from the back of his head so that his entire face was covered, leaving only the eyes visible. He stood carefully, legs braced, his left arm through the two handles of the heavy bronze and leather shield holding the long thrusting spear with its lizard sticker butt spike in his right hand. I and the other ten marines stood like him, Kleitus, Lysias and me in the stern, the rest in the prow nearer the point of impact.

The distance was short now. The Thetis had slightly changed its course, heading for the gap between the third and fourth Persian ships followed by the Hera's Grace. Lysias turned his head to look behind him at the General, who nodded. Ariston shouted to Theodorus,

"Get your rowers moving. Ramming stroke."

The shouts and fluting increased in pace and the ships picked up speed. A trireme needs to ram at a speed of not less than ten knots. If it's under that, the impact will break up the attacking ship, even one as tightly corseted as ours. But the Athene Nike, swift and graceful, surged forwards. I remember thinking the wine dark sea looked like a polished mirror when Miltiades started to sing the battle hymn, the paean. It was taken up by the marines and rang across the short space of water between us and the nearest Persian ships, which had now adjusted their course and were heading directly at us.

I pulled my father's great war helmet down and over my face. Inside the helmet it was dark, sound was muffled, vision restricted. It made me feel alone, isolated and confined. I watched as we passed between the two Persians, felt rather than saw some arrows fly between the boats, heard Theodorus roar out the stroke. Then just as we seemed to be through them with a lurch we swung to the right; now the stern of a Persian ship, suddenly big, filled the horizon, its archers loosing shaft after shaft at Ariston and the General in their seats. At the last moment at a command from Ariston the rowers ceased their stroke.

Then we hit. The deck shook and I experienced for the first time the moment of impact: heard the terrible sounds as the ram cuts and smashes its way through the light planking of a doomed ship, ripping out its guts, smashing the rowers on the bottom tier to bloody pulp. For an instant that seemed to last forever the two ships cleaved to each other. This was the most dangerous time in the ramming as, if we failed to disentangle, they would board our prow while their sister ship boarded our stern.

"Back oars. Back oars."

At Ariston's shout the rowers moved to reverse stroke and with a grating and splitting sound the ram came loose and we pulled away leaving water pouring through the ragged black hole that the ram had opened. The impact had thrown one of their archers into the sea and he disappeared under the boat. We backed water rapidly and swung about, and now we were head to head with the other Persian ship, which had also backed water in order not to overshoot us. There was now only one possible course of action, to ram the second ship head on, the impact of which would probably shatter both hulls.

"Ramming speed."

We surged forwards and I braced for impact and death. A slight change in course, at the last instant we veered to the left and I heard Ariston, Theodorus and the General and Lysias all shout at once,

"Dock oars."

Then almost all our oarsmen on the right rowing benches pulled their oars in as far as they could. This was accompanied by a screeching and shattering noise from the Persian ship as our reinforced prow sheered through the banks of Persian oars still in the water. Their rowers were still at full stroke in an attempt to ram us head on. The damage done to human flesh and bones by this manoeuvre is terrible to see. Their left tiers of oarsmen were smashed by the ends of their own oars, arms mangled, ribs staved in and crushed necks and heads broken. The screaming was terrible. I could see blood splashing through their oar ports as we bumped and scrapped along their side. The manoeuvre caused terrible loss of life and injury crippling their ship, but it also slowed us. While our stern rubbed and grated against theirs and the freedom of the open sea beckoned we were grappled. Ropes, iron grabs, even hands tried to tie our fast ship to their ruined one.

Back then ships of the Persian navy carried a greater complement of marines so the scene that faced us across a few feet on their stern platform seemed packed thick with armed men. Then for a moment there was a panic as often happens in combat. The men who an instant before had been frenziedly trying to secure our boat so they could board hesitated and we stood facing each other. In this moment as we stood tentative I saw a Persian archer notch a shaft to his bow, saw it take flight at short range, heard the buzzing like an angry wasp as it flew past my ear followed by a soft thud and an intake of breath behind me. I watched as he fitted another arrow. In my ear, someone, Miltiades I think, shouted,

"Stick him, somebody."

And then it started. In instinct I launched my thrusting spear at the archer as if it were a javelin. He

101

loosed the arrow at me and moved his head. I heard his arrow hit home to my left at the same time as I saw my spear point take the man behind the archer in the neck, below the chin strap, and blood spray like a fountain from his throat. Kleitus lurched into me forcing me back and I lost my footing on the slippery deck.

Then they came over the side. Miltiades took my place next to Lysias and locked shields. Both of them pushed forwards, weight behind their heavy shields, catching the Persians jumping onto our deck off balance, stabbing with their sword points deep into the stomachs of the staggering marines. Then our ship lurched and moved on, our sailors having cut the ropes with axes and fended off the Persian boat with their oars, leaving trapped three surviving marines who had leapt onto our deck. I had drawn my sword when one of them, a heavily bearded man in the gear of an officer, jumped into Lysias. Their shields clashed, Lysias staggered back, his sword running red, the wounded Persian remained upright.

"Finish him, Mandrocles."

I stepped forwards, weight behind my shield. The officer must have been unsteady from his wounds. I caught his shield with mine and thrust over the rim of it into the gap between the helmet and the shoulder guard like my father had taught me. The sword slipped in easy and he staggered back, shield down, his body defenceless; I could see the look of surprise in his eyes like a man wakening from sleep. I pushed my sword through his gut just below the rib cage and he went down; first to his knees then onto his side, hands scrabbling at his belly.

I looked round and it was all over and in less than the time it would take a man to drain a cup of wine. Lysias and the General wiped their swords on the tunics of the dead Persians. Theodorus was calling the beat, and Ariston set course for Lemnos. The two enemy craft blocking the path of Thetis and Hera's Grace had no appetite for battle and let our ships sail between them contenting themselves with letting a few arrows fly.

But behind us like flies on a cow's eyeball, five Persian ships surrounded Kouphotate. There was no evidence of fighting. It was as if Metiochus had wanted to be caught and I was glad of it, they were welcome to him. I had never felt life so keenly than in those last few minutes. I had seen and felt only what was right in front of me, nothing else existed.

When I pushed my father's helmet back off my head it was like re-entering the world and the rest of the boat and its crew came back into focus. We threw the dead Persians from the deck. A wineskin was passed around and that taste of rough watered wine was the taste of life of survival: nothing could taste better. Those with appetite ate some salt fish and barley groats. The oarsmen rowed in relay so that everyone got a chance to eat. We were able to do this as only two of the Persian ships had a chance of catching us and it was apparent that these didn't fancy it.

We cleared the deck of the dead and removed the stains of their dying. We had only two dead; Kleitus and an archer. Strangely I had watched the man who killed both of them loose the fatal arrows. He, I think, survived and was probably now helping to clear the decks of his crippled ship of its own more numerous dead.

Five of our rowers who failed to pull in their oars in time had been badly broken up. It was probable that three would die and certain that the other two would never row again. I think for a time after I lost my wits. I found it difficult to regain my sense of normality. It was as if I existed in a different world as I stood and

103

watched my companions work the boat. I was brought out of my reveries by Miltiades, who jabbed my left shoulder with his finger.

"Wipe Kleitus' blood from yourself, Mandrocles. Or soon you'll smell rank."

I hadn't even noticed that my left arm was covered in blood from when Kleitus had fallen against me, an arrow shaft protruding from the eye slit in his helmet.

" Clean yourself up and let Cimon up on deck."

There was a pause then he said,

"And Mandrocles, you fought well today like one born to kill; that will serve you well in future."

He meant it kindly but the words troubled me. I recognised that it had come easily to me and once the waiting ended so did my fear but I felt that I'd put a shadow between what I had now become and the boy I'd been.

I remember little else about the day only that by evening the chasing flotilla and the Kouphotate were far beyond the horizon. Whatever Miltiades thought about his son's conduct we could only guess, but my hope was that we would never see him again. Later we made landfall on Lemnos but dared not land as the island was in stasis and not safe.

So with only one choice left we set course across the open sea direct for Athens and somewhere behind us was the Great King and all hell trailed in his wake.

PART TWO

CHAPTER 11

Dazzling sunlight flashing from the shrine on Cape Sounion in the distance tells the returning Athenian that he's almost safe home. This was the first time I'd seen it and I recall the water was stirred by a breeze as we pulled past the headland. We followed the Attic coast towards the city, passing the pirates' nest that the island of Aegina was in those lawless days and in the early evening sunlight we pulled into the bay of Phaleron.

Above us perched on the great rock were the walls of the citadel built in the age of heroes before the kingship of Theseus. Hard to believe but in those days Samos Town, the capital of Polycrates, was a finer town than Athens. It had richer houses and palaces, longer walls and the wondrous tunnel built by Eupalinos and, of course, the great harbour. The Athens I entered that day for the first time bore little relationship to the wonder that Cimon started and that Pericles the onion head will finish and no doubt take all the credit for.

Back then the city didn't gleam with marble columns financed by the tribute of our wars and empire. The Acropolis didn't sparkle so bright in the sun that it hurt the eyes to stare. The harbour at Piraeus that would house the greatest fleet in the world existed only in the imagination of Themistocles. But even so, I loved Athens from the first. I felt it almost as a pain in my ribs and I sensed that here I would decide my fate, meet my friends and lovers and die. Precocious, you might think, for a youth of sixteen summers, reader, but inside you will understand those feelings, you will have felt the same about something when you were young.

Our little flotilla of four sea damaged ships, low in the water with the weight of the General's wealth, waited in the bay until assigned a place to moor. As I waited I listened to the noise from the shore, gazed at the trail of dust that marked the road up to the city and dreamt of what was to come.

In those days ships moored in the wide open bay of Phaleron where the river Khephisos empties itself into the sea. There was no order here then, just a collection of shanties and sheds along the shore where ships were beached, radiating from the road. As if we were expected a crowd had gathered drawn by rumours of the General's return. A crowd divided into factions like always in this city, noisy and raucous, for Athens was in turmoil, divided, angry, but mostly fearful.

It was rumoured that the aristocratic leaders of the ancient tribe of the Alkmaionidai were plotting to restore Hippias, once their enemy. They would welcome the Persians and restore the tyranny with themselves as leading men. The demos and new democratic leaders were in a lather of fear at the prospect. All of this you could feel on the water front at Phaleron. We waited impatiently on the ships, the smell of the land and the city strong in our nostrils. We knew that what happened next would determine our fate. How would the General be welcomed?

He had no natural faction for support. Not from the aristocrats: the Alkmaionidai, who had driven Hippias from the city, were family enemies. Now it was rumoured that through secret diplomacy, they were reconciled with Hippias. For them the rise of the demos was a greater threat than the return of a Persian backed tyrant. Miltiades' break with Hippias over the Ionian revolt was too serious to patch up and he could in any case expect no mercy from the Great King.

And certainly none from the democrats: he was from an ancient aristocratic family that was not sympathetic to the demos, he therefore had no party and few, if any, friends. His only advantage was his great experience and reputation as a Persian fighter but would this be welcome in a city gripped by fear of a Persian invasion for which he could be blamed?

These thoughts must have played in his mind as he sat silent in the trierarch's chair and waited for some sign from the city. Time passed, the sun had almost gone and the day began to grow dark. Cimon, growing bored of the boat began to pester his father to go on shore. The General stood and looked to the beach. This drew a response of cheers and insults from the crowd. He turned back and said to himself as much to as to us,

"I am Miltiades of the Philaidai. My ancestor Philaios first set foot on these shores just after the sack of Troy. I am the leader of one of the oldest families of Athens, descended from ancient heroes. This city was built by our efforts."

Whatever claim he intended to make was interrupted by a great increase in the noise from the land. We turned to look and saw that a strong party of armed men had pushed their way to the sea's edge, facing the boat. A tall man with a greying red beard hailed the ship.

"Welcome, brother, we have come to escort you to the family home and give you safe passage through the common herd."

The General smiled for the first time in days and shouted back,

"Not before time, Stesagoras. Since when has it been polite for a younger brother to keep his elder waiting for so long? I thought we would miss our dinner."

"There's time for that later, brother, for now it's important that you get your land legs quickly for we walk back to the city. The way is crowded with many who wish to see you, some friendly, some not."

We set off in the midst of our escort and I thought that our welcome at Athens was not that much different from our flight from Khardia and that perhaps life in the service of the General would always be like this. We pushed and shoved our way off the beach and onto the city road; the crowd from the beach followed. The way was crowded, some shouted greetings to the General and reached out to touch him, and others jeered but stayed out of the range of our weapons. Shortly after joining the road we met a party of well dressed men also with armed retainers. For an instant the two parties stood staring, each blocking the other's way. The man at the front of their group strode forwards and into the light of our torches. He was of medium height and well dressed in a long simple robe, his face bore all the hallmarks of aristocratic disdain. He had a bulbous forehead and receding hairline that made the front of his head look unnaturally large.

"You will find no forgiveness for your crimes here, Miltiades, and no welcome either. I'll give you a couple of days to reacquaint yourself with your family and whatever friends you have left. Then if you do not get back on your boats and leave I will have you brought before the Archon and the people to be prosecuted for your crimes."

"And why, Xanthippus, should I worry about anything said by a man who takes kubda like a pornoi who sells herself for three obols?"

The man flushed at the insult but kept his self control.

"Two days, Miltiades."

He stood back and we moved on, but once the General's anger was roused it was slow to die. He shouted back at Xanthippus and the crowd,

"These Alkmaionidai will sell you to the Persians. Soon they will arrive and who will lead you? Athens has been their whore for long enough. I have returned to give you back your honour."

We began the long walk up to the city and a strange walk it was. Night had fallen but the whole population had turned out to see us. Strange faces stared out of the night, briefly illuminated, then, as quickly, fading from the light of our torches. By the time we reached the city itself none of us was talking. We were too tired and in my case too disturbed by the strangeness. I think it affected us all. Elpinice was quietly crying to herself and Cimon, half dead with fatigue, had begun to stumble. Theodorus picked him up to carry him and he made no protest. I saw little of the city as we stumbled along ill-lit, badly paved streets and dirt tracks. The houses and buildings showed no light and had no windows on the street, just blank walls and the occasional stout door. I remember crossing a large open space flanked by a foul smelling drain and hearing Miltiades say,

"Ah, the sweet perfume of the Agora."

Such was our glorious entrance to Athens and my first sight of the city that was to become my home.

At the end of a lane between the Agora and the Acropolis, we stopped in a small square, facing a house standing on its own. Like all other houses in this city it had blind walls and a shabby but strong doorway. The door opened as we approached and we passed through into a courtyard. Like all rich town houses of those days the exterior was deceptive. The courtyard was flanked by a covered walkway and at its centre was the family shrine next to a pool with a beautiful statue of the goddess carved in the ancient style.

A house steward led the children away whilst senior members of the household greeted and paid their respects to the General.

"How strange it is to be back in our home. At times these last few years I felt I would never see it again. If things had gone better in the Chersonese I probably never would have. I certainly never expected to arrive here as a fugitive."

Not normally a reflective man, these words of the General dampened the already subdued and tired atmosphere. No one replied so he continued,

"Why was there no official greeting? I have fought Athens' wars singlehanded these last years, and bring the city the islands of Imbros and Lemnos."

Even I knew that neither of these statements was strictly true; he had taken an opportunistic gamble on which side to back in the revolt, the wrong side as it proved. So, as a consequence, we had been forced to flee the islands he had conquered by the Persian fleet. All we had brought to Athens were the four triremes and what we had managed to put in them. Was it likely that the Athenians would welcome such an enemy of the Great King into their city? I think these were the thoughts of all of us that hung in the night air of the courtyard.

Finally, Stesagoras broke the silence.

"Brother, you must know that Themistocles is Archon for this year. He favours the demos and his family, poor as it is, has no love for us."

"A worthless man, but still he is only one of the nine."

"Indeed, but he is the named Archon, the one who matters."

"Themistocles. Have things been brought so low? A man of no family, little better than a merchant or potter. The offspring of some no account coupling with a foreign woman in a poor clan scratching a living in the arse end of nowhere. If such a mongrel can be elected Archon it is lucky for Athens I'm back."

"Brother, you are tired. I have some simple food and drink ready. Take some, and then sleep. Tomorrow we can decide what course of action is best. Perhaps you could travel to the family estate on the bay of Marathon."

"Bugger the bay of Marathon; I've not fought my way back here to hide away playing the country squire on our estates at Brauron. You'll have me threshing grain and fucking goats next, like some peasant farmer."

There was a silence. Stesagoras had the patience to restrain himself, perhaps through sympathy and love for his brother. Miltiades, red in the face with the veins of his neck sticking out in his fury, struggled to regain self control. When he spoke again it was in a softer tone, low and even.

"No, I've done all the running I care to do. If I ever return to our family lands in Marathon it will not be to hide there! Anyway perhaps Themistocles' archonship need not be the end of the world. He's a thinking man for all his dull and stupid appearance so I've heard. He can have no more love for those treacherous Alkmaionidai than I have. They led the revolt that drove out Hippias and now that they've lost their grip of the demos they're sucking up to him again. I saw Xanthippus' cousin on Samos with the tyrant Aiakes. They tried to bribe me at the Heraion, and later in the town, and when that didn't work, to kill me near the docks at night. If it hadn't been for the boy here that would have been the end."

He paused for a moment, walked across to me and put an arm around my shoulders, a most unusual gesture for him. I flinched involuntarily but he didn't seem to notice.

"I wasn't meant to die then and I'm not meant to skulk in a farm now – the gods have something else fated for me. See, I even have my personal luck bringer. I've only been back in the city a few hours but I can sense the fear, this is a divided city – it's like a

113

balance, not knowing which way to go. It will be me who tips the scales."

"Brother, you heard Xanthippus; he plans to bring you before the Archon to be tried for tyranny. He speaks on behalf of his brother-in-law Megacles, a vengeful man who heads the most elevated family in the city, rich and powerful."

"Yes, a powerful family, waiting to sell the city to the Persians and re-instate Hippias as tyrant. Now do you think Themistocles won't be as aware of that as we are? Strange also, don't you think, that there was no sign of the Archon or any of his representatives at Phaleron to greet or even arrest us? Perhaps that means that he's in the same bind that we are, walking the balance. Perhaps the man of the people isn't as secure as we think. He has an impeccable record as an enemy of the Persians; any return of Hippias spells the end of him and his strange, misplaced, ideas about government."

He walked inside following his brother and picked up some bread and a wine cup from a table laid out with food and drink.

"Mandrocles, take some food and wine then go and sleep. Perhaps tomorrow or the next day we'll go and pay the Archon a visit. Now go, I have things to discuss with my brother."

A slave showed me to a small sleeping cubicle near to where the children were housed. But as exhausted as I was, I could not sleep in this strange place. Now that the chase was over and we were in Athens, things seemed no safer. Some months ago I had been a farm boy, now I was in the service of a dangerous, unsteady master driven from home to exile. I had killed two men. Towards dawn I fell into a feverish nightmare where I saw the look of surprise and anger on their dying faces as I killed them over and again. Then I was on the

Athene Nike in a wide bay next to a short strongly built, bull necked man. He turned towards me and I saw that he was laughing.

"Yes, I'm lucky too Mandrocles, but you know that don't you?"

I turned from the faces of the men I was still killing and said,

"Yes Themistocles."

With that he walked through the side of the ship and into the sea; after that, darkness and sleep.

CHAPTER 12

The way things developed we didn't get two days, or need to arrange a visit to the Archon. It seemed that we'd stirred up the bees' hive. They must have been up all night to organise their move against the General because a summons came just after first light for him to appear before the named Archon at his seat of office in the Agora. I was awake and watched the brief exchange from the shadows of the courtyard colonnade.

An elderly man clutching a staff that marked him as an official, a herald of some type I presumed, stood by the pool facing Miltiades and his brother where they were drinking a breakfast cup of hot, spiced wine. The man, despite his haughty demeanour, was clearly nervous.

"Miltiades, son of Cimon, you are summoned to come before the named Archon at the Royal Stoa."

He paused. Neither Miltiades nor his brother bothered to answer, just continued to sip from their cups in a relaxed manner. Put off his stride the herald continued in a more hesitant manner.

"Yes, the Royal Stoa, which you will find in the agora opposite the…"

He got no further.

"Don't presume to give me directions in my own city; my family is one of the most ancient in Athens, we practically built the place. Return to your master and tell him Miltiades, son of Cimon, will attend him when he is ready, which will not be until after he has breakfasted and set one or two personal matters in order. Now go, you will find the door behind you."

The man bowed briefly then quickly turned for the door. I could see that the colour had drained from his face.

The General and his brother went back into the house. I was hungry and went to the kitchen to find breakfast. Cimon was already there eating a frugal meal of olives, dried figs and some hard flat bread.

"This is my family home, Mandrocles. Strange isn't it that this is the first time I've seen it."

I took a stool next to him, he looked tired and out of spirits.

"Father visited me this morning to tell me he was going to engage a tutor for me. So I'll waste my days with letters and learning which I hate. I want to explore the city but it seems that things are ordered differently here. I wonder how my horses at home are."

He made no comment on his father's summons by the Archon but then the minds of children work a different way from ours. There was noise in the corridor and the large frame of Theodorus filled the doorway.

"I've brought you honey cakes from Palemedes in the Ceramicus, the best you will have ever tasted."

The boy's gloom vanished at the bosun's appearance and soon he was licking the sweet sticky honey from his fingers. They were, and still are, the best honey cakes in Athens. I still eat them, although now they're made by Palemedes' great grandson, who has a bakery that doubles up as a bar in Piraeus. Close enough for me to be able to walk for some cakes and a cup of hot, spiced Samian in the mornings for breakfast and a gossip with other old veterans of the fleet.

Motes of sunlight entered the kitchen from the hole in the roof above the fireplace, which, as the weather was fine, was uncovered. I sat in a daze, staring at the patch of light on the earth floor and the sunlit specks of dust which floated above it whilst I listened to Cimon and Theodorus talk about the Athene Nike and the voyage. I felt that I had arrived home and that I would

117

play a part, however small, in great events. It is part of the nature of a young man, for such I considered myself, that change is cause for optimism. Now I've seen that change I'm not so sure. I was disturbed by Theodorus' speaking my name.

"You should take more care over your possessions, Mandrocles. I've brought that cup you're so proud of; you left it in the stowage."

He passed me a sack with the drinking cup in it and at once I thought of Metiochus and wondered where he was now. Wherever it was couldn't be far enough away for me, and I was sure that his part in our story was not finished. I took the cup and stowed it underneath the cot bed in the cell where I slept. A shout from the courtyard rang through the house; the voice was the General's.

"I go to pay my respects to the Archon. Mandrocles, you will come; we may need your luck. Theodorus, bring some of your best lads and follow on behind. I think our enemies will be out in force."

He wore a simple robe of roughly fulled wool over his tunic, like any ordinary citizen of the city, but despite this no one would have mistaken him for anything other than the man of power he was. We left the house and walked into the street to begin our procession to the Agora. The day was warm and I noticed that the family herme, a statue of a bearded man with a vigorously erect phallus set up in a niche in the wall, had been garlanded with a new crown of laurel leaves. Miltiades walked at the head of our party with his brother, followed by the kinsmen. I attached myself to these but was ignored. So, free from any obligation to make conversation, I was able to observe this first step in the General's plan to win over the hearts of the Athenians.

118

The way took longer than I'd expected. Before long we ran into citizens lining the route to get a glimpse of the General. Some he recognised and exchanged words with, most were pleasantries but there were also curses and shouts. The closer we drew to the Agora the slower was our progress and the thicker the crowd.

At the south eastern entrance to the crowded square the kinsmen and Theodorus' sailors formed a protective wedge about the General and his brother and we gradually pushed our way through. I therefore had little chance to take a good look at this heart of the ancient city. As a young boy, with my father, I had tended to the beehives set on the meadows where Mount Kerkis swept down to the sea. The swarm of people and the buzz of noise in the Agora reminded me of those bees. Athens is like a giant hive where the bees are always aroused, buzzing with excitement or anger, never still. They may produce honey like that in the cakes but they also sting.

We followed the main route, which crossed the Agora diagonally, pushing and shoving, exchanging greetings and insults. People swore, cheered or spat according to their inclination, scuffles and fights broke out as we passed. I noticed that the road we took, constructed of compacted gravel, was quite smooth and that made our progress easier. Later I was to find out that we were following the sacred Panathenic way that runs from the Dyplon gate to the Acropolis, the oldest road in the city, dating back to the age of heroes. We pushed on through the noise, heat and dirt until suddenly the crowd thinned out and we stopped.

The dust raised by so many scuffling feet sank lazily back to the earth and I looked around. We'd arrived in an open space at the opposite side of the square. To our right was a low walled square structure with bronze statues. Theodorus, catching my gaze, said,

"That there's the sacred heart of the city, the 'altar of the twelve gods', that's why they've all settled down a bit; and that over there is the Royal Stoa, headquarters of the Archon, where we're headed."

I followed his direction to the left and saw in front of us a small building of white stone fronted by eight simple columns with a roof of reddish baked clay tiles. Our party was adjusting their dress, brushing the dust from their clothes and expelling it through their nostrils and mouths. The smell of dry earth and sweat pervaded the atmosphere around us along with a silence, unusual to Athens that hung in the air. Standing at the foot of the tan coloured steps that led up to the columns stood a group of similar size to ours, obviously awaiting our arrival. The General adjusted his robe and settled his appearance as best he could then said to his brother in a voice deliberately loud for all to hear,

"Well, look who's here to welcome us, the whole vipers' nest and some we might not have expected."

I recognised Xanthippus from the night before by the elongated shape of his head. We moved towards the steps, Miltiades at the front. He moved in a relaxed way, as if on a stroll through the gardens of his estate. As we drew level with his accusers he looked directly at a tall, lean bearded man of middle age.

"So, Megacles, have you come to see what a man who fights the Great King looks like – used as you are to only mixing with those who kiss his arse?"

Megacles started an angry response but we never got to hear what it might be as a figure emerged from between the columns at the top of the steps. Even I didn't have to be told it was Themistocles. Someone less like an aristocrat it would be hard to imagine. He looked far more like Theodorus or Ariston. Squat and powerfully built with a bull neck, he resembled one of the gnarled heavy bruisers who compete in the wrestling contests at the games. It was in every way the man who had walked into the sea in my dreams. His face radiated pugnacity and aggression, from the bristles of the short black beard that covered his face, to the harsh staring eyes set beneath prominent brows. This was my first waking glimpse of the new type of leader of the polis, or politicians as they now call themselves. In fact I suppose he was the first and I wonder now if he ever realised the revolution he'd started when he had the leisure many years later to reflect on it as an exile to the court of the Great King.

Miltiades, followed by his brother, moved towards the steps; he gestured to me to follow. There were only a few steps but it seemed to take forever to get to the top. Three men detached themselves from the other group and walked parallel to us towards the columns. Themistocles spoke: on first hearing his voice was a surprise – it was light and graceful and carried well; authoritative, yet at the same time almost seductive as if an aged centaur had opened its mouth to speak but the voice had been that of the god Apollo.

"Miltiades, son of Cimon of the Philaidai, you are brought here before the named Archon in the presence of the demos to be accused of certain crimes. Megacles, son of Hippocrates of the Alkmaionidai, you have come here to level accusations before the Archon in the presence of the demos. Each of you step forward into the chamber with one companion. Stesagoras, son of Cimon and Xanthippus, son of Ariphron will do. Aristides and the youth will remain here."

He turned and walked back inside followed by the four who had been named. I noticed that as they followed the Archon neither the brothers nor their accusers deigned to look at each other but stared straight ahead. Taking this as my model I stood and waited without casting a glance at the man named

121

Aristides. We had no great time to wait but, despite the sun, a chill breeze had sprung up and rapidly my sweat streaked body was chilled. Below us the crowd grew restive feeling cheated perhaps that whatever was happening was out of sight and that there had been no public disorder or bloodshed. At length they came out and walked past us down the steps and into the crowd, which divided into two factions. I followed close behind the General, who set off back the way we had walked in the morning. At the end of the Agora by a fountain house of rough grey stone of great age, he stopped, climbed the steps of the building and turned to address his supporters.

"Friends and freeborn Athenians, in four days' time I am to be tried by the court of the Areopagus, the court of the aristocrats. I am to be charged with failing to protect the grain supply from the Euxine region to Athens, and with acting as a tyrant in the Chersonese. But you and I know what this is really about."

He paused for effect.

"I am being charged with daring to fight the Great King. You understand that it's not only my fate that will be decided in four days, but the fate of Athens and of all the Greeks who wish to be free. You understand that the choice which faces you is between a general who has fought the Persians and knows how to beat them, and a clique of aristocrats who would sell our city to them and have them reinstate the tyrant Hippias.

"Let us hope, friends that in four days it is the patriots and true men who carry the day or our city will share the fate of Miletos and you freeborn Athenians will become slaves. I am sure you don't want to bow to barbarian soldiers as you walk through your city so I urge you now to return to your districts. Tell your good friends how low some in Athens are prepared to stoop for their Persian masters."

He stepped down to shouts of support and we continued. Some of the crowd followed, the rest dispersed to their districts, probably to wine shops to plot and spread the General's message. By the time we reached the house we had lost most of our following. The General and his kinsmen went to confer in the men's court. For some time I kicked my heels in the small square in front of the house for the simple reason that I had no idea what I was supposed to do. On the ships things had been simple; here I had no role, too young to be counted as a man, too old for a child. All that waited for me in the house was a small dark sleeping cell, my father's armour, the drinking cup and a narrow pallet bed.

So I sat in the shade by the door and scratched patterns in the dirt with a dust dry twig from an olive tree, long since dead; far from home with no kin; my future to be decided by the whim and fortunes of an adventurer in a city full of enemies. That same morning I had been full of hope but such is the mercurial nature of youth, in the distance I felt I could hear the laughter of the gods. I thought of Theopone, of my mother and brothers, even of my father, and after a time my tears formed a little trickle of water in the dust patterns I scratched.

I was distracted from my loneliness by the opening of the door. The domestic steward, with some of Stesagoras' house slaves, emerged with two women, both dressed in the drab, ungirdled mantles worn by respectable women in Athens called the peplos. Both also wore a separate headpiece with a veil covering the face as is the custom in the higher and stricter families. The slighter of the two broke away from the group and came across to me, pulling the veil above her face as she moved; it was Elpinice.

"Mandrocles, they're sending me away to the country estate at Brauron."

We stood face to face, she half a head shorter than I but still tall for a girl. I saw that her eyes were red and the track lines of tears streaked her face.

"Don't let them leave me there to become an old maid amongst the rustics."

Our faces were so close that for a moment I thought she would kiss me, but her female companion pulled her sharply by her arm and she moved away. As her veil was pulled back over her face she called out,

"Mandrocles, do not forget me."

I never have.

CHAPTER 13

Next day I was killing time polishing my father's hoplite armour. Cimon was being instructed by his tutor, some type of cracked philosopher from one of the islands, when the General shouted me out.

"Mandrocles, you're not here to be a gentleman of leisure like the suitors of Penelope, you've work to do."

I stepped out into the court and was pleased to see a group of sailors, including Ariston and Theodorus.

"You can go and help keep an eye on these rogues while they take soundings in the city. It'll give you a chance to see your new home. Here, take this."

He passed me a small purse with some coins inside. He'd already been taking soundings. The previous night had been disturbed by comings and goings into the early hours of the morning, filling the house with whispers, muffled conversations and the quiet opening and closing of doors.

That day the sky had the brilliant blue of a winter's morning and the white stone of the courtyard sparkled. My fears of the day before vanished. Theodorus draped a heavy, scarred arm around my shoulders and once again part of the ship's company I walked out into the street.

"First off, there's a little duty me and the lads have to perform up there".

He gestured towards the Acropolis, perched high above the city.

"Give you a chance to visit the citadel and get a view of the town."

The rock of the Acropolis hung almost directly over the house. In the evening light it glowed golden but in the morning sun it gleamed and dazzled. We made our way along the twists and turns of the lanes that led round the base of the rock towards the entrance high

125

above. In those days this part of the city comprised mainly houses and yards scattered about the slopes at the foot of the rock. These had developed over centuries, constructed mainly of whitewashed mud brick, with red tiled roofs. This part of the city, on the approach to the Acropolis, was destroyed later during the invasion but was then rebuilt, so in my memory I can hardly distinguish the new from the old. But I remember that morning and my walk towards the great ramp. Some of the men bought honeycombs from a street vendor, which we shared out and ate as we walked. The taste and smell of honeycomb has always been amongst my most intimate associations with Athens. Soon we reached the ramp that led to the gaps in the ancient wall that fringed the citadel. By now the streets were busy and we pushed our way through the crowd and up. The ramp was a huge stone wall with a paved surface, wide enough for three carts to travel side by side. At the top of it we passed through the ancient wall constructed of giant rocks onto a flat platform where the entrance, an ornamental building supported by six great pillars, came suddenly into view.

This was my first glimpse of the entry to the sacred sites. I know that you, reader, will think of the new temples and buildings that now stand there, their marble columns gleaming in the sun marking the beginning of our greatness. Also the ones that at present exist only in the dreams of Pericles onion head and which he tells us will be the final stamp of our supremacy. You will think that our old temples and shrines which the Persians destroyed were crude and antique. But let me tell you, the wonder, simplicity and magic of the old Acropolis had something that made you catch your breath. Something plainer, grimmer perhaps, but inhabited by the breath of the gods and built by men more in touch with the dark nature of the earth. Remember, all that is new is not necessarily more blessed. Cleverer, flashier perhaps, but I think less all the same, and for me nothing was as true to that as the old altar of Athene Nike which stood to the south of the ramp by the citadel entrance. This was what the sailors had come to visit and to offer thanks for their safe return in the goddess' own ship. We paid a small fee to the old crone who tended the shrine and stood in reverence before the altar. On the altar there was a simple dedication inscribed:

"Altar of Athene Nike, Patrokles made it."

We stood for a moment in silence then left our offerings and entered the citadel with the scent of the shrine's incense thick and bitter in our nostrils. Today the citadel is one great building site, full of sweating slaves and metics, where rubble and foundations sit next to the flashy gleam of new and ornate buildings. What you see now is more a statement of men's hubris than their piety. But that first day, in the crisp morning air of bright winter, it was impossible not to feel the presence of gods, long dead heroes and perhaps something more ancient hovering near but unseen.

We picked our way through the mass of statues, many more than life size, graceful youths standing among basins on plinths containing sacred water for purification rites. To me the most beautiful figures were the statues of women and girls sculptured and painted so finely that it seemed that their robes moved in the breeze. Also there were many figures cast in bronze, men, women, even dogs and horses. It was as if we walked through a forest of stone and bronze painted in bright colours. Scattered among the statues and bronzes were simple square temples fronted by plain columns but with pediments decorated with the carvings of gods, ancient heroes and creatures of the night that never the sun shone on.

127

We paused before the statue of a woman mounted on a plinth dedicated to Athena; beneath it was an inscription that read,

"Given by Melagar, ship's captain."

Ariston pointed at the dedication.

"My father raised this in honour of a vow he made after he survived the shipwreck of his own boat. The wreck and the vow ruined my family. Now, unlike him, I steer other men's ships."

We moved on to an open space with a much larger temple that dominated the rear area of the citadel. By now only Theodorus and Ariston remained with me, the rest having separated to talk with friends and acquaintances and pick up gossip from the city.

"This is the temple of Athena, Mandrocles. We go in to give our thanks to the goddess then we can go back down and visit the wine shops of the Ceramicus."

The pediments of the temple were decorated with carvings of the battles between the gods and heroes. At the centre was a large statue of the goddess herself, clutching a snake in her left hand. I stood for several moments staring at the goddess, silently praying that she would continue to give me the luck that had been mine since I first stepped onto the deck of the Athene Nike.

Ariston took me by the shoulder and turned me away.

"Don't gaze too long on the goddess, boy, or she may decide you lack respect. Remember our city's goddess can be cruel and vengeful. You don't want her to notice you too much."

We left the temple and its scent of bitter herbs and incense and for a time I stood in the sunshine on the old wall that circled the citadel and looked at the thousands of roofs of the crowded houses below, massed together, divided by narrow, twisting lanes, then over them to the sea sparkling in the Bay of Phaleron, where our ships were beached. I thought for a moment that somewhere out there towards the south was the Persian fleet; this then brought to mind an image of the face of Metiochus and I felt for the first time the chill of that bright winter's day. I jumped down and ran after Theodorus and Ariston, who were making their way back towards the entrance and the path back down to the city.

We pushed our way down the ramp, the men were louder, more rowdy now the debt to the goddess had been paid and the rest of the day was now theirs to enjoy. They exchanged banter and insults with passers-by. Some of these exchanges concerned our being men in the service of the General. It was clear to me that there was talk of little else in the city. Would the General be convicted and exiled, and if he wasn't would he lead us into war with the Persians? But we men in his service knew that whatever the Athenians did to the General the Persians would still come to Athens. The Great King would have his vengeance.

At the foot of the Acropolis we joined the Panathenic way and followed it through the Agora to the Ceramicus, once the district of potters, now an area of bars, brothels and the homes of the poor. We stopped in a small square near the old city walls next to a cemetery: many of the bars were simple trestles, with wine and water sold from carts. Their owners or bar girls shouted invitations to wine, and more. Ariston steered us through the crowd towards a more substantial shanty.

"Here, this'll do. The Bald Man: not too dirty, wine's decent, pretty slave girls. Just have to make sure we don't get cheated on the measures."

Inside it took some time for my eyes to get used to the dark. We were in a small room with a wooden counter at one end and next to it a small brazier for cooking food, the smoke escaping through a hole in the roof. The place smelt of stale wine and burnt fat with an undertone of fish. There were some tables with rough stools at them, an earth floor and a pot in the corner to piss in. Sitting round a table furthest from the counter were three men in green tunics, sharing a jar of wine.

Ariston drew Theodorus' attention to them.

"Look, some of the dregs that do the dirty work for Megacles."

"I see them."

Theodorus walked over to the men, who stopped drinking and were looking across at us. He rested his hands on the table, leaned across to face the man sitting in the corner.

"Hey, Eubulus, cistern arse, that's the table we want. You've got as long as it takes us to order a drink to get out of here, this table's reserved for Persian fighters, not their bum boys."

There were more of us but Theodorus alone would probably have been enough, and it seemed they wanted to be away. To help them decide he stretched out a brawny arm and swept their jugs and cups to the floor, then stepped back. The men got up, cursing and brushing the spilt wine from their tunics and made for the exit. As they left Eubulus turned and said,

"Enjoy the drink while you can, the odds are with you now but the city's not safe for Miltiades' jackals."

The tavern keeper was being pacified by Ariston as Theodorus shouted across,

"Get us two chous of wine, bald man, cut two to one and make sure it's cut right and I'll give you four obols, which is one more than it's worth."

The bald man signalled to one of the girls, who began to set up the mixing bowl and the cups whilst the other one swept up the mess of smashed cups and wine.

130

Her mantle although cheap was clinging and I passed the time trying to make out the outline of her thighs and buttocks. The tavern owner was complaining to Ariston about the cost of the breakages. Theodorus shouted to him,

"Bring us some food and what we pay will cover any losses. Come on, cheer up, man, we're thirsty and you'll soon find a way to cheat us."

He nudged me hard.

"Don't waste your eyes on her, Mandrocles, across the street is where the flute girls train. If you like later we can try to get one of them to take you behind the tombs."

We pulled another table across and sat round. There were nine of us left of the group that had set out from the house; three senior rowers from the Athene Nike and the bosuns from the other three ships. The girls brought across two large jugs of wine, a tray of drinking cups and some olives. Theodorus pulled a jug across to where he sat in the place previously occupied by Eubulus.

"I am today's drink master but it's not a fucking symposium so, after the libation, I give you one toast only."

He poured a large measure into one cup for the libation, passed it to Ariston seated on his left; Ariston took a sip and passed it on. When it arrived back with Theodorus he drained the remains and then filled a separate cup for each man.

"The toast is 'let the gods give Miltiades, son of Cimon, the justice he deserves'."

He shouted this so that the words carried to the street outside the tavern, then added in an undertone,

"They'd better, because the city is going to need him. Now drink up because we have at least two more chous to finish after these."

131

I sat back and sipped my wine, which was rough but not too bad. Some of the men played with dice whilst the bosun of the Thetis told a rambling, bawdy tale. Later the girl brought across a wooden tray loaded with small fried sprats, a pot of high smelling sauce and some hard bread and onions. She laid them on the table whilst trying to dodge the hands reaching up the skirts of her mantle. We finished the first jugs and two more arrived. Men came and went, at some time we numbered over twenty. My head began to swim and the smoke from the lamps made my eyes smart and stream with water.

So I got up, left the table and walked out of the tavern unnoticed. Outside I could still hear the noise of oaths, shouts, laughter and bits of song from my companions. I walked for a bit and then, feeling the need to sit, I wandered across to the nearest of the tombs in the cemetery. It was quieter here with trees scattered among the tombs. I moved off the road and sat on the plinth of an ancient memorial with my back against the leaning column and waited for my head to stop spinning. After a while I noticed that I was not alone in the cemetery. Working girls were bringing clients to service standing up behind the tombs. I watched them, feeling a mixture of frustration and timidity. I left and walked back towards the tavern. By the city gate I noticed a number of women, some of them quite young, standing around as if killing time. Then one detached herself from the group and went with an elderly man through the gate and into the cemetery. For a moment I wondered whether I could find my way to asking one of the prettier girls to go with me. This had been noticed and there was a shout from one of the group of women,

"Special rates for you, pretty one."

This moved her companions to raucous laughter. Feeling shame, I moved off quickly and almost barged into a tall man leading a group of three scantily but expensively dressed girls carrying reed flutes. He pushed me aside and they walked past, but as the last girl passed she looked straight at me, smiled showing a row of perfect white teeth and said with a laugh,

"You did well to steer clear of those diseased hags; you'd have been scratching for weeks."

The noise led me back to the tavern. Ariston was standing in the doorway.

"You've been gone some time, boy, I wondered if you were coming back. If you wanted a woman so much you could have taken a turn behind the curtain with one of the bar girls like some of the lads have been doing."

Inside Theodorus was leading a drinking song and banging on the table as the others shouted back the response to each line. The table was covered in spilt wine and the patterns made by the dregs that had been flicked in the game of kotobos; in the centre were the remains of a plate of greasy looking sausages. One of the sailors was vomiting in a corner.

I sat and watched until they finished. Then Theodorus stood, slapped some coins on the table and walked out, followed by the others. Outside the light was fading, someone called for torches, which the tavern keeper produced from behind the bar and lit. Then, with Theodorus at our head, we began our route home. I walked at the back with Ariston. After a time I realised we were in a district of narrow lanes meeting in dusty squares where we'd not been before. I asked him where we were going.

"Well, the General told us to find out what opinion in the city was like and we're not quite finished doing that, so it looks like Theodorus is just going to make one last call."

We arrived at a small square, more like an opening between streets. In the centre was a crudely carved wooden statue to the local deity, its paint faded with age, and at the corner a tavern with the image of a red cockerel painted above the door. Theodorus stopped outside it, handed the torch he was carrying to the man next to him, and shouted,

"Any of you bastards in there got any argument with General Miltiades then you'd better come out."

A group of men appeared at the entrance. One man pushed through from the back of the crowd and I recognised Eubulus. He came up close to Theodorus so their faces almost touched.

"It's not us so much that are against him. It's the Archon and the elders, see? After his trial I doubt we'll be seeing as much of you pirate boys."

"It seems the gods haven't smiled on you today, Eubulus."

Quick as lightening Theodorus grabbed Eubulus' head by his lank black hair to steady it, and with his right fist smashed his cheekbones and jaw. The others went quickly back inside.

"Well, looks like it's first blood to the General."

Theodorus flexed the fingers of his right hand and leaned over Eubulus writhing on the ground trying to put his damaged face back together.

"Nothing personal, but we've fought the Persians and when they get here you'll need us so you'd better start to learn that. Because, if you're going to survive, then one day you'll have to stand with us in the shield wall or row a trireme. Here's some money to get that face fixed."

He threw some coins in the dust and then turned back to us.

"One more drink on the way home, lads, but I don't think they'd welcome us in the Red Cockrell so we'll find somewhere better."

CHAPTER 14

For two days the house was full, ablaze with talk in corners, secrets, comings and goings. I was ignored so I owed what little I learnt to Aristagorus, the cracked philosopher who tutored Cimon. The trial divided the town but it was clear that Miltiades commanded a great deal of popular support.

Against us were the Alkmaionidai and their supporters: powerful men with cliques who could influence the city's ruling council, the Areopagus. But they lacked support on the streets and more to the point had few options. They couldn't be seen as appeasers of the Persian king, in the pocket of Hippias the exile and traitor, and they hated and feared the new men, leaders of the demos like Themistocles. They were cunning enough to realise that times were changing fast and they had to accommodate to this but couldn't agree how. So they were dangerous but divided with no common policy.

The factor that united them was Miltiades. He was anathema, the enemy of their bloodline who now wanted to lead the city in disastrous opposition to the Great King. This gave them a clear strategy as, fearing the Persians, no one in the city would be mad enough to want to risk war with them. Even better, despite his anti Persian stance, he was more hostile to the democrats than they were. He was not only a noble and oligarch, but had also been the son-in-law of Hippias, who had vowed to destroy the democrats on his return.

They held the best cards so it seemed the only chance for Miltiades was to play his single good one. To present himself as an experienced freedom fighter and his trial as part of the struggle for the freedom of Greece, with himself as freedom's symbol. The real charges levelled at him might, therefore, become submerged in the confusion of the times.

The negotiations in this house and others across the city were conducted against a background of tavern brawls and street fights. In these, the crews of the General's ships played, and for the most part seemed to enjoy, a leading part. I was refused permission to accompany them again so I skulked in the house, watched and waited. I spoke to Aristagorus, who told me the house was visited at odd times in the day and night by well born men with military reputations. Not only respectable men such as Callimachus and Stesileos, but also some of the new men, leaders of the demos, men close to Themistocles. In this atmosphere the city churned like liquid bronze in a melting pot, never settling, and in the house of Stesagoras the lamps burned all night.

They were still burning as the day of the trial dawned, and they were needed. The day was cold and grey, clouds scudding down across the hills brought sudden downpours of rain blown horizontal by the wind. Despite this, in that cold grey dawn the streets were full, people crowded in doorways and in the shelter of walls. There was expectation and unease in the air but not violence, unlike the day of our procession to the Agora.

Yet, as on that day, we set out in the same order; today though there was no need for the guard of sailors so, before we reached the place where the council of the Areopagus were to make their judgement, the General dismissed his men. His brother questioned whether this was a wise or safe decision. Miltiades replied that it would not be caution that would win the day but reputation and bravery, and that his reputation was that of a leader, a man of courage.

So leading our small party himself, he walked through the streets, shouting greetings and thanks to the onlookers and giving the appearance of a man enjoying a morning stroll with a few friends. The walk was uncomfortably long though as the court of the Areopagus was set on Ares Hill where long ago Ares, the god of war, had been tried for the murder of the son of Poseidon. By the time we reached the court we were cold and drenched.

The court of the Areopagus is not designed to make a man feel comfortable. It's built over the cave where the furies, who the ironic Athenians call the kindly ones, live and are worshipped. The responsibility for this worship was the original duty of the Areopagus when it was established in ancient times.

What I remember most was the smell of damp woollen clothes and the steam rising from the shoulders of the assembled company. There was little dignity in this gathering: it smelt like a flock of wet sheep crowding the byre. Also, the chamber was smaller than I had imagined it would be. Seated across the hall from our party, but close enough to recognise clearly, were Aristides, Megacles, Xanthippus and many others of the Alkmaionidai faction. Sitting amongst them, which surprised me, were some of the men who had in the last couple of days visited our house. When I looked to where the council members were seated I recognised some of our visitors there too.

The General and his brother sat bolt upright and stared impassively at their accusers. So in the damp fug of the chamber amidst muffled conversations, sneezes and coughs, we waited for it to begin.

At last Themistocles entered and without pausing began a brief address.

"I, the named Archon, Themistocles, son of Neocles, of the deme Phrearrhioi and the tribe of

Leontis, call, as is my right, upon you, Megacles, son of Hippocrates, to make the accusation against Miltiades, son of Cimon, so that the council of the Areopagus can make true judgment in the interests of the demos."

There was muttering from many members of the council at these last words, unhappy at having their ancient privilege linked to the demos; it seemed that Themistocles had added these last words of his own volition. There was an unexpected hush in the chamber as Themistocles sat and Megacles rose to open the prosecution.

You, reader, will know that there are as many versions of what was said that day as there are olives on a tree or tits on the Ephesians' perversion of the goddess Artemis, but I was there and I remember well, not every word of course, but all the important ones. I will set down here the true account and it is well worth your attention.

Megacles stood. You know how full of themselves the Alkmaionidai are, speak as if their words are too good for the rest of us, but he spoke well and to the point. He even pretended to have a little respect for the demos and its jumped up new men despite their being from no notable family. He made three points, the first being that the General and his family had always been thick with the Pesistratid family, the tyrants that had ruled Athens until the Alkmaionidai had liberated the city. That he, as leading representative of the Alkmaionidai, was continuing the glorious tradition of the tyrant slayers Harmodios and Aristogeiton, whose great statues stand now in the Agora to the glory of the city, that his responsibility was to continue to ensure the city's liberty was secure. He was prosecuting Miltiades, son of Cimon, because apart from having been given the Chersonese to rule over as a tyrant by the Pesistratids, before their rightful overthrow he had ruled unlawfully and suppressed liberty. Now Megacles drew himself to his full height, pointed a finger at the General, who up to this point he had ignored, and shouted,

"I accuse you, Miltiades, son of Cimon, of the crime of tyranny and impiety through flouting the will of the gods."

He then proceeded to mention almost in passing that Miltiades had been the son-in-law of the overthrown tyrant Hippias.

His last charge was that in leaving the Chersonese to flee to Athens Miltiades had neglected to fulfil his duty to protect the trade route in grain, so necessary for Athens, from the Black Sea region beyond the Chersonese. Everyone in the chamber knew how much Athens depended on that wheat, yet even to a youth of my age this last charge seemed odd considering the activities of the Persians, not to mention its contradiction of his earlier condemnation of the General's governance of the Chersonese in the first place. However, he finished to considerable acclaim and shouts of approval. I noticed that the majority of the council seemed to be nodding in agreement and Megacles' kinsmen and supporters congratulated him as he sat down, shaking his hand or patting his shoulder.

Yet during his speech he made not one mention of the Persians or of the ambitions of the Great King. Themistocles, I noticed, had sat impassive through the presentation giving no hint of his sympathies. He now rose.

"Miltiades, son of Cimon, how do you answer these accusations?"

Then it was the General's turn. I know that what I set down here as the General's speech is a true account and not just an old man's memory. I know this as I possess some notes. These were given to me by a man who was later to become a true friend, a writer of tragedy, close to Themistocles, who was on that day acting as his scribe. Now when I read those notes I can see again the court chamber and the General standing straight backed and proud.

The moment he rose to speak a violent gust of wind and hail rattled the tiles on the roof and swept through the chamber, so he paused until it passed. Then in the silence that followed, the chamber seeming preternaturally quiet, filled only with anticipation, he began.

"I am a soldier, a defender of Athens and freedom. I fought my way through the Persian fleet to get here and in doing so lost my eldest son. I've spent my life away from the comforts of the city whose interests I serve. As you know, I bring the city a gift of the islands of Imbros and Lemnos, taken by me, through force. You know my ancestry is as old as any in the city. My ancestor was Philiaios son of Ajax, who came here after the fight at Troy, so I need take no lessons in service to the city from the Alkmaionidai. Rather, I and my family, remember both my father and uncle died overseas in the service of this city of the goddess, suffered for the city, unlike the Alkmaionidai who enriched themselves from it.

"But I stand here before you today, not to defend myself from these childish slights, which I know you honoured and distinguished members of the council see for what they are, being yourselves intelligent men who serve the city of the goddess Athena. No, I stand here today to warn you of the danger we face, to offer my support, and my life if that is required.

"I notice that my accuser did not once mention the real reason for this trial: the threat of the Great King to our liberty. Why is that I wonder? Could it be that there

141

are friends of the Great King amongst the ranks of my enemies, men who might benefit from that friendship?"

At this there was a level of commotion amongst the friends of Megacles, but Themistocles signalled for them to be silent.

"I thank you, Archon. I see that, as always, the truth has the power to wound but if what I say is too strong for their delicate stomachs, I will move on. My role here is not to attack my enemies, even though it seems that if they could, they would restore the tyrant. For them, having seen and disliked the effect of the new liberties enjoyed by the demos, a tyrant would be preferable.

"Yes I admit it, I, as you know, was a friend to the tyrant Hippias; my father was favoured by his father before him. But there is a great distinction; we enjoyed his favour when he was the legal ruler of Athens. It has never been the practice of my family to dispute the will of the city."

At this point he paused, and looked towards Themistocles. He then extended his arm towards the Archon. These gestures had been deliberate and were missed by no one in the crowd. He held this pose for a moment then continued.

"I serve the legal government of the city; I serve its laws and its gods. I think it was for this reason that the tyrant Hippias attempted to have me murdered on the island of Samos. Yes, it's true: my former father-in-law attempted to kill me because he knew that I would attempt to prevent the tragedy of the sea battle at Lade which destroyed the Greek fleet and which led to the rape and destruction of Miletos. Perhaps you are wondering why he would want me dead and not just silenced, or bought off.

"I will tell you the plain truth. He wants me dead because I understand how to fight the Persians; I know how they can be beaten.

Listen to me carefully and remember that had the Ionian allies followed my advice that day at the Panonium, then we would not face the troubles we do now. Their fleet would still be a powerful force and our ally. But they didn't listen, they were blind to the truth and you all know what happened as a consequence. The fleet was destroyed, and so the city was sacked and the rebellion crushed. But there is far worse, as I think you are now beginning to realise. The Great King was not content, and he would not be content, until he punished those who aided or encouraged the rebels."

He paused for a moment and looked around him as if he was fixing each man with his gaze and speaking to him alone. Then with intensity and gravitas, his voice filling the chamber, he spoke again.

"I need not remind you, fathers of Athens, that you decided in this very chamber to send a fleet of twenty triremes to aid the rebels, that those ships crewed by Athenian heroes did great damage to the Persian fleet. That they gave hope to our Ionian allies. That this fleet was present at the sack of the city of Sardis that so incensed the Great King. That this Athenian fleet was a symbol of freedom; and that the Great King could not tolerate.

I need not remind you that the Great King has a long memory and that his bitter gaze is now turned towards you, yes, towards you and this city, and then, but only then, towards Sparta and the rest of Greece.

Don't be foolish enough to think that by condemning me you will avert that gaze and the wrath that follows. The only way you could do that would be to offer him the earth and water that symbolise surrender, and you know what that would mean for all

143

in this room. All, except of course, the Alkmaionidai and their friends. But, for the rest of you, particularly you new men, leaders of the demos and the polis, politicians I believe you now call yourselves, there will be no mercy. For you, the time when you had a chance to make an accommodation with the Great King is long gone. You, like me, can either run or you can fight. You know that I choose to fight. I sacrificed my territory and my family and I fought my way here.

Why? Why did I do that? Because, be under no illusion, I knew that my enemies here would try to destroy me as they are doing now. I did it because of my duty, my sacred duty to the city of the goddess."

At this there was a peal of laughter and derision from the other side of the room and someone, Aristides I think, shouted,

"That's as likely as the pornoi paying the three obol fee to her customer."

This brought laughter from some in the room, but not many, I noticed. Themistocles ordered silence and Miltiades nodded towards him as if in gratitude that he could continue.

"No, you laugh all you like, treat it as a joke. But don't laugh at this because I can bring you the one thing that no other man in this city can. I have fought against the Persians for many years and before that I fought for them. I know how they move, how they organise, I know their weak points, and I know how to beat them. Now listen even more closely, I know how to make this city, its leaders and the demos great. I understand that perhaps you may think that war can be avoided and that is your preferred…"

Here he hesitated before deliberately using another of the new words,

"…policy: but when that policy fails, as it will, and when the Persian army lands on our beaches, who amongst you will want to be the man who tells his children that he voted to exile the city's one hope of victory? Who amongst you will want to be the man who voted to offer earth and water to the Persians? The man who condemned the city to slavery and many of your council members to death? Who in this room would want to betray his deme, his tribe and his polis? No one in this room, I think. Even my accusers, even they, for they, like the rest of you, have ancestors who have shed blood for this city.

We are all Athenians and that being the case I conclude my argument, fathers of the city.

Except to say that, although the reach of the Great King is long, it will take him some years to mount an expedition strong enough to threaten us. During that time we have space to make plans with our allies, such as the Spartans, who will be similarly threatened. We have time to appoint a suitable panel of generals and devise a plan that will bring victory. In these coming days, fathers of the city, my experience, which today you can make yours, will more than repay your wisdom."

Then he sat down and there was silence, silence that lasted so long it seemed it would never end. At last Themistocles announced that we must withdraw so that the court could consider its decision.

As the entire world knows, they made the decision that saved not only Athens but all Greece. So we walked home through the rain free men, which I wouldn't have believed in the morning. Through all this Miltiades showed no emotion, he maintained exactly the same dignity walking back from the court as he had walking to it. Furthermore, he refused to allow his supporters any public celebration, in fact he behaved as if it was a sacred day and all levity forbidden.

But the day held one more surprise. The evening continued wet. My sleeping cell was covered in cold puddles where the roof leaked. My bedding was damp and my head reeled with the events of the day. Sleep wouldn't come. At some point the noise of the wind and rain ceased and I got up and wandered out to the courtyard. I thought the rest of the house slept but there were voices under the colonnade so I stayed where I was, silent in the shadows. Miltiades and his brother sat drinking wine and talking, and the talk was punctuated by soft laughter. The first voice I heard was that of Stesagoras:

"I thought at one point you'd pushed it so far that you'd lost it, brother, like the old fool in the satyr plays."

He mimicked Miltiades' voice, saying with as much pomposity as he could manage,

"I did it because of my sacred duty to the city of the goddess; in a pig's arse you did, you must have known that would provoke our enemies."

"Yes, I almost laughed myself at that point but I couldn't resist it. You know how seriously they take themselves, standing there like they've got a silver oil lamp up their backsides. But it worked didn't it? Those old fools on the council lapped it up, they loved being called fathers of the polis. Still that joke of Aristides was funny though, the one about the pornoi paying the fee. I almost liked him for a moment."

There was silence in the garden as both men stopped to drink, then Miltiades spoke again.

"And did you see Themistocles' face when I fed him that line about serving the legal government of the city and its gods. Even better when I made common cause with the new politicians, and they fell for it. If this venture fails I could still make a decent living as chorus leader in the plays at the spring Dionysia festival."

"But he's no fool that one, a very dangerous man and a clever one – must have been, to have risen from such a no account family."

"Which is why we can't afford to have him work against us; he understands we have to fight, that's why he ran the court the way he did. He thinks he needs us now if there's to be war. Maybe after that he'll think of a way to settle us."

"So what do we do about the invitation that came tonight? Do we go?"

"A strange thing that; didn't see it coming, a symposium at the house of Phrasicles."

"Who's thick with Agesilaus, brother of Themistocles."

"But we go of course; should be of interest. Haven't been to a decent drinking party since the one on Samos after which Aiakes tried to have me murdered. Would have worked too but for my lucky keepsake. Yes, we go. I'm interested to see if Agesilaus sounds us out, or maybe if Themistocles himself turns up."

"Then perhaps you need to take your luck bringer with you again."

"What, Mandrocles? Yes, perhaps I will. Drink up, it's been a long day."

So in that way I came to attend a gathering at which I would meet a long standing friend and also the man who later had the power of life or death over all of us.

CHAPTER 15

Following his acquittal the General thought it vital that he and his family be seen to conduct a normal life in the city. So, despite the slight risk, the next day dawning fine, he gave permission for Cimon accompanied by his tutor to visit the Agora just like any other aristocratic youth. He told me to go with them.

"While you're there, Mandrocles, get yourself a decent mantle to wear, you're coming out with me tonight. Aristagorus will show you where to buy one, he's going to get something more fitting for Cimon too. You should have seen the old fool's face when I told him, you'd have thought that Zeus would fling a thunderbolt and bring down the house there and then, started to lecture me on the necessity for frugal living and the sacred tradition of the women of the home weaving the wool for the men's robes. Until I pointed out that we'd sent the women to Brauron and a few other things beside. I don't think he'll be so keen to question next time."

Whatever the General had said to Aristagorus certainly had an effect, he was even sourer than usual but at least he was quieter. However, by the time we reached the Agora he had recovered sufficiently to begin a lengthy discourse on the duties of a gentleman. This he believed lay in maintaining a state of eunomia, or good order, which the great Athenian Solon had made a principle of the city's governance more than a hundred years before. He illustrated this with endless examples that lasted all the while we measured and judged the cloth at the stalls. Cimon, normally bored by this, paid enough attention to make the mistake of asking Aristagorus a question. I was walking just behind them, partly listening, partly looking around.

The fine weather had returned and the sun had begun to give a measure of warmth. I gazed around inhaling the stench of the Eridanos river that rises pure and fresh on Mount Lykabetos but is so polluted by the time it flows through the Agora that it stinks like a foul drain. I noticed that many walls had graffito freshly painted, some calling on the Athenians to fight the Persians. The atmosphere in the city felt less oppressive than when we'd arrived. We were moving out of the area of stalls with Aristagorus droning on.

"But the new principle established at the fall of the tyrants gave, I think, too many freedoms to those of low birth. I refer of course to isonomy, the principle of a balance of liberties, but even that does not go far enough for some; soon, I fear, birth will count for nothing. There is change and disorder in the air."

He paused, his thought process diverted,

"There, look."

We followed his gaze towards the statues of the tyrant slayers in their prominent place. These were the original statues made by the sculptor Antenor, later stolen by Xerxes, not the replacements of Kritios that you can see today. For me the originals, although perhaps simpler, were nobler, and the more striking for it. But that day, as Aristagorus had noticed to his disgust, they had been freshly crowned with laurel. His exclamation had drawn some attention to us and Cimon was recognised for who he was, causing some citizens to shout greetings to him. Some men bellowed his father's name like the paean is chanted at the start of battle. Cimon acknowledged this chanting of his father's name with a modest wave of thanks and a smile.

Why, you wonder, do I bother to recount an unimportant stroll in the Agora when there is so much of importance to record? But have patience; that day I saw the first sign of the public attention that was to follow Cimon all his life, and I saw the first display of the naturalness, dignity and courage that he was to wear like a robe all his days. It is customary now, as you are all too aware, to hear Cimon portrayed as an ignorant drunkard, booby I think is the word Pericles used behind his back. Perhaps that's what you think. But if that's the case I'll wager that you never knew him, you were never led into battle by him, and certainly never felt the power he could exert over all he met, from the bottom row on a trireme to the Spartan Ephors. Because if you had, you'd know the disparaging terms were lies spread by lesser men behind his back. Even by Pericles who, for all his faults, I admit is not a lesser man. But those who saluted him that day in the Agora recognised something of the greatness that was to follow. But not for long: Aristagorus quickly pulled him away and walked us at a sharp pace back home.

That afternoon a little before the light began to fade, we left for the house of Phrasicles. The fat red winter sun was already sinking behind the Acropolis and there was the first hint of chill in the air. Miltiades and his brother dressed simply but richly, walked at the head of our party, straight backed and radiating high birth and command. Me following, uncomfortable in a new stiff-feeling robe. Then behind at a dignified distance, Theodorus and a party of roughnecks from the boats as escort, smartly dressed and behaving with unusual decorum. The way was not long but by the time we had reached the house the sun had gone and the cold mists of winter had gathered.

Outside the door torches were lit and we were welcomed in across the courtyard, our shadows flickering like the lamps, and into the andron where the symposium was to take place. The house and room was furnished in simple but expensive good taste. Our host offered greetings and we were shown our places.

There were fifteen couches in the room, spread around the walls, and most were already occupied. Phrasicles was a tall, slender man with carefully curled long hair and a slightly androgynous air, not the type one would have imagined as a companion of Themistocles. He led Miltiades to a couch at the far end of the room opposite the door, the place of honour. Stesagoras was placed along the side wall and I was directed to the least favourable couch by the door. Whilst the slaves removed our sandals and poured warmed, perfumed water over our feet, I took in my surroundings.

The room was lit with finely fashioned lamps, fragrant with the scent of rose and burning incense that released a heady aroma that I could not identify. My nearest neighbour was placed to my right, the door being to the left and, therefore, leaving a gap between myself and the neighbour on that side. But before I was ready to greet him, slaves brought in drinks that they set on the low tables by each couch, whilst others poured water over our hands. The food was good and I think of great cost as it included dishes of eel in a light sauce, some fine fillets of tuna along with a variety of shellfish. There was a murmur of appreciation and thanks to the host. Such fish was only within the budget of a rich man. Then everyone began to eat at once. The eel that night was the best I think I ever tasted but I've never really had the purse to allow me to be a connoisseur so I'm not the best judge. But I do know that the tables were rapidly cleared.

I'd learned by this time the name of my neighbour, Aeschylus, a land owner and farmer from one of the country regions. He was a well made dark haired man of about thirty, handsome in a hawkish type of way. He didn't say much but observed everything, including the fact that the second most honoured couch on the other side of Phrasicles from the General was unoccupied. The tables were cleared and refilled with small plates of dried fruits, almonds, little honey cakes and sweets, along with dishes of salt. These were eaten more slowly to the background murmur of small talk. Then the tables were cleared, the floor swept of shells, bones and other debris, our hands rinsed again by slaves and the main business of the evening began.

There was sound of a commotion outside and our host rose to greet the new arrival. It was not just the deliberate timing of the late entrance, but his obvious enjoyment of the reaction it provided that distinguished Themistocles. I noticed the General exchange a look with his brother. Themistocles half blustered, half laughed his way through an apology to his host, who accepted it gracefully and presented him to the company. He greeted Miltiades with a stiff politeness but to my surprise had time to turn and wink at Aeschylus, who raised his eyes in reply.

While Themistocles was being seated the jugs, cups, water and wine were brought in and set up. Both of the great men insisted that the host Phrasicles assume the role of symposiarch, the master of ceremonies; thus we began. Despite the normal procedures the mixing of the wine and water in a large krater before transferring it into a jug to pour, and then the making of the libation to the gods, no one could have been under any illusion that this was no normal drinking party.

Phrasicles announced a four krater night with an aged Chian cut five to two. He made the first toast, to the Archon and the General, and then announced without any consultation that with the first krater we would discuss the nature of our polis and how it should be preserved.

These days I don't get invited to many drinking parties. I can't remember the last one but I don't suppose they've changed much. This one followed the normal pattern but the discussion was a set up. It was a set up to see if Themistocles and the General's views on what was needed to preserve the polis could accommodate each other.

But it was done cleverly. Phrasicles started with an abstract speech based on the ancient poets' views on virtue and honour, ending with Nestor's speech to the Greeks at Troy, reminding them that it was when times were hardest that they must gain strength from the courage and virtues of their elders and ancestors. Stesagoras picked up the theme with examples from Hesiod, assuming the importance of defending and nurturing the land that bred you and its ancient traditions. Then, as if he had been primed, my farmer neighbour leaned forward and called out.

"And from your city do not wholly banish fear. For what man living freed from fear will still be just?"

He paused and I thought that this seemed a bit poetical for a farmer when he continued,

"So, how would our ancestors have reacted to the activities of the Great King and his recent rape of Ionian Greek cities?"

One short sentence but men forgot the wine, the philosophy and sat up straining for what came next as it was clear some kind of challenge had been set down. Themistocles broke the silence.

"You ask a sharp question, son of Euphorian, but one that removes from us the comforts of a pleasant evening. However, it is perhaps the question that nags at the back of all our minds so let's discuss it. Lucky then that we have one here better qualified than any to give an answer. Better because his ancestor was Ajax, one of the heroes to whom our host alluded so eloquently, and also because he himself knows and has fought the Great King. We would be honoured by your opinion, son of Cimon."

It was a cunning statement, flattering yes, but one that would elicit, if there were to be, the basis of an understanding. Not only from what the General actually said, because most of that could be anticipated easily enough, but from the way he said it. Would the patrician ex tyrant choose to make common cause with the new men?

Miltiades leaned back as if in reflection then he prevaricated further by drinking at length from the beautiful cup decorated in the archaic style.

So, for a while we sat in an expectant silence, broken only by the low spluttering of the lamps and a distant faint voice from the slaves' quarters. I think he used this pause to buy time to decide how to reply knowing that it is during such moments that men's futures are decided. At last he put down the cup, leaned forward and began.

Beginning with a compliment to the host, he delivered an authoritative analysis of the Great King and his ambition to expand the empire of the Persians. He cleverly mentioned the common heritage of the Persian lands with the Trojans, almost suggesting that the desire of the Great King was to exact revenge for that ancient war. He spoke at length of the failure of the rebellion, its poor, disunited leadership, lack of discipline and tactical sense. He then moved on to the fate of the cities which had resisted the empire. He did not mention the sack of Miletos but it was there in our minds, knowing that this too could be the fate of Athens. He concluded by saying that it was his belief that with strong leadership the Persians could be beaten because they would be fighting against Athens and Sparta together on the Greek mainland where they would have extended supply lines. This would be much tougher than defeating a revolt within their empire.

He spoke powerfully and I could see from the faces of the company that he moved them, not least Themistocles. He did not, however, make any effort to praise Themistocles or the government of Athens, or make any attempt to forge links of friendship, and I could see from Stesagoras' face when he finished speaking that he, at least, had expected more.

It seemed that Themistocles too expected something more. By this time the second krater had been mixed and as Phrasicles moved to suggest the next subject for discussion, Themistocles cut in.

"Forgive me, for I know it is your right as symposiarch to lead the talk, but as we have the good fortune to have a man of such worldly experience as Miltiades, son of Cimon, amongst us, I wonder whether we could now seek his opinion on our new system of government in Athens."

"I feel I must refuse this invitation, Archon, otherwise I will have dominated this symposium and denied others their opinions."

I could tell that the General, having given his military assessment of the situation and spoken from a reservoir of experience, was reluctant to hold forth on a topic that covered less firm ground and which he felt distasteful.

"But that would also deny us your opinions on the workings of the polis."

Miltiades resented being pressed in this manner and it was clear was unused to it.

"I would rather restrict myself to military matters and matters of state than the dabbling of those I believe now style themselves as politicians."

He could not help himself from putting a scornful inflection on this last word. Themistocles, however, showed no sign of discomfort.

"However, we have already diverted once from the tradition of the symposium, and to deny us your wisdom on our form of governance would, I feel, result in many of us leaving the gathering disappointed, which would not do justice to our host."

This was unexpected. I saw that even my neighbour, the farmer, seemed surprised. Miltiades flushed red, his pride and quick temper were, as we all knew, notorious. Themistocles settled back into the cushions of his couch, a faint smile playing across his lips, and reached for his refilled cup.

The General with an obvious attempt at self control blurted out,

"And on which particular aspect of that governance would you like my opinion, son of Neocles?"

Themistocles replied in a smooth, almost teasing manner,

"Why I think we would most value your opinion of the principle that distinguishes Athenians from all others: isonomy, the balance of rights and powers that leads to a form of government that serves the needs of the demos and the wishes of the gods."

As Themistocles spoke the smile never left his lips. Stesagoras was trying to signal to his brother to control himself, the farmer was trying hard not to laugh. For myself, although I didn't understand much of the talk, I could see that the General was being pushed, tested. I'd seen enough of him to know that where his temper led, violence followed, and that nothing angered him quicker than the failure to offer him due respect. If there was anything in the world guaranteed to provoke him it was the look of amused insolence on the Archon's face. It was the perfect provocation to that swift and violent anger. He put down his cup but with such force that the crack resounded around the andron.

"Oh yes, isonomy, I've seen it scratched on walls. I'm not sure what it means though, something about rights and responsibilities of citizens whatever they might be. Am I close, son of Neocles?"

"Well, not quite as close as you could be, son of Cimon, but then you've been away from the city a long time. Isonomy is the principle that gives the rights that allow men to make the city strong and thus balance health and happiness."

"Yes, I'm beginning to remember. It was the word that the Alkmaionidai Cleisthenes used to justify the re-ordering of the city after the fall of the tyrants. It replaced the principle of Eunomia didn't it? I always thought that the old principle of good order had served us well enough, better than misrule at any rate."

There was a collective expelling of breath round the room at the accusation of misrule. The smile vanished from Themistocles' face.

"Then perhaps you've been away for too long, son of Cimon. Many states have embraced the principle of demokratia now and it is isonomy that gives the balance and makes the difference between freemen and the slaves of the Great King."

Themistocles started this sentence as if forcing the words through clenched teeth but ended it shouting, the great veins of his bull neck standing out like ship's cables. I wondered what signals I'd missed that had led to this fury so quickly. As the words "slaves of the Great King" were shouted out the General reached to his waist as if for a sword and, in doing so his elbow caught the already damaged cup, hurling it to the floor, where it smashed in myriads of shards. He rose from his couch as if to seize hold of Themistocles. Phrasicles rose quickly to stand between them as I waited for the

157

knives to be used. Amidst the uproar Stesagoras and the farmer leapt from their couches to keep them apart.

CHAPTER 16

There are moments when it seems time stops. Like the frieze on a temple pediment depicting some awful forgotten event, they stood there intense but scarcely moving. Phrasicles, Stesagoras and Aeschylus in the position of supplicants to the cruel, but unmoved gods. Themistocles and the General stood face to face, each close enough to feel the other's breath, eyes locked. It was Themistocles, surprisingly since he was Archon, who first moved, allowing the rest of us to breathe normally.

"Come, Miltiades, let's not show our disrespect to our host; the fault was mine. I broke the tradition of the symposium."

He turned and went back to his couch, as did all the others, Miltiades was last. I wondered how the General controlled himself when he felt he had been publically slighted. Perhaps part of the answer was the track of blood that led to his couch. In his rage he had stepped on a shard of the broken cup, there was a jagged tear in the heel of his left foot leaking blood across the andron floor. Not a good omen. Stesagoras accompanied him back to his couch followed by Aeschylus, the farmer, which seemed strange. Slaves arrived with water, dressings and brooms to sweep away the remains. The house steward brought the General another cup of a similarly fine provenance.

During this Phrasicles spoke to the rest of us:

"This is time for our third krater and I think we have reached the end of our formal discussions, so to help us enjoy the remains of the evening we will have some entertainment."

He was about to clap hands to summon whatever troupe of players was waiting to come in when the General spoke.

"Forgive me, Phrasicles, but I, like the son of Neocles, would crave your indulgence a moment."

My eyes, like all others at this moment, switched to Themistocles, whose position on his couch stiffened as if he were about to rise again. From the corner of my eye I thought I saw the farmer make some slight gesture to him but I can't be sure. Whether he did or not, anyway Themistocles stayed put and the General continued.

"You asked me what I thought of the principle of isonomy and I don't think I did myself justice with the answer. You are right, I have been too long away, and there is much I need to learn.

"But I am still an Athenian and have fought all my life for Athens. I said at the hearing at the Areopagus that I owed my allegiance to the legitimate government of the city just as it is my duty to offer my life in its defence. That I meant this, my ancestry alone tells you. I will stick to my duty, unlike some."

Here he hesitated for a moment, realising his mistake and that some now expected a statement of denunciation. So he continued more quickly.

"None of whom are of course represented in this honourable gathering, but I think we all know of whom I speak. That being the case I will defend my city, its government and its isonomy for that matter, to my last breath and the representative of this governance is with us in this room to hear me pledge this."

Without any other gesture he sat down and picked up his new wine cup. In the brief pause before Phrasicles clapped his hands everyone distinctly heard Themistocles shout,

"Nobly said, son of Cimon."

Three girls carrying double flutes entered the room followed by one with a small harp. All were dressed in light and wispy gowns which hid little, all were beautiful. They were followed by two boy dancers, both naked, of whom I took little notice although some of the gathering, including Phrasicles, did. The symposium then drifted into the traditional and most enjoyable stage. Sadly I didn't know the rules back then and failed to take advantage of what was on offer.

The girls began to play a theme, repeating it over and again with variations. They were skilled and moved with grace, providing a background for the boys, who performed a dance mime in the centre of the andron. For as long as it was necessary for politeness to honour the taste and expense of our host, we all watched the display in near silence. When the rhythm of the harps and theme of the flutes ceased things changed.

The symposium broke up into groups, some played dice and kotobos, others ogled the flute girls and tumblers as they drank. At the head of the room, concentrating on nothing else, their voices covered by the music, laughter and shouts, Miltiades and Themistocles talked in earnest. Stesagoras had joined them and shared Themistocles' couch. Phrasicles as host stayed in the group but seemed to play no part in the conversation. It seemed his role had been fulfilled – he had supplied the reason for the meeting, and was not now needed.

I could not take my eye off the girls, one in particular, who seemed familiar. The farmer Aeschylus noticed.

"You seem interested in the girls, Mandrocles, particularly that one."

I blushed but continued to watch.

"You are quite honoured; these girls are run by Androcles. He only keeps the best in his stable. You wouldn't get one of these to bend over behind a tomb in the Ceramicus for you."

He was teasing me but I was glad of the information. As I watched, the performers began to distribute themselves around the couches, some summoned by guests. The wine had loosened behaviour. The girl I wanted, the most beautiful, was beckoned to play for the man who was placed next to the couch that Stesagoras had vacated. She seemed to float across the room to play for the finely dressed, long haired but fat man who had let his robe slip down over his left shoulder in the current fashion. She stood by him and I noticed him slip his hand through one of the slits in her robe and begin to rub it up and down between her thighs. She didn't react but then, to my shame, turned her head and directly returned my gaze, as a slight smile crossed her lips and for a second I thought I saw her tongue slip out between them.

"You've missed your chance with her, boy, and if you stare much harder your eyes will be on stalks. Let Diphilos have his fun, there'll be chances for you later if that's the way your taste runs."

I took my eyes away from the girl, who had begun to play again whilst fat Diphilos fingered her, and made room on my couch for Aeschylus. It was clear that his tastes ran the same way as mine and he genuinely only wanted to talk. I realise now that he was trying to sound me out on the General and had been deliberately seated next to me. Back then I think I just felt grateful; I was little more than a boy of no importance in a room full of men, all of whom counted for something in the city. In truth I was surprised to have been allowed into the andron having expected to spend the night waiting outside with the escorts.

"So what have you made of tonight's rich fare, Mandrocles?"

"If by rich fare you mean the exchange between the two great men rather than all this, then I don't know and I'm not sure what sort of game is being played."

"Game indeed, young man, a good name for what we have watched, but then who can untangle his path out of the maze of the thicket, dark it is everywhere."

This last phrase I didn't understand and asked him to explain.

"It doesn't matter, just a line of verse I must have picked up somewhere. Look, tell me of your time with Miltiades. The stories of your escape from the Persians and the sea fight are the talk of the city."

He ordered that our cups be refilled then sat back to listen as I told him the tale. By the time I had finished the symposium had moved on. My flute girl and one other still stood playing, however, the others were sharing couches being groped and more by the guests. One of the boys was with Phrasicles, whose carefully styled hair was now tangled in disarray. Stesagoras was back on his original couch talking and drinking with Diphilos and another. Of the General and Themistocles there was no sign. My head was unclear, I needed to piss and on getting to my feet I found I was unsteady. Aeschylus put out a hand to support me.

"Careful, boy, the cut of the wine was stronger than you're used to, I think."

He was right but my pride was injured. In fact the room had started to swim before my eyes and the noise of the party seemed to grow and recede as if in waves.

"I'm in no need of help; I've fought from the deck of a trireme so I've no need of help from a farmer who's never left Attica."

Drunk as I was I realised that I'd caused offence and made a fool of myself and I could feel my face colouring as I lurched out of the door. Looking back, apart from my petulant and childish reply, I needn't

163

have worried as everyone else in that room was drunk. Well, everyone who mattered. Once outside the door I realised I was about to vomit so rushed into the courtyard where I heaved up my guts behind some bushes in the shadows.

I stood for some time taking deep breaths. It was cold but bright; the stars sparkling, the moon fully risen. I lacked either the confidence or inclination to return to the party so I remained in the courtyard hiding behind the bushes like some assassin. After a time I became aware that I could hear the murmur of voices approaching from the other side of the courtyard. Not wanting to be discovered I stayed still and silent. Two men were walking along the colonnade heading back towards the andron. They paused for a moment.

"So we have reached agreement, it must be war."

"Yes, war. We work apart but to the same purpose, any differences to wait until after."

"Shall we swear it?"

"For men like us there is no need to swear. Apart we fail, we fail, we die, no need to swear, it's not as if it's a play."

They both laughed and walked off. I'd grasped the importance of the agreement but not why they'd laughed. I remained outside a while thinking, until the cold drove me inside. In the passage leading to the andron fastening herself into a winter cloak was the flute girl who had played for Diphilos. She saw me and laughed lightly.

"So, Mandrocles the beautiful, worse for wear I see."

I didn't know how to reply, feeling shamed, but she took me by the hand and led me into an adjoining chamber where there were vessels of perfumed water for the guests' use. She stood before me and looked me up and down.

"You can't go back into the room looking like that."

She took a cloth, dipped it in the water and began to dab, first at my face and then at some of the stains that I realised covered the front of my tunic. It was done with gentleness, tenderness almost; the first I had experienced since I last saw my mother, which now seemed in a different life.

"There, not that much better, but it will do. Be more careful in future."

She laughed again.

"Oh, and Mandrocles, did you take my advice to stay away from diseased hags?"

I remembered where I'd seen her before and managed to nod in answer to her question.

"Good boy, then I suppose it's safe to give you this."

She reached out a hand to the back of my neck and kissed me softly on the lips. I still sense the scent of her breath.

"My name's Lyra. I think we might meet again."

Her hand trailed across my cheek, she turned and left me in the room with the slowly vanishing presence of her perfume, trying to recall the feel of her lips.

Back in the andron it was still noise and revelry. Those guests who remained were gathered around Themistocles and the General engaged in a raucous game of dice. The loser of each throw had to pledge the others in a draught of wine. This the General enjoyed; his face was red as he roared out his own pledges and shouted his laughter at the others. I noticed that my companion, the farmer, was no longer present. I regretted this and was sorry that my last words to him had been those of a drunken silly boy. I'd liked him despite his trickery and the hidden understanding between him and Themistocles. I'd hoped to apologise and part as friends.

I settled into the cushions of my couch across the room from the games, to watch. The drink had proved too much for a couple of them, who ceased to play. One fell from his couch and lay on the floor snoring. At the end of the last pledge, Themistocles and the General played a game flicking the dregs out of their cups to see if the pattern of lees on the floor would give a hint to the future of their enterprise. I could see no pattern. The General was drunk, his brother helped him from the room, Themistocles played drunk but I think was acting; his eyes missed nothing.

We were escorted to the door with pledges of friendship and as our escort led us out I felt a hand on my shoulder and found myself face to face with Themistocles. Close up I was half a head taller, which I remember being surprised at.

"You will perhaps learn from tonight, Mandrocles, never to drop your guard. Still you miss little and that's good, for I think our paths will follow the same course for some years. You may turn out to be useful and I think I might like that. Go well."

He turned and we left the house. Outside the torches were still flaring. Leaning on his brother the General sang broken fragments of a drinking song that we had sung earlier. The night was otherwise silent and we trudged back through the cold of the sleeping city accompanied only by the disconnected snatches of bawdy songs. In my head though, the odd line of Aeschylus repeated itself over and over:

"But who can untangle his path out of the maze of the thicket, dark it is everywhere."

CHAPTER 17

That winter was bitter, so cold that for days snow lay on the hills and we woke in the mornings to a light dusting on the streets. The ships at Phaleron were beached and apart from farmers bringing their animals, milk and cheese to the city the roads were empty. The city lived indoors waiting for a thaw. Yet it seethed with rumours: rumours of a great Persian army, of agents within the city walls of treachery, of the overthrow of the demos by an aristocratic faction. It seemed that people were now more in fear of the city being split by faction, more scared of their neighbours, than of the Great King.

But even shut down by the winter, news did trickle in from the outside world and the Great King's empire. Artaphernes, his brother, had brutally crushed the last traces of the revolt, subdued the islands and was restoring order to Ionia. This we'd expected but worse was to follow: the Great King had let it be known that he would destroy all Greek states that resisted him, and Athens in particular.

Athens would burn like Miletos and a plan for the systematic subjugation of all Greece was being drawn up. Even now the talented and brave young General Mardonius, son-in-law of the Great King, was gathering a vast army. With this he would invade Thrace, then Macedonia as a precursor to an invasion of Athens from the north.

In my long life I've learned that there is no combination like external threat and the fear of internal treachery to stir up and make mad our already volatile city. During this time the house of Stesagoras became the centre of Miltiades' campaign to build a strong political base and persuade Athenians that they must fight or die. Of Themistocles, however, we saw nothing yet it appeared that the two men had stuck to their agreement to work for the same end, but separately. Strange how a cynical pact between two enemies hastily cobbled together at a drinking party can shape the future of the world.

Whether they met in secret elsewhere I can't say. Miltiades' movements were hard to track, he confided in no one, not even Stesagoras. For several days at a time he'd disappear but this was never commented on. Visits to the house, however, were of greater interest and at one of these I saw my first Spartan: Brasidas a kinsman of King Cleomenes. He was a tall, long haired man in a rough cloak who carried with him an air of distrust, dislike perhaps, for all things Athenian. He even brought his own drinking cup – a rough ridged thing called a kothon – and insisted on having all his heavily diluted wine served in it.

"Almost as if he thought we were going to poison him. Still he's the best of them, and a good friend behind the typical 'look at me I'm a tough Spartan' act. They just don't know how to behave away from home," the General said after he'd left. He had little time for most Spartans, thinking their reputation for austerity and heroism some type of posturing. Cimon, however, for all his wildness and lack of discipline, was impressed and followed the man round the house whenever he could, questioning him on the Spartan way of war. To be fair to our taciturn guest, he indulged the boy with long serious answers and seemed more at home in his company than in that of grown men.

Then one day, as the worst of the winter seemed to be passing, the General told me to fetch my cloak and accompany him. The sun shone through a watery blue sky and it was possible to sense the coming of spring. More people were about and the General was hailed with greetings and shouts of encouragement as we walked through the Agora. At the southern end, at the foot of the hill where they're now building a temple to Hephaistos, there used to be an area of old buildings and vegetable plots. At the far end, down a muddy track that wound its way between more rough huts and sheds, we arrived at a large barn. We picked our way through the goat droppings and puddles of mud to the entrance hearing the sound of raised voices from inside, growing louder with every step.

Inside, a group of strangely dressed men stood in a semi circle facing a peculiar looking individual who was striking strange poses and shouting. His long and curled hair seemed to have been coloured an unnatural looking copper brown and his robe had more dye in its border than all our clothes put together. He was shouting.

"You're meant to be begging mercy from cruel implacable gods, not asking for a parcel of fucking honey cakes. How have I been stupid enough to hire such donkeys, deaf mutes would have been better. The donkeys themselves would have been better. The donkeys certainly move better. Gods, Aeschylus would wet himself if he saw this. I've passed turds that show more emotion than you. Listen, you, you in particular chorus leader, chief donkey, donkey leader, this is how it is supposed to sound."

He took a step back, took a deep breath and struck what seemed to be a ludicrous attitude with hands held high above his head and began to chant in a deep, far carrying voice:

"Oh the unhappy, citizens wretched,
Blood grudge and vengeance, the discord grates,
Our hearts black now. Women's breasts beating
Husbandless children doomed by cruel fate
Spurned by our friends, by the gods deserted
Struck down Butchered, at the cursed ruined gate."

169

He paused, struck a new position and shouted again at the miserable looking men:

"Then you, chorus, you bleating sheep. You're meant to have witnessed horrors so you answer like this,

'We see mother's torn breasts
Husbands, happiness, gone
We weep for the city
Whose friends didn't help it
Aiee sharp grief in waves
Endless like the sea
Cry out Miletos' fate.'"

He paused and the silence was broken by Miltiades clapping his hands.

"Bravo Phrynichus, there won't be a dry eye in the Agora after they've heard that."

Phrynichus turned and the expression of disdain he directed at his chorus was replaced, instantly, by an exaggerated gesture intended to portray incredulous delight.

"Great thanks, Lord Miltiades, you do great service to visit us in our attempts to honour the gods and the city of the goddess. But you are right, there will be no Athenian who watches this whose heart will not be wrenched apart, whose eyes will not fill and..."

Here he repositioned himself and thrust out his right arm towards us before continuing in a louder voice suggesting a great emotion,

"Whose ire will not be raised by the Persian desecration of the once great city of Miletos?"

I'd never seen a man behave like this and wanted to laugh. The General wasn't laughing, but did allow himself a smile.

"And bravely done too, Phrynichus, I am sure that the choregus will be well pleased with your efforts; the prize is as good as won"

"It should be won but these days people are easily seduced by gimmickry and novelty of the type that young Aeschylus peddles; it is hard to maintain traditional values these days."

"But with the Archon's brother as your choregus I wouldn't worry too much, it seems to me that Themistocles is not a man to back a loser."

Phrynichus led us away from the chorus, who seemed relieved by the break, and said in a softer voice,

"But I wonder if some of this verse is not too strong meat, is it wise to stir up such passion in our citizens? I made the changes that the choregus suggested but it seems to me that the play suggests that our city shares the blame for destruction of Miletos. That the Persians will do the same to us and that the goddess Athena wishes us to fight. Now if the theme were to be the sack of Troy, as I'd originally intended, there'd have been no problem. But to set it in Miletos, so recently destroyed and the grief so raw; will that not cause problems, move people to grief, guilt, anger? Even those hopeless donkeys of the chorus over there can't fail to get that across."

"But my dear Phrynichus, that's what will win you the prize, it's got to be strong to beat Aeschylus and anyway, everyone's done Troy to death. But no one except you, Phrynichus, has ever set a tragedy in modern times. No one has dealt with something which threatens us all. Think, Phrynichus, with this play you won't only win the goat as prize but you'll be able to take the play on tour to some of the rural deme theatres. Think of the money you could earn with something as strong as this in places like Thorikos. Those onion breaths will treat you like a god."

This speech worked well, no one could be as persuasive as the General when he wanted to be. He made the listener feel the most important person in the world and it was equally as effective when directed to a crowd. It didn't matter if he believed or even cared about what he was saying. What mattered was that you, the listener, believed. Perhaps if he had believed or stayed true to what he said he would have become the greatest man Athens ever produced and all our futures would have been very different. It worked on Phrynichus though; you could almost see him thinking about the congratulations, the gold coins and most of all, of the celebrity.

"You are right of course, Lord Miltiades, it's just a pity they haven't finished building that new theatre in honour of Dionysius up by the Acropolis. That would have been fitting, a new theatre opened with a new type of tragedy, a play for the modern age. Still we must get on. Please stay and watch us work if you have time."

There was a rough bench near one of the walls where we sat and watched while he shouted and bullied the chorus through their lines. But something had changed. The persuasive mood of good fellowship had left the General.

"When you watch this, Mandrocles, these tragic plays, this goat song, you see on stage what we know to be true. We're playthings of the gods, alone in an immense space where there is nothing. You've heard goat song, the noise they make as we hold them still for the knife before sacrifice. I think that's all the gods heard when Miletos was sacked. We left the fleet, remember, when the fleet was beaten, Miletos was doomed. We laugh as we walk the goat to slaughter. We laugh at the goat's struggles, its death song. The gods laugh at us; they think no more of us than we do of the goat as we walk to our slaughter, all of us you, me, Darius, Cimon, Metiochus, wherever he is. We struggle, the gods laugh, we die, they laugh, we enter the void, become nothing. I don't think we even become shadows wailing in the mists of Elysian Fields."

He stopped and for a moment I thought I saw the beginning of tears, but he quickly rose from the bench.

"We may as well use this time as best we can. I don't want Athens to become Miletos, so they'll have to wait a while longer for that little joke. We can though do our best to ensure that there'll be a whole Persian army entering the void before us. At least then we write the conclusion to our own tragedy."

On the few occasions I heard him talk like this I thought to myself, which is the real man? But I think this was the man he wanted to be. As we reached the door a group of men were noisily coming in disturbing Phrynichus' concentration and causing him to stop and turn.

"Ah, Praterius, Theristis, friends, come to see a real poet at work, eh? It can only improve your scribbling."

As the last man came in he paused and his face changed.

"But not you, word thief, I don't want to see my ideas turning up in the experimental rubbish you peddle."

This last man I recognised, it was my friend the farmer from the symposium. He showed little emotion at this hostile greeting, merely grinned before saluting the General and then me with a broad smile.

"He's happy to see the other scribblers, but not me. I'll take it as a compliment."

The General, who still seemed deep in thought, caught him by the arm.

"I have things to do, Aeschylus, and as you've now got some spare time, take Mandrocles with you and explain our spring festival to him."

Without a word to me he strode off towards the Agora. Above us large, white clouds scudded across the sky but between them were patches of blue. The sun shone through with piercing light making us squint in the brightness. Aeschylus took my arm.

"Walk with me to the Ceramicus, Mandrocles. We'll have something to eat. I know a kapelion where they cook good spiced sausage and the wine's not too bad. I'm glad I've run into you, there's someone who wants to meet you and after we've eaten there may be time to make the introduction."

The kapelion he took us to was in the same area of narrow streets and poor shacks as the Red Cockrell. For a moment I was alarmed that it was the Red Cockrell we were headed to and wondered, if that were the case, would I be recognised as one of the gang with Theodorus when he had so badly broken up the face of Eubulus? I needn't have worried; we ended up in a similar place within spitting distance where Aeschylus was obviously well known. The sausages were good, moist so that the greasy juice they oozed flowed down our chins, but to my disappointment there were no bar girls, just an ex sailor with a bald head and one eye swaying from drink behind the small bar. Aeschylus wiped his hands on his tunic, started to speak then began to laugh, choking on the mouthful he was swallowing. I waited till he recovered.

"I've not been fully honest with you boy, the gods forgive me."

He began to cough again until he managed to hawk up and spit out a gob of gristle, leaving me to wonder if he was going to try to seduce me. How would I fight him off without offending the General or Themistocles? He must have supposed as much as by the time he was recovered enough he said hastily,

"No need to look so worried, Mandrocles; my tastes don't run in that direction, unlike many in my profession. No, I'm not a farmer, well, not an active one. My brother Cynegeiros takes care of all that."

"Yes, I think I've worked that out. You're a poet like Phrynichus, aren't you?"

"Watch your mouth, boy, if you want us to be friends; only the gods can decide who is truly a poet. I'm only learning to become one, searching for the voice that explains and moves. The true voice, not the rag bag of old tricks and speeches that Phrynichus trots out."

He paused to clear his throat and took a mouthful of wine.

"But it's true, I'm interested in what he is rumoured to be writing this time, and why the Archon wants me to withdraw my original entry for this year and substitute something lesser. This year's Dionysia is about something more than competing for a goat and honouring the gods, and Phrynichus' play is at the heart of it. Whatever it was that Miltiades and Themistocles cooked up during the symposium in that idiot Phrasicles' house is beginning to come to the boil."

"I thought you were Themistocles' man."

"I'm no one's man. Poets can't be and even if I were, I'd never know most of what he thinks or does, he's a deep one. I think I travel the same road he does though. He has ideas for the city, some I think I know, and others I can't even guess at. But, given a chance, he'll make us what none of us has yet even dreamt of. Is that poetical enough for you?"

"Is that what you meant by that strange remark about untangling a path through a maze the other night?"

"Oh that, perhaps. I never really know what some of my lines mean, they feed off each other, start in one direction and end up somewhere else; take on a life of their own. But that was from the withdrawn play, one that the Archon previously supported. It's a good line so it will either wait until that play's time comes, or it'll find its way into another; nothing good's ever wasted."

You, reader, will understand that as a youth of sixteen much of what he said I failed to comprehend, but more to the point I wasn't really interested so, more to change the subject than anything else, I asked him,

"So, are you well known enough to get your plays to win at the Dionysia like Phrynichus?"

"No, I've not yet won the prize, but maybe one day."

Even now, so many years later, and him dead, I still blush to think that in that bar I sat with the greatest dramatic poet the world ever produced, except Homer but certainly including Sophocles, the current darling of the theatre, and was bored. One thing did interest me though.

"Why is the General interested in Phrynichus' play?"

"Well, I'll say this for Phrynichus; it seems he's writing a play about a real event that will eventually have consequences. It's about the Persian sack of Miletos, you should be interested, you were closer to that than either Phrynichus or I was. Themistocles' brother is the choregus who put up the money but Themistocles is behind it. He reckons that once our citizens are brought face to face with the horrors the Persians inflicted on that once great Greek city, they might feel a little anger and maybe guilt."

"Is that why you were prepared to change your play, so that this one would seem stronger?"

"Partly, but also we're changing the way men control their own destinies in this city, how they make the decisions that give us laws leading to a better life, the way the gods intended. This idea of rule of the demos, it's the future, boy, and Themistocles is leading us to it. So, between that and the Persians we've got our work cut out. Drink up; we've somewhere else to go."

We followed some muddy lanes until we emerged in a small square near to the cemetery. Across from the training school of the flute girls was a line of whitewashed tenements built of mud brick and timber with red tiled roofs. Aeschylus walked to the end building and banged on a strong and metal studded wooden door hung with a wreath of herbs as a charm against the evil eye. The door was opened by a bruiser with the battered face of a retired boxer. He recognised Aeschylus and even seemed pleased to see him. His lips moved to form what on other men would have been a smile. It wasn't a pleasant sight and he repeated it when he pocketed the coins that were passed to him. Behind the door was a small courtyard with a kind of beauty unexpected in such a place. At the far end of the yard sitting under a veranda was a group of girls eating sweet cakes and laughing. One looked our way then spoke to a girl with her back to us. She turned as Aeschylus called,

"Lyra, I've brought someone to introduce to you although I know you've already spoken."

She stood up and floated across to us wearing a simple woollen robe that was as modest as her gauzy one had been revealing. I stood mute, unable to think of any words or to meet her gaze.

"Has the beautiful young hero of Miltiades' sea fight not the courage to look at a woman, or doesn't he like what he sees?"

It was teasing but kind and inviting at the same time. Aeschylus had drifted off to talk to the other girls. I saw him take one of the cakes.

"You were more forward last time we met each other, have I changed so much these last weeks? Come, I have a favour to ask. In ten days the Dionysia begins.

177

I wish to see the trilogy by Phrynichus and his satyr play. Would you escort me? It would mean sitting at the back with the women, metics and slaves, but I would be very grateful."

I think I mumbled something in acceptance.

"You can collect me here. Give a coin to Demetrius on your way out, then he'll remember to let you in."

CHAPTER 18

Following the giant phalloi swaying above their heads, the procession romped through the Agora; the crowd threw spring blossom as the leaders dodged the swipes of young green branches wielded by the bacchants. That was how the god was brought home to open the great Dionysia festival in those days. The winter was over, the promise of warmth, plenty and long light days lay ahead, and that was it; simple and direct. Not like now with the ordered procession, ceremony, and ancient ritual that's all been made up these last few years. Back then when we held the festival in the Agora, it was simpler, and truer, closer to the routines of the life of the land that sustained us.

That year, the first day of the plays in the house of Dionysius offered a trilogy and a satyr play by Pratinus the elder. The General went with his brother and friends, I was confined to the house to look after Cimon and help the stewards. At times you could hear the noise from the crowd in the house. That evening the General returned late but in good humour. He had been cheered and sat in one of the seats of honour with the Archons. He summoned me.

"Tomorrow, Mandrocles, it's the turn of Phrynichus, go and watch but stay out of trouble, I've asked Aeschylus to go with you. If there's trouble get straight back to the house. Get up early, you'll need to be quick to get one of the seats with a decent view."

He gave me some money and dismissed me leaving me to wonder what he meant by trouble, although of more concern to me was the presence of Aeschylus as I had intended to check if Lyra had been serious about her offer. Since seeing her I'd thought of little else and imagined myself with her as I tried to sleep in my narrow bed at night.

179

Next day I was up early, the sun shone and the house crackled with activity and excitement. Everything relaxed for the Dionysia. The festival ruled the city, if rule is the right word; misrule would be better suited. The streets and taverns were packed as crowds from the surrounding countryside poured into Athens for six days of entertainment and licence in praise of the gods for their liberation of the land from winter. But the central glory of the festival, in the midst of the drinking, eating, rutting and fighting, was the three consecutive days of plays. Even now if you ask any Athenian what is the finest time of the year, the days to live for, he will say the plays at the spring Dionysia.

I found Aeschylus in the kitchen sitting by the fire pit, dunking bread into a cup of warm, spiced wine.

"You ready, Mandrocles? Don't want to keep your woman waiting. Brush your hair before we go though, at least try to make a reasonable impression."

It was typical of Aeschylus, to have remembered my promise to Lyra. Funny what we remember, it's my clearest memory of that morning. We must have pushed our way through the streets already crowded even at such an early hour. I'm not even sure if I can still picture being received at her home or what she was wearing, what she said, how her hair looked, how she smelt. I think we bought some cakes from a baker's stall on the way to the play but that could have been another year. What does come back in every detail, as if I can taste it, is the theatre.

In those days the plays were staged in part of the Agora called the orchestra. For seating they set up ikria, great timbers with planks attached to them like steps, and that's where the audience sat, packed in and shuffling for room. In front of these ikria was a space for men of great office and distinction and in front of

180

them space for the dancing and words. Behind this there was the skene hut where the props, costumes and masks were kept and where the actors changed.

We found space on the ikria near the back with a reasonable view. It was like being back on the ship as the planking swayed and the timbers creaked and shifted with the weight and movement. It didn't seem too secure to me but no one seemed bothered. In fact two years later a section of ikria collapsed during a play and people were crushed to death. After that they moved the festival to the new theatre of Dionysius on the southern slope of the Acropolis.

We sat through the early morning as the theatre filled and the sun rose along with expectation. Peddlers sold food and drink, jokes were shouted and the noise increased. I saw Theodorus with men from the Athene Nike in front of me, nearer the stage area. Then, to cheers, the great men processed in and took up their places. I saw the General, Themistocles and Xanthippus; it seemed the whole city and most of the countryside was there. The prayers were spoken; Phrynichus came on stage, asked for the gods' blessing and explained his three plays. I sat between Lyra and Aeschylus aware of the feel of her body close to mine and his pointed criticism of most of what Phrynichus said.

Then the plays started, they were the first I saw and I've loved the theatre ever since. The chorus and actors wore thickly padded tunics under their costumes and masks and so seemed larger than life. Simple I know, compared with what you're used to now, but I was gripped from the first. The first two plays went smoothly enough but the third one, the "Sack of Miletos" that we'd seen rehearsed, was different. The audience were all too familiar with the destruction of that city.

181

Before the chorus took to the stage there was a buzz in the crowd, there'd been rumours in the wine shops for days, that this play was something different. In the front row I saw the General shout something towards the block of seats where Megacles and Xanthippus sat with their friends. Themistocles had left his seat and was nowhere to be seen. On stage the flute ceased playing and the chorus delivered their opening lines. After a short while Aeschylus shoved my arm to attract attention.

"This is something I never thought to do, he's writing about what's just happened, this is no myth or tale of the gods, it's not in the tradition of the festival. It's not in any tradition. Who put him up to this?"

Lyra spoke across us,

"Keep quiet, hold your poet's jealousy, it's got real power, look around you."

We did. In the audience, even at the back amongst the metics, slaves, bad women and those of no account, people were shocked, some weeping. Then I too got swept away in the words and emotions. Phrynichus, who took the part of main speaker, was giving his account of the death throes of the doomed city and all Athens, lived it through him, the gut wrenching mixture of grief, fear and guilt. Much of it I can still recite.

"Wine to vinegar, cities ruin
Burnt the tower, razed and waste
They will not come now – Athens's heroes
No black ships strong on the wave
The bloody slaughter scars our soil
Our young dead now, thrown from walls
Maidens ravaged, crones lamenting
Youths are gelded in the blood pit
Blood driven on the wind of pain
Altars smashed, defiled, besmirched
Images broken, shrines unclean

182

The well of grief, spouts desolation
Our great city, gracious freedom
Now cast down salt sown, dead flesh
Watch, O Athens Watch, remember
As Persian spears pile dead on dead
I see their eyes now fast upon you
They see clear the goddess rock
Disasters stream will pour upon you
You'll lie like us for dogs to tear
No high heaped tomb, no funeral dirge
Betrayers you will know despair."

The howling sound began somewhere near the back. At first I thought some animal had got into the stands, but then as it spread I recognised it for what it was, grief. The audience was wailing. I turned to Aeschylus his face was in his hand, tears falling onto his robe. On stage the actors tried to continue, faltered and then stopped. Phrynichus took off his mask and made as if to speak directly to the crowd, perhaps to calm them, but he had no chance. A bull of a man sitting close to the front rose and roared at him,

"Bastard, you try to rub our faces in the shit of disgrace."

His shout was taken up by others as grief changed to anger. Fruit, beakers and other missiles were thrown at the stage, but also at the stand where Xanthippus and his friends sat. Then the first blows went in and fighting erupted along the rows, and the whole structure of ikria began to sway. I looked towards the General's seat, if he was threatened I should join him, but Theodorus and the lads were already there and escorting him to the exit.

Two men were fighting in the row behind us; one fell partly across Lyra, blood seeping from her ear. I

183

shoved him off and she clung to me, Aeschylus shouted in my ear,

"This is turning ugly, time to go, keep hold of the girl, use your weight, and shove your way out."

We began to fight our way down the rows of planks. It was if the gods had cast us all into madness. People were crushed, eyes were gouged as some pushed to get out while others inflamed with rage, kicked, bit and punched as the noise of shouting, wailing and screaming rose. The actors scattered and ran, the last to leave Phrynichus, blood streaming from a gash on the forehead. With Lyra between us, Aeschylus elbowed and butted the way out, dragging the girl while I hit out at anything in our way. Some had either fallen or been hurled to the floor and these we trod on as we and others fought our way out. Near the exit the crush was so dense that it was hard to breathe and impossible to free the arms to strike. Somehow Aeschylus forced a route through the scrum. It became easier to move and we could see the open space of the agora. In front of Aeschylus a large man with a close cropped head and dirty tunic sensed him close behind and turned quickly. He must have recognised him as he shouted to others close by,

"Here's one of the players with his whore."

He grabbed at Aeschylus, missed and caught Lyra's gown, pulling and ripping it. His red face was close enough for me to smell the rotten stink of his breath. Aeschylus tried to pull him off, an arm round his neck so I was able to smash my fist into his face, feeling the collapse of the bone and cartilage in his nose, then hit him again as he fell. We pushed through and ran for it, one on either side of the girl, pulling her along, then turned into a side alley and leant against a wall to catch breath. Behind us in the Agora was the noise of chaos, shouting and screams but it seemed we hadn't been followed. Aeschylus dusted off his tunic then placed a hand on my shoulder.

"Take the girl home, the way back will be safe enough."

"But what about you?"

"I'd better go back; see if there's anything I can do to help my fellow poet."

He paused,

"Don't worry I know how to take care of myself in a crowd of Athenian citizens."

He gave me a lopsided grin and was gone. Behind me I could hear the noise of anger and violence and, more ominously, the smell of burning. For a moment I considered following him. There was a gentle pressure on my arm.

"So are you going to see a lady safely home, or chase after your friend and enjoy the riot?"

I looked at her as she stood, a smile playing about her lips that I could not quite understand. Her hair had come loose in the struggle and fell thick and luxurious on her shoulders, her eyes questioning, wide and clear and the plump smiling lips slightly parted. Any thoughts of Aeschylus and danger of that instant disappeared. I took her hand and we moved rapidly away from the violence, noise and increasing smell of smoke. We went to her room.

It was, I know, the first real act of love I had ever felt. I had coupled excitedly with Theopone as a boy on Samos and tried it out with a pornoi in the Ceramicus, but not like this.

She lit a soft lamp in her room, then in the flickering play of light and shadow, loosed the pins in her gown and let it fall rustling to the floor at her feet. She brushed her hands through her hair so it fell in a shiny wave and stepped naked towards me. I noticed the slight bounce of her breasts as my heart hammered. She

185

then put one hand behind my neck and pulled my face towards hers and I felt her small tongue dart between my lips. The other hand went beneath my tunic as I reached for her.

"Not so quick, we have plenty of time; this isn't the Ceramicus three obol trip."

She gently bit my lip then disengaged and crossed to the bed, lay on her back, her arms behind her head, her knees raised and splayed. I saw the patch of dark hair with the other pink lips open.

The first time didn't last long, in fact I spurted almost immediately, at the soft touch of entry, but the second, the second, was almost a voyage, learning the paths and the rhythms. How to cause sensation, how to delay the moment; it was like the way one learns how to entice a ship into a mooring. In fact when I spent the second time I saw the sea blue and endless somewhere behind my closed eyelids. We stayed on the bed till evening, made love, drank some wine she kept cool in the cellars and the world was defined by our sticky bodies and the rumpled sheets. Since then I've spent many such afternoons but that was the first so I still taste its sweetness now, while the rest have blurred and faded.

When I left it was dark. I could smell her essence on my hands and her perfume on my skin. I was lightheaded, weak jointed, but complete. But I felt hunger and made towards the tavern of the bald man but stopped before entering. For inside were raised voices and on the air hung the smell of burning. My head cleared and I realised that my mood was out of step with the city, there was anger in the streets. Whilst I had lain in the bower of Aphrodite there had been a reckoning.

CHAPTER 19

All the lamps were lit in the General's house. I was met at the door by Theodorus.

"Where you been, boy? The General's been calling for you, better get to him and watch out, he's angry."

He was. Flushed, red faced, a sign I recognised as symptoms of his excitement and ill temper. He sat on a campaign stool across from his brother and, to my surprise, Themistocles, who nodded at me in a companionable way. The General barked at me,

"Where have you been Mandrocles?"

The second time I had been asked that question in as many minutes.

"Anything could have happened down there today, we wasted time looking for you, you were supposed to have been at the theatre getting an education, not wasting your time drinking and whoring."

How he knew what I had been doing I couldn't guess, but I was impressed.

"Things are getting too hot here so the Archon has advised a change of air so we're going to spend a few days in the country on the family estate. Gather your things, we leave before dawn."

Before I could move off to my cubicle Themistocles asked.

"What did you think of the play, boy? How did it make you feel?"

"Sick, angry, and I think ashamed."

"And why the shame?"

"Because we stood by and let the city perish, we let the beating heart of Ionian Greece and freedom be crushed by the Great King."

"Good, well let me tell you that my fellow citizens felt that and something else besides. They haven't fought the Persians like you have."

187

At this point I felt a warm glow of satisfaction; Themistocles could give that to a man. He smiled at me then continued,

"Athenians felt fear: they know that they're next on the Great King's list. A pity that the rioting couldn't have waited till the end of the play, because the last lines make it crystal clear, bit of a waste that."

He turned towards the General,

"You remember those last lines about the goddess of the city seeing across the seas to where a Persian invasion fleet is gathering to sail to Athens, and instructing the Athenians to fight to protect her shrine and Greece's liberty. That was a poetic masterpiece. If they'd managed to control themselves until they'd heard that, then my cunning, but fearful, fellow citizens would have realised what they need to do.

"You know Miltiades the idea for that last scene spoken by the goddess was mine. What a fine and moving job Phrynichus made of it, a pity he had to flee the city and his house was burned. Still, I'll make it up to him; we know how to reward patriots. So best if you clear off quickly too, until the anger, shame and fear burns itself out. It'll give you time to play the country squire and plan your next move. When you get back we can decide what to do about those heel dragging buggers in Sparta."

I mumbled goodnight and stumbled off to bed.

We left long before first light and by midday had crossed the peninsula. The soil of Attica is thin, scarcely covering the bare bones of rock that protrude like the exposed roots of great stone trees. This soil, where ploughed or in groves of olives, is littered with flinty crushed fragments of rock, unlike green and fertile Samos. It surprised me that it could raise a crop at all, just bring despair and back breaking labour for the farmer. Rock is the essence of Athens, from the great mass of the Acropolis, harsh in the sunlight, to the scarred and flinty uplands and hard won fields.

Now, to our left, was the Bay of Marathon with the heights of Mount Pentelitus behind it. Before us was Brauron, ancestral home of Miltiades. The soil here was just as thin but the feel was different. We passed the herme with its jutting beard and erect phallus that marked the boundary of the deme, and passed into a more ancient land. It was here, in the age of heroes, that Miltiades' family had settled after the fight at Troy, displacing the old ones, scarcely human, who had fled to the hills to live their lives, goat footed along with centaurs, lapiths and other creatures that appear only at night when men are in bed. We passed the most sacred sanctuary of Artemis, which even then was still in use and busy. I would like to have stopped but the General was in a hurry, eager to visit the home of his boyhood. So we rode on in the spring sunshine, the smell of the charcoal burners' fires in our nostrils, rode through the still visible but crumbling ruins of earlier times. The family estate was little different from the holding of any freeman farmer who can afford hoplite armour, just a little bigger. As we rode into the yard I noticed that the General was impatient, almost happy to be back. At the door stood the elderly farm steward Ephialties and a tall young woman, modestly veiled.

Ephialties and the woman walked into the yard to greet us, followed by the house servants and slaves, arms opened in the old tradition of greeting and service. I noticed an ancient crone, toothless and barely able to move, tears running down her withered and shrunken cheeks. Miltiades slid down his horse's flank and walked past Ephialties and took the crone in his arms in embrace. When he released her I noticed his cheeks were wet. Only then did he give his attention to the steward and the woman. She, with traditional dignity, gave a slight bow, then withdrew but not before fixing me with an open stare. At last I realised who it was, amazed what a physical transformation little more than six months can bring. I felt a shock of excitement but was brought to my senses by a series of instructions from the General.

Reminded of my status that put me somewhere between a personal retainer and poor, but distant, relative. I carried out my tasks before taking my gear to the outbuilding where I and a number of others were to sleep. Here life was simple. I ate with the servants, accompanied the General when he rode out and helped work the land. The inside of the house I hardly ever saw despite all my efforts to catch a glimpse of her. Still, a couple of weeks of outdoor labour restored the muscles I had grown on the Athene Nike, and then wasted in Athens. Twice only in that time did I see Elpinice and on the second of these it was she who sought me out.

"It has not been easy to get to you, Mandrocles. I think you could have made more of an effort."

Her eyes sparkled with her old mischief, her face was uncovered and my knees were weak.

"Today my father goes to dine with a relative between here and Perati, too far to return till tomorrow. He will take only Lysias and an escort. If you would like to see our groves by moonlight then be outside the gate after the lamps are out."

I spent the rest of the day in agitation in case the General decided to take me with him as part of the escort. I needn't have worried. Just past midday his party rode by where I was clearing a ditch, without a glance. It seemed to me that the lamps would never go out that night and I was outside the gate before the dusk had turned to night. It was one of those clear late spring evenings when one can almost smell summer in the air, rising from the fields and woods. She came at last, gracefully through the gate, to my delight not in the peplos and veil but barelegged in a simple tunic. She smiled at me, her teeth flashing white in the gathering darkness. I stood undecided on how I should greet her, but she took my hand and kissed me lightly on the cheek and then set off towards the woods that fringed the low hills above the estate.

That night passed quickly yet nothing really happened. We walked amongst the trees; lay in a grove overlooking the sea, talked of our lives and hopes. Today I can't recall much of what we actually said. I can see glimpses of her slim form and white ankles. I remember holding her with her head on my shoulder as we lay beneath the branches. I think I can remember the scent of the grove and a faint trace of salt wind from the sea, the rustle of the wood, the breath of the gods. I knew that this was not a night for rutting and although aroused I never tried. Instead I felt closer to someone than at any time before or since. We kissed but mainly we talked and listened. I think that because we both knew that neither of us was free to choose our future we treated the night as if it was all there ever would be. One thing that she said has stayed with me though.

"We are both stuck with this life Mandrocles, but if you serve my father well, or fight with courage in the war, you can change your future. Even if you're killed you will have had the chance to experience great things, to have truly lived. So despite my high birth my life will have no more excitement than the women slaves on this farm. I will not be allowed to choose who I love: I will be married off to some rich old man. You will help to change the world marching in my father's army. All there is for me is to worry about you as I decay and wither on this or some other estate."

She's an old woman now. I'm sure, reader, that all you will know of her is her notoriety and reputation as odd and hard, but what I still see is the beautiful young wood nymph I lay with that night. Even now on the odd occasions we meet I don't see the terrible old woman who berated Pericles in public, I see the girl.

Just before dawn we wandered back to the house, hand in hand. At the estate boundary she turned as if to kiss me. Instead she sniffed my skin then breathed out in my face, turned and ran to the house. Sometimes when I awake from the dream that I want desperately to return to I can smell the ghost of that sweet breath.

Two days later the General told me to be ready at sun up to ride out with him.

"I'm taking you, Mandrocles, because you have good eyes and take things in quickly."

We rode through the early hours, heading north from Brauron, keeping close to the coast until we reached the Bay of Marathon. The area was scattered with farms and stretches of olive grove and woodland. Where the land was uncultivated it was overrun with wild fennel, a contrast to the rest of Attica. We left the road and moved up into the foothills of a mountain until we had a good view of the full sweep of the bay.

"Tell me what you see, boy."

"A wide bay, a good place to harbour a fleet. Well sheltered."

"Good, what else?"

"A river empties itself into the sea; it looks like it's changed its course several times."

"Anything else?"

"At the far end there's a small lake separated from the sea by a large wide sandy beach."

"Do you think that would be the place to beach a fleet?"

"Depends on what your purpose was; the beach would be good for running the triremes up on it."

"And what if you wanted to land an army?"

I was surprised but decided not to show it.

"I'm no general, but yes, a good place, shelter for the fleet, plenty of space to deploy an army, fresh water, and good fertile land to forage in."

"And what about fighting a battle?"

"Well, if it were possible to land safely there's just enough space to deploy troops in battle order. Not much space for cavalry though."

"What about the ground where you lead them when deployed?"

"Well, no one likes to fight with their backs to the sea and although the beach is good, it looks like everything else inland is marsh. So, an army fighting at that end would lack space to manoeuvre if things went wrong."

"Yes, the Great Marsh lies between your army and the road."

"But the advantages of the bay as a beachhead for landing an army outweigh the risk of having to fight here because of the problems of the marsh I think."

"Good Mandrocles and that's why this is where the Great King will land his army when the time comes."

We dismounted and hobbled the horses. I produced a skin of watered wine, flat bread, hard cheese and onions and we sat to eat. I asked him the obvious question.

"So how would we stop him landing here?"

"We wouldn't. I've kept this place in my head ever since the shambles at Lade when I knew I'd have to run to Athens and we'd have to fight. He'll land here to organise and deploy his army for the march on Athens."

"So we defend the city from the Acropolis."

193

He laughed and reached out to ruffle my hair, then realised the intimacy of this gesture and stopped.

"No, if he gets the army to Athens we're lost, the city will be betrayed by Alkmaionidai, we'll fall apart through treachery, and won't fight."

"What about our Greek allies?"

"What Greek allies? Don't count on the Spartans, the Thebans will go over to the Persians and no one else is big or strong enough. Look, Mardonius and his army have already taken Thrace and are invading Macedonia as we speak. As they work their way south Datis commanding the main Persian fleet is moving from island to island across the Aegean. Like a boy using stepping stones to cross a stream. His final stone will be Euboea, just across the water there."

He paused for a moment to eat and drink, and then continued as if to himself.

"No, we want him here; we have to beat him before he gets out of this bay because until then he's hemmed in by these mountains with no space to deploy his superior numbers. The real question is how we manage to get an Athenian army away from the city and persuade it to fight here. We'll think about how to beat the Persians here when we've managed that. It's a big gamble but if we don't take it there'll be no more of Themistocles' demos, just an Alkmaionid aristocrat ruling the city like a Persian satrap."

He got up and brushed the crumbs from his clothes.

"Come on, we've just got time to pay our respects at the shrine of Heracles before we arrive for dinner and bed at the house of a friend of mine in the village."

I followed him down the hill impressed that he'd carried this place in his head since Lade. All Athenians have carried it in their hearts ever since.

CHAPTER 20

We stayed at Brauron till the harvest, kept in touch with Athens by a stream of friends and clients. The news was never good, the same two themes: Persian conquest and Greek treachery, as the General had predicted. Rumours dictated the pattern of our lives and invaded our dreams. Rumours of the Thebans negotiating with the Great King, and darker rumours concerning the Spartans. These last were less precise but all the more frightening as a result, changing all the time to become a chimera, a nightmare hard to interpret draining the courage from the city.

The plan had been to stay on the estate until the next spring when fear would have spread, leaving the people desperate. Then the General would return and stand for election as one of the twelve strategoi or generals charged with defending the homeland. The combination of anxiety and the politicking of Themistocles would make this a certainty. I put up with this as it gave me a chance to snatch some moments with Elpinice. But these moments were rare and for the rest of the time I was little more than a farm worker. Except for one night visit, with the household, to the shrine of Artemis, the moon goddess, in Brauron, my life was in most ways no different from my existence at home on Samos. I missed Athens, its wine shops and friendships. On hot nights I lay awake and ached for Lyra's touch and the excitement of the streets around the Ceramicus. I also wondered what my strange friend Aeschylus was doing and if he was at work on a play to present at the next festival.

Then one evening, as the sun was sinking red into the sea across the bay and I was returning tired and dusty from the fields, I saw some good quality cavalry horses tethered outside the house. Inside, there was the sound of raised voices. I was not admitted so collected my food from the kitchen and took it back to my sleeping place. It seemed to me as I ate the flat bread dipped in oil, that unless I was of specific use to the General, and as long as we stayed here in the country, then my life would be like that of the peasants. My status was above theirs but not sufficiently to make me a full member of the household. Lonely and bored, it was long before sleep came.

I was woken early, before first light, by the sound of voices then by the sound of horses' hooves moving out of the yard. Soon after, I heard my name called. I dressed hurriedly, dipped my head in the water barrel and ran across the farm yard to the door.

Miltiades was up and dressed in his travelling clothes.

"Get your gear, Mandrocles, then say goodbye to my daughter."

This set me back on my heels.

"Don't think I haven't noticed the two of you making sheep's eyes at each other. Come on, don't look so surprised, you'll grow out of it; you know she's not for the likes of you. Anyway it'll be a sorry man who carries her into the chamber as his bride. We move out before the sun's up."

He stalked back into the house laughing. Whatever had happened in the night had restored his good humour. Having had permission I went to the corridor where the women slept. Elpinice was dressed and waiting.

"Go well, Mandrocles. You know what my father said was true, but we'll see each other again long before I'm married. Give my love to Cimon."

Ignoring her maid and guardian she kissed me on the cheek then pushed me away. I carried my gear to the cart, then mounted my horse and waited for the order to leave, eating some bread and honey in the saddle. The General came out accompanied by the crone, his old nurse, who was crying as she had been at our arrival. As he turned to mount she pressed some charm or token into his hand. The sun that had sunk red into the sea the night before announced its presence by a soft, pale glow behind the mountains and we rode towards it.

But it wasn't Athens we were heading for but the Athene Nike beached in the Bay of Phaleron. Things had happened whilst we were away, things which even frightened Themistocles. I learned of this on the route, and also why the General had remembered me sufficiently to take me along. I thought at first it had been to keep me from Elpinice while he was away, but his primary concern had never been for his family and I know that my place in his life was nothing compared with his place in mine.

Looking back, I wish his reason for taking me had been to protect the virtue of his daughter. There would at least have been some bitter satisfaction to be gleaned from that. Better that than his real reason, which was to use me as bait or bribe: no, my role on that trip was to be not much better than that of a catamite. It was a plan he could have lived to regret bitterly had my sword thrust been a fraction straighter. But, I am ahead of myself.

We rode quickly that day, and, as always, the General needed to talk about his plans. It was his way of reaching a decision. He didn't need any response, just a listener and one who was bright enough to understand but of no importance and couldn't profit from the confidence. Themistocles' agents in Sparta had learned of a secret Persian embassy to the Ephors and perhaps also to King Cleomenes although that was harder to believe. This was a high level delegation and included, among highly placed diplomats, Metiochus, the wayward or treacherous, depending on your inclination, elder son of Miltiades, spawned by the daughter of Hippias, resident traitor at the Persian court. This was a shrewd move on the Great King's part, subtle and ambiguous, playing a game with both the General's reputation and his actions. Themistocles needed to send his own secret ambassador to counter the Persian influence but he didn't dare ask any of the obvious high born Athenian candidates, Xanthippus, Megacles or their like.

So he decided to risk the General, not because of any diplomatic skills, although the gods know he was cunning enough, but because he was the strongest advocate for war having burnt his boats with the Great King. Yet this was also risky as the presence of Metiochus meant that perhaps the Persians might use him as a means of buying Miltiades.

When you remember the Persian embassy to the Spartans, you will recall what you heard in our histories. In these the Spartans are noble heroes who die fighting and "lie here obedient to their word", as that arse licking worthless versifier Simonides put it after Thermopylae. In these tales the Persian heralds turn up demanding the earth and water from the Spartans as a token of submission. The Spartans throw them down a well saying

"You'll find plenty of water and earth down there."

A good story, and it may well have happened, but that was for show.

In reality there is no race more duplicitous and self serving than the Spartans. Those show-pony buggers with their carefully arranged long hair and flashy red cloaks only ever act in self interest and only fight near home. Despite all that boasting about Thermopylae and that conceited epithet written by Simonides, no one was more gratified by the pointless death of Leonidas than the Spartan Ephors. The truth is that without our fleet fighting beside them in those treacherous narrow waters, they couldn't have held. I should know; I was there. They chose to fight at Plataea on home turf but not at Mycale in a more desperate fight.

If you want to know how that second war was really won and what it felt like, then you only have to see Aeschylus' play "The Persians", or if you can read, borrow a copy. He knew; he was there. But none of that would have counted if it hadn't been for Marathon, without that, no free Greece, nothing. And where were the Spartans, the showy, heel dragging buggers then, when the world held its breath as the Persian empire turned its full might on a small city?

No, it all begins and ends in treachery. I've lived long, seen much, and understood little. Yet in my soul I feel what my friends the poets came to realise. The gods don't care, they have no interest in us, and the bits we worship we make up. There is no comfort or purpose or design, the struggle is all. Young Sophocles goes even further; he says the best we can hope for is never to have been born, to have never existed. The world's like that, nothing's what it appears and nothing proves that more than the reputation of the Spartans.

We pulled away from the shore as the sun was setting and before we drew level with the Isle of Salamis, the moon had risen sufficiently to illuminate our wake, dividing the wine dark sea. We sailed at night through phosphorescent waters in the manner of men with things to hide. In these waters, with little wind and a full moon, there was little danger but no sailor likes the sea at night. However, as our mission was secret, to have taken the land route across the isthmus and past Corinth would have led to immediate discovery. From Salamis we sailed direct across the

199

Saronic Gulf to make landfall on the spur of the Peloponnese north of Epidaurus. From there we followed the coastline rounding the headland, passing between Herminone and the rocky mass of Hydra. During the days we beached the ship out of sight and layup. At night we sailed out from behind waterless Spetse, crossing the Gulf of Argos to Leonidikion, finding a deserted cave to hide in during the day.

Then instead of following the road to Sparta we continued south down the coast along the almost deserted badlands at the edge of the Peloponnese. Then, rounding Hell's mouth we sailed at night into the bay of Laconia. This voyage in the Athene Nike was like no other, the men didn't know the purpose of our journey, but they were uneasy. Sailors are superstitious, even Lysias, Ariston and Theodorus were jumpy. Miltiades was taciturn and out of temper. There were no jokes or songs, just anxious watches on dark waters. We avoided the Spartan controlled port of Gytheion and landed in a creek up the coast, more like pirates than Athenians. There we beached and hid the ship hoping that its goddess Patron would not take offence. The ship's company would camp here to await our return while a small party of eight of us set out for Sparta. We cut across country to avoid Gytheion and joined the road leading to Sparta some leagues north.

After all the skulking and hiding, the road to Sparta was surprisingly easy and I remember the weather, perfect, as it can be in that harvest season when summer kisses autumn. It was a road one could travel comfortably in one day and arrive as the sun still hung above the mountains. The land was lush and fertile. We met few on the road but saw many toiling in the fields.

Sparta is a surprise, not like a city at all. Such public buildings as it has are not gathered round some agora or acropolis, but dispersed. In fact there are few buildings of note, not even temples. The one temple of any real worth, the sanctuary of Artemis the Upright, is rich in military dedications but home to a cruel cult where young boys are flogged to death. This is done, it is said, for the benefit of the state for reasons lost in the past. What right thinking people would put a temple to such use?

Sparta is more like a group of small villages, roughly joined together surrounded by an outer ring of farmsteads and hamlets. You might think it was the ancient Arcadia of the hero tales, but you'd be wrong. This was not a place at ease with itself. The Spartans ruled through fear. They long ago subdued the neighbouring Messanian lands, whose occupants they treated little better than slaves. Their lack of city buildings grouped together behind defensive walls was a public symbol of their arrogance. The message it gave was, "we have no need of walls, none can threaten us, our army is invincible". The town, such as it is, lies on the Eurotas river in the shade of the Taygetos Mountains. Although at first sight it might look idyllic, its history is drenched in blood; it's a place of fear and evil. One of the consolations of being near the end of my days is that never again will I have to set eyes on Sparta.

Once we drew near to the city Miltiades' behaviour changed. He ordered that we stop by the side of the road, take the clean robes we carried in our packs, and change. He reckoned that if we had been in danger it would have been while travelling on the deserted sections of the road some distance from the city where we could have been killed in an ambush. He was sufficiently proud of his reputation and confident of his Spartan guest friends to consider himself well protected once arrived in the city.

It was hard to judge though if one had arrived in the city or not. No one took much notice of our party of eight although it must have been apparent that we were not Spartans. We stopped in what appeared to be a small square fringed with some rustic houses. Miltiades summoned a local boy who had been playing with a small dog by the side of a midden. He gave the boy a coin and sent him off to deliver a message that he made him repeat back several times before he was satisfied it had been learnt.

"Better make yourselves comfortable, lads, we could be here some time. It's unlikely that we'll find anyone here. They're either in the mess, training at the gym or track, or up in the hills. Anywhere in fact, but at home, and looking at these hovels who can blame them."

The evening was pleasantly warm and we were tired so it was no hardship. I had heard tales of Spartan maidens exercising naked but all we saw was the occasional glimpse of a heavily built woman dressed in an earth coloured robe of the coarsest material. She came out from the back of one of the houses, gave us an unfriendly stare, and crossed to one of the other houses.

"If that's what the wives are like, no wonder the men spend all their time in the mess halls buggering each other."

We laughed at Theodorus' joke but Miltiades warned,

"Don't make too many jokes where they can hear them, they tend to be a little touchy. Spartans don't understand humour unless the joke's against others."

We saw he meant it and were silent. I sat musing in this dispiriting place. I've always loved laughter, the crowds, and theatre and apart from the comrades who fought beside me, my friends have mainly been poets.

Unless, that is, you are of a modern disposition and include women. There were no plays or poets here; unless you could race, hunt or kill something, it had no value. But we didn't have to wait long. Soon the boy returned leading two armed men.

CHAPTER 21

They were well built with a gaunt look, and I recognised Brasidas, our house guest in Athens, who had impressed Cimon so much. He took us to the communal men's hall where all Spartan citizens over the age of twenty are obliged to eat with their tent companions, the men who they would line up with in battle and upon whom their lives depended. Here, the crew members of our party would also stay until such time as we could leave. Miltiades, Lysias and I were separated out and taken into the eating hall where the communal meal, which the Spartans call the Syssitia, is taken.

They eat this on wooden benches at a low table in groups of about fifteen. We were split up and I was placed with a group of older men and some youths who made it clear I wasn't welcome. Throughout the meal, such talk as there was excluded me, apart from the odd, scornful laugh at my expense and, on an occasion when I was looking around at the other tables, a wooden spoon was thrown at my head but glanced off my shoulder. This I ignored, there was no other course of action.

You will have heard of the famous black broth of Sparta. Think yourself lucky you've never had to eat it. It's served out of a large greasy pot and consists of some lumps of indeterminate meat cooked in blood and seasoned with vinegar and some salt. It tastes worse than it sounds, the only point in its favour being that there's not much of it for each man. This is to prevent the men from being spoilt and becoming effeminate. With this we had coarse barley bread and large quantities of what, for them, passed as wine, heavily watered.

The idea behind these halls was that if the men were hungry they could supplement their rations with whatever they could scavenge or steal. Nothing bought, or home produced, was allowed. None of my companions had bothered to scavenge anything; perhaps they found the black broth and bread sufficient. So I sat in silence trying to shovel down this stomach shrivelling muck. I could see Lysias on his table, as miserable as I; but on the central table Miltiades was talking freely and showing every appearance of enjoying the meal.

Everything that's good or makes sense about life is inverted in Sparta. A place that chooses a regime that keeps thousands down so that a small group can waste the richness of the land in this type of posturing vanity. One day soon there will have to be a reckoning between free Athens and these bastards.

I don't know what they talked about on Miltiades' table but it's clear from what he told us that night as we settled into sleep that Sparta was as divided over the Persian threat as Athens. He also confirmed that there was a Persian embassy in the city and that tomorrow we would have an opportunity to meet the Ephors.

These are the board of five, elected through popular acclamation each year and the real power in Sparta. They supervised all levels of Spartan society from the personal behaviour of individual Spartans, to the conduct and performance of the two kings. It was to these men that foreign embassies appealed. It had been their decision not to send help to the Ionian Greeks in their revolt against the Great King. Even though King Cleomenes spread the tale that it had been his decision to reject the petition of the Ionian leader Aristagorus because his precocious eight year old daughter Gorgo had judged that Aristagorus was a corrupt man. This daughter was now married to Cleomenes, younger half brother of Leonidas; one of the young Spartan leaders who Miltiades thought favoured war with Persia.

The next day the General, Lysias and I were kept waiting outside the simple chamber, open to the elements, where the Ephors met to conduct the affairs of state. By the time we were shown in the General was in a state of great irritability, bordering on anger. It was obvious that we had been kept waiting because the Ephors had been busy with another delegation and pains had been taken to make sure we had been kept deliberately apart. The previous group had been taken out by a different exit but a trace of them still lingered. In the chamber there was a distinct but fading scent of perfumed oil hanging in the air. A scent that I remembered from Miltiades' palace in Sestos where I had been the couch companion of his son.

Before I set down what happened in that chamber, reader, let me tell you my first impression of the fabled Spartan Ephors who arouse such fear in the free parts of Greece. In a way I was disappointed because, apart from the elaborate dressing of their long hair, and the red Spartan cloaks they wore, they were just five men of late middle age. Strange how the truly frightening appears commonplace, how evil can be so banal. They sat in a row, each holding the traditional Spartan walking stick with the T shaped cross piece at the top, which I felt to be pure affectation. They wield power whilst pretending to be ordinary citizens, with the simple habits of rugged farmers. These men, on a whim, could depose a king, have a boy flayed to death, have their spies report on the conversations between man and wife or send the army to war. They listened in silence as Miltiades stated the case for Athens and Sparta to stand together to defend the homeland from barbarian invasion. Then the Ephor sitting in the centre spoke.

"Sparta is, as always, aware of her duties and responsibilities and will act according to its laws and customs, respecting the wishes of the gods."

Miltiades, keeping self control, replied,

"Then, fathers of Sparta, we can rely on your rejecting the demands of the Persians for earth and water?"

"That has already happened. The bodies of their heralds now lie at the bottom of a well contaminating its once sweet water."

"But, there is talk of a second, more highly placed delegation in the city, and this might attempt to disturb the ancient friendship of our two cities."

"Miltiades, son of Cimon, we have heard your petition. We know our responsibilities. It was not us who unwisely sent a force to support the revolt. Where is that force now? We shall act, as ever, in the interests of the general good. You Athenians would be better to think of the misfortune you have caused instead of looking to us for salvation. The Spartans will do what is needful, having first listened to the counsel of the gods."

During this speech, which like most Spartan speeches I have heard, was full of self regard, strange their invented reputation for brevity, the other four Ephors sat as if bored, waiting for the audience to be over. Miltiades, realising that there was little else to say, nodded at the Ephors and we walked out. Outside he gave voice to his feelings.

"Typical of the Spartans; hiding behind their gods with no intention of giving a straight answer. Whoever they saw before us got a longer hearing. They'll act as always out of self interest and will only fight if it suits them. Still, it's clear they're undecided. Tonight I dine with my old friend Cleomenes, that's King Cleomenes to you, Mandrocles. I think he might have different ideas concerning our Persian friends."

I'd never seen a king before but that night I suppose I saw two, as within a year Leonidas would have taken the crown from his half brother. Cleomenes had a reputation for ruthless manipulation and had recently manoeuvred his co-regent King Demaratus into exile and had him replaced by a more compliant partner, Leotychidas. However, when we saw King Cleomenes, the symptoms of the drunken madness that was to be his downfall were already visible. I remember little of that night other than the fact that Leonidas acted as if he was already king. Now, following his death at the Hot Gates he is the symbol of the perfect hero throughout all Greece. It is almost an act of blasphemy to criticise him so I will say only this. His dealings with the Persians were no more straightforward than those of his brother and it was difficult to see what he really believed. But if I'd been Cleomenes I'd have kept a very close eye on my half brother.

I wasn't at the meal; I accompanied the General but was left to wait in the kitchen, where I noticed that the food being taken in by the slaves was not black broth. It was far more delicate and, from the noise of the meal, I imagine that the wine was better and not as heavily watered. When Miltiades emerged he was accompanied by his host, walking arm in arm. They were either drunk, or pretending, either was possible.

But if the General was drunk he was soon sober enough to say that he felt that Cleomenes could be trusted to fight the Persians if they invaded Attica, and that the Persian mission to the Ephors had been received no more favourably than we had.

What happened next, like most important events in life, took us by surprise. We were walking back through Pitani, the most desirable of the four loosely connected villages that make up the town of Sparta, when a group of men with an armed guard noisily left a house some yards ahead of us and set off in our direction. I was thinking to myself that this must be a most unusually social night for Sparta when, by the light of the torches, I recognised one of them. If this meeting had happened in daylight when neither father nor son had been drinking, then the future of Athens may have taken a different path.

Metiochus recognised his father first, pointed him out to his nearest companion, a trouser wearing barbarian, and pushed past his escort shouting a greeting. I don't think he intended to offend his father, he looked pleased to see him, but as he approached I saw his eyes find me and his expression changed.

"Greetings, father, what brings you to this place the gods have deserted?"

Miltiades was pulling himself together from the shock of seeing his son. He reached out a hand in greeting, perhaps a move to embrace, but Metiochus continued.

"I see you've brought the catamite; I thought you'd decide to keep him for yourself. Come to us at the court of the Great King, boys like him are commoner than two obol pornoi and much prettier."

He meant it as a joke, but to Miltiades, half drunk, it was a terrible mistake. The General, in front of a foreign escort and faced by barbarians, could not tolerate an attack on his dignity and honour. Any control in his wine fuelled brain vanished. Lysias tried to hold him back but too late. He pushed forward; shouting at his son, red faced, spittle flying,

"You mincing pansy, don't dare talk to me like that, tarted up with your barbarian bum boys."

He almost choked for a moment, overcome with rage, red faced, spluttering and spitting on the ground

209

to clear his throat. Metiochus raised his hands, a gesture of apology, and had just mouthed the word "father" when the General found his breath.

"Traitor and coward, the boy Cimon is a better warrior than you, even Elpinice makes a better man than you."

Then it was confusion. A guard tried to get between them, but weapons were out. Miltiades smashed the handle of his dagger into the man's face, and then stabbed him through the cheek. It went as street fights do; swift movements, sudden grunts and shouts. At the centre, father and son raging, stabbing at each other between the bodies of their struggling escorts. Finally Lysias managed to pull the General back. Metiochus' Persian friend was trying to do the same but with less effect. Then Metiochus shouted,

"Take the chance, old man, take the King's mercy or be a fool leading a fool's army, the Athenians despise you, they'll…"

He got no further, in answer to some urge I tried to finish him. I shifted my balance for the killer lunge and went for his heart. His companion jerked back and my blade was deflected by his shoulder. Then everything moved again. He was pulled back and my second thrust caught someone else, the Persian I think, and at a place where the blade goes in deep and easy. Then they were gone, back the way they came. The two on the ground didn't move. We paused to look to our wounds.

Lights had been lit in some of the houses but no one came out into the lane. The General, his mood changed, slumped onto a mounting block by a house wall.

"So he really has gone over to them, to his traitor grandfather. When I heard he was here I thought we might get him back. Not now."

Then he stood up and walked into the night towards our lodgings. We followed.

Two days later we left the city with King Cleomenes' promises of support against the Persians ringing in our ears. I don't think the General believed them, but we had achieved something. Our brush with the secret Persian embassy had embarrassed the Ephors. The embassy left the next day, perhaps worried they might join their compatriots at the bottom of the well.

The voyage home was as sombre as the voyage out had been. The General said little but the crew took care not to get in his way. It was only when Athens came into sight, the rock of the Acropolis gleaming in the autumn sunlight that he spoke to me.

"I know you tried to kill my son, Mandrocles, and I know why and had you succeeded the fault would have been mine. But I confess to you that among the reasons I'd hoped to give him to return home, you were one. I'm sorry for it. It broke my word to your father."

This was the only time I heard him apologise to anyone but I think he did it to purge himself. He put his hand on my shoulder,

"But if you'd killed him I would have killed you, and then we'd have lost your luck."

He turned to look over the bowsprit and murmured softly.

"Don't have children, boy, they bring nothing but pain."

And I never have, at least any that I'm aware of; or care to recognise.

PART THREE

CHAPTER 22

Fugitives in increasing numbers drifted into the city. They brought nothing with them unless you count wounds, but they carried fear. They carried fear and spread panic like contagion. Fear from the Agora to each small square and every household. It spread through all districts and was swallowed with the wine sold at the drink booths in the Ceramicus. What all had feared but dared not name was here: the Persians.

Their army was moving south from its conquest of Macedonia; and worse, there was rumour that a great invasion fleet commanded by Datis, the admiral of Darius, had left the Cilician plain and made landfall on the island of Rhodes. Everyone claimed they knew someone who had spoken to a man who knew a man who had just returned in a fast ship from Rhodes who had seen the fleet. They knew that this armada was made up of the entire Phoenician navy and that every single ship had been needed to accommodate all of the army of the Great King. Everyone knew that the Persians had hundreds of horse transports specially built for the elite cavalry that swept away and destroyed the Ionian Greek armies. It, like their invincible infantry, would be brought to Athens. They even knew the route the fleet would take and where it would land. They knew these last details because they knew the Persians were in daily contact with traitors in the city, the friends of the exiled tyrant Hippias: the Alkmaionidai, the high aristocracy of Athens.

They knew that when the great fleet of Darius arrived in the Bay of Phaleron to set siege to the city, that these traitors within, enemies of the demos bought by Persian gold, would rise up in the night and massacre all the patriots as they slept in their beds. Their women would be raped and sold into slavery and

215

all the male children, down to the smallest baby, put to the sword. Everyone knew this as they had all met a man who had been told it directly by the house steward of Megacles, or a groom in the stables of Xanthippus, or a pornoi who was the lover of the gatekeeper of Aristides.

"Most of it's pure balls of course."

Themistocles paused to look out into the courtyard as if to check that no one was listening. He paused to warm his hands against the fire lit that unseasonably chill afternoon. The light of the flames threw his bull necked shadow onto the whitewashed wall. But it didn't show the lines of anxiety on his face. For all his bluster and confidence he was a lonely figure, uncertain and unsure. The worry of trying to preserve and extend the democratic revolution weighed on him. He knew if we couldn't hold off the Persians then he and the new democracy were dead and he doubted that we could. But he took a swallow of wine and continued in his normal bullish manner.

"There's no immediate danger from the north since Mardonius managed to get his entire fleet wrecked in a storm off Mount Athos. Then, luckily for us, got himself wounded in a skirmish with one of the tribes of goat fuckers living in the mountains that pass for Greeks up there."

He took another swallow, emptying the cup.

"But the stuff about the fleet seems accurate enough. Our agents have confirmed it; we should know the size soon. It's the rumours that worry me most, the ones about the enemy within. I know as well as you that Xanthippus and those other lordly bastards are as worried about this as we are. There will be some who've sold out for gold or for hatred of us, but for Xanthippus and his friends it's their honour and reputation that matters. I'd never say this in public, but

I'm pretty sure that if it comes to it, they'll fight with us."

"Well, I'll just have to take your word on that; remember it was those same lordly bastards that put me on trial on pain of death or exile."

Miltiades put down his cup,

"Haven't you got any better stuff than this or do you actually live all this friend of the demos stuff that you spout in public assemblies?"

He got no answer to this other than a wry smile. We were in Themistocles' house near the Hangman's gate on the fringe of the Ceramicus. The General had complained about having to visit this house and even asked Themistocles why he'd chosen such a run down, unrespectable district to live in. The answer had been that it was only a short walk from the Agora and that he chose to live near to the people in whose interests he governed the city. I always liked to listen to Themistocles and watch him when I got the chance. In public his speech was plain, even if he did tend to exaggerate, and he pitched it at the level of the ordinary citizens with the right to vote.

He himself was from an undistinguished aristocratic family, but in public chose to hide this fact. He, like the rest of his class, owned estates and better houses but he knew that he would never have an aristocratic power base. His family would never be able to compete with the Alkmaionidai or the Philiads, from whom Miltiades sprang. So his power base was the demos amongst whom he lived and whose manners he, to a certain extent, adopted. Such politicians are now as common as fleas on a dog, but he was the first and the best.

We had come to his home to report on the thinking in Sparta and the results of our mission. Since that journey, Miltiades' manner towards me had changed again. He was more familiar and I was treated more like a squire. I think the incident with Metiochus had wounded him more than he let on and in a way he saw my attack on Metiochus as an act of love or loyalty in his defence. Despite his cunning as a strategist, in matters of emotion he was simple; you were either with him or against him. My father had once saved his life; so, by accident, had I, and now I'd tried to avenge Metiochus' slighting of him.

His eldest son he'd disowned; his younger son was still a child, so I think I temporarily filled a need. From me he got absolute obedience and fidelity. After Sparta I was with him right until the end and so able to share in the greatest day for Athens and Greece. In fact you ask anyone who was there what the great moment in their life was; the reason for which were born; the thing that gave meaning to their existence. They'll all say the same. Ask my friend Aeschylus, the city's greatest poet.

I see, re-reading this that I digress. Such is the way, I suppose, of old men; pardon me, reader. Anyway the General's analysis was enough to chill the blood.

"I'm not sure what comfort we can take from the Spartans. Cleomenes knows it'll come to war, he was happy enough to throw their heralds down the well, but what type of war? He knows that Darius will want to settle with us first and I fancy at the back of his mind he doesn't think we can win here. I tried to convince him that if we stand together and hit the Persians before they can fully disembark and deploy, we can beat them. I told him I know how to do it. When he left he offered reassurances that Sparta would come to our aid but he was drunk, too drunk. There's something wrong with the man, something's shifted too far in the balance of his mind and I don't trust Leonidas. He said little but I got no reassurance from him, he's thick with the

Ephors. There's something strange there. If I was Cleomenes, I'd be very careful."

He paused to spit the wine he'd just tasted straight into the fire, which sizzled and the flame burnt green for an instant, then he continued.

"If it's left to the Ephors we're on our own. There's trouble coming in Sparta – the city's divided. Fortunately for them they're far away behind the Taygetos Mountains, harder for the Great King to get to. So they'll wait and see what happens to us and then make their minds up.

"I don't want to insult your hospitality, son of Neocles, but you must have something better to drink than this."

"No, you get the same as all my visitors, the worthies of the demos, simple drink for honest men."

How he managed to keep a straight face as he said that demonstrated what a powerful actor he was. The General, to my surprise, saw the funny side and laughed.

"Well at least when we empty our piss pots at home we'll know where to send the contents."

Themistocles grinned.

"And we'd be honoured to receive the gift of such an illustrious household, but for the moment we have more urgent matters to attend, we need to organise the city and put it on a war footing."

He paused for a moment in reflection, then continued,

"Have you managed to fix it so you get elected as strategos of your tribe for the coming year?"

"Of course, it's in the bag, who else could they choose? I'm the tribe's leading man from the oldest family and despite your democracy some things are still arranged in the good old ways."

219

"I've no doubt, but enjoy it while it lasts, change is coming, and the demos are the future. It's taken root and you'd be well advised to think about that."

The words were said kindly enough but they marked the chasm between the New Athens as Themistocles saw it and the old Athens that the General would like to restore. Future events would prove neither man got it exactly right, and in a funny way, Pericles onion head is now their joint heir. But on that day with the threat of invasion imminent they knew they needed each other, couldn't afford to fall out, so the exchange passed over and Themistocles continued,

"But in spite of your great influence and reputation you won't be able to fix making yourself the first of the Ten."

Then, as now, each of the ten Athenian tribes elected its own strategos or General each year. Like the system of the Archons, one of these took the role of the first strategos, the Polemarch.

"This year it's Callimachus, so for reasons we both understand he'll be Polemarch for the year we fight."

Miltiades smiled.

"He's a good man, respected, brave, and experienced, he eventually came on my side in the trial. He'll be a lot easier to influence than those silly Ionian buggers before Lade. He knows when to fight and when to run. Besides he will be one of ten and I suppose you've fixed it that you'll be strategos for your tribe."

Themistocles chose not to answer directly, even in private he preferred not to be seen to interfere with the workings of the new democracy.

"Callimachus is very much his own man and he's much closer to Megacles, Xanthippus and the rest than he is to us. He'll want to make up his own mind and, brave as he is, he's old fashioned. He's more likely to

220

choose to defend the city than to march out and attack a much larger army supported by the best cavalry in the world on open ground; and, with respect to your great reputation as a Persian fighter, son of Cimon, it's what I would do or what I would be forced to do as we haven't got a strong enough fleet of fast triremes. Given the fleet, I'd fight at sea; see how the heavily laden Phoenician ships cope with that. The sea, that's where our future lies, but we have to build ourselves a well defended port. My idea's for the Piraeus…"

Miltiades cut him off.

"I've just escaped from the Persians on a fucking trireme; I've fought from the deck more times than you've walked through the Agora. The Phoenicians are the best sailors with the best ships and, as you've so rightly pointed out, they're on the other side and we've not got the ships.

"If we fight here and defend the city we'll be starved to death if we're lucky. But it's more likely we'll be betrayed from within and you and I will be hanged from that gate near your 'fashionable' house and your friends in the demos who survive will watch and cheer. It'll be like the fight at Troy except the barbarians will win and it won't take them ten years.

Anyway I don't intend to play Hector and be chased three times round the Acropolis by Datis or Artaphernes before dying in the dirt."

He stopped, red in the face, looked at Themistocles and to my surprise they both started to laugh. Themistocles shouted to his steward.

"Bring a full jar of the Samian that we keep for family feasts, our new Hector has earned it."

I sat there thinking how similar they were, but even then I think I understood how the politician was the more subtle. Miltiades' character was obvious to all, he could manipulate situations but he was, to his last

221

ounce of blood, an aristocrat. His loyalty was to himself and his family; he would fight the Persians because he had no option.

Themistocles was more difficult: a brave man, a great war leader, he changed the future of Athens and probably the world, but he was unknowable. You could follow his actions but never understand the depths of his mind. He was the future but on that day neither of them knew that. On that day it is probable that neither of them thought they would survive the year, that's the quality of courage.

The best Samian was brought in and Themistocles mixed it with pretence of aristocratic ceremony. He would have made a good actor in the satyr plays; he looked enough like Silenus not to have needed costume or make up. They toasted each other whilst the steward organised the slaves in lighting the lamps and setting out food; plates of olives, strips of different fish and good bread. After tasting the wine and taking some from each dish Miltiades started to talk of hunting and, until the jug was finished, they reclined and swapped stories and boasts as if they were old tent companions. I'd seen enough of both to know that if they hadn't had a common interest and that their lives were at stake, there would have been little to keep them together. In normal circumstances they'd have been enemies and neither would have hesitated to kill the other.

By the time we left it was dark and we needed torch bearers to see us home. The paths were muddy tracks in this part of the city and the quality of the buildings poor. I noticed fugitives and refugees huddled on patches of spare land in tents and shelters made from materials they had scavenged from the city dust heaps and middens. Some even crouched in doorways for the night. As we passed the shadow of Hangman's Gate the General said softly, perhaps to me or maybe to himself,

"Within a year we'll probably both be dead."

I was about to answer when he went on,

"But if we come through, if we win, then within months it'll be odds on we'll be fighting for power."

I realised then that it was an interior monologue about his dance of love and death with Themistocles. He paused and we trudged home to his brother's house in silence.

CHAPTER 23

As the poet Hesiod says, the world moves uncaring through its seasons and some days are lucky and others are not. So it proved, for soon we didn't rely on rumour to scare us with reports of the Persian fleet. Neither did we need fugitives to bring us news of cities that offered the Great King earth and water before purging themselves of democrats and patriots. Piece by piece the picture of the coming nightmare was put together, fed to us during the dark days and cold nights of that winter.

By the start of the sailing season rumour was replaced by certainty. Our own ships had seen the great fleet and tracked its progress. It had left Rhodes undamaged and progressed from Kos to Samos, my old home, now a nest of traitors, where Aiakes was restored to power. The fleet took hostages as it went, to ensure good behaviour from the islands. Next it made landfall on the island of Naxos; here the Great King had a score to settle. Ten years earlier at the start of the Ionian revolt Naxos had successfully withstood a four month siege laid by a Persian army and fleet of two hundred ships. Our hopes were founded on the ability of the Naxiots to hold again and at least delay the fleet until the late summer and autumn storm season would make it unsafe to sail. This would give us another year to build an alliance and hope that Poseidon would destroy the fleet in his own time.

That hope was dashed. A trireme, running before a squall, and crewed by exhausted sailors, beached at Phaleron. Bad tidings travel fast and these tidings spread so quickly they must have been shouted across large distances. We became aware of it, not through being told directly but by a wailing noise, almost imperceptible at first, starting outside the walls but spreading inwards until it filled the city, its shrillness penetrating the gates of the houses. Naxos had fallen, and fallen without a fight. No heroic tales to pass on to their children this time. Those with either the sense or the ability to leave the city had fled to the hills to hide. Those that remained, offering no resistance, were either enslaved or killed depending on how young or useful they might be. The city and its temples were burned.

In Athens people made plans to flee the city, but where could they go? Athens was the destination of fugitives, not the departure point, there was nowhere else. After Naxos things changed. Even the most stupid or optimistic now knew that soon the Persians would arrive and they also knew that this time if the Naxiots didn't even consider defending their strongly protected city then the invading army must be too strong and through the fear this engendered, the talk of treachery grew.

But the city of the goddess Athena is not like other places. The logic that the city's philosophers spout doesn't actually work here. Athenians are quick to rouse, intemperate and volatile. So without any intervening stage the mood changed from panic to a slow burning anger.

Back then this irrationality was useful. Now I fear volatility will lead to our doom. But then, I, like the city, was younger and I shared the anger. For those who wanted to settle with the Persians the city was a dangerous place. Each morning at daybreak half naked, broken and bloodied bodies were found in the dark corners of public squares, or dumped in the stinking waters of the great drain and the Eridanos river. So, in a short time it was not possible to find anyone advocating dealing with the Persians and the rumours stopped.

This didn't mean that the plans of the traitors ceased, we all knew that within the great families there

225

were those who would betray the city to the Persians. But there were now none who cared or dared to openly work up people's fear. So, almost overnight we all became patriots. In this atmosphere the General, who, as he predicted, found it easy to have himself elected strategos of his tribe, became the focus of resistance. But the pattern of life in the city was changing, people began to live each day as if it was their last and as a consequence the wine booths and brothels did great trade.

That summer, it became a habit of those with time on their hands to walk down to the coast to look for sails in the distance, to visit the bars and food stalls for gossip in much the same way they did on feast days. For some it could be said that the threat of the Persians gave interest to their lives and helped them to ignore other problems. Not that any sails in the bay would have caused surprise as we had watchers on Cape Sounion and Salamis who could ride to the city to raise the alarm long before the enemy ships came in sight.

On one of the first warm days of the year, when the coming of summer could be sensed, I was in bed with Lyra when Aeschylus came to find me. We were lying, our limbs entwined after the act of the little death, letting the sweat dry on our bodies. Lyra, as she was accustomed to, had been teasing me, saying she looked forward to the Persian occupation of the city. The Persians would pay better and were better lovers, having learned to practise erotic arts in their temples in the east. We usually talked like this; casual remarks and teasing were common in such a relationship. It was not easy to show affection; although I know she cared for me more dearly than she would admit.

For me to have declared love for a pornoi flute girl would not have been natural, but I think I did feel something close to that. Not, of course, what I felt for

Elpinice but intense and unsettling all the same. Sadly I've never been much of a luck bringer in my personal life, the only two women I would ever have taken to wife were either too high or too low born and I've never had a taste for boys so another type of close relationship was denied me.

At the third bang on the door it opened and Aeschylus came in.

"I've spent half the day looking for you, Mandrocles, get dressed we're going visiting."

Lyra sat up with a pout, reaching for the sheet, giving the poet a good look at her breasts which he seemed to enjoy. With him she played the part of a whore whose job is finished and barely acknowledged me on leaving but I could see that she was angry to have our time together interrupted. Angry or perhaps upset. In the play acting nature of our friendship I've never been too sure. We walked through the Ceramicus but didn't head for Phaleron Bay as I expected.

"Where are we going?"

"To Piraeus, my brother's there with an old friend of yours."

I'd never been to Piraeus. I didn't think there was anything there but a few fishermen's shacks and said so.

"Until recently you'd have been right but now those in the know think that Themistocles is going to have a port built there. Cynegeiros, my brother, has bought some land there, cheap; he's got a business man's head on farmer's shoulders. Until the work on the harbour starts, he's got goats on it. But he's not the only one investing, if the city survives he thinks he'll make a killing, sell it on or build bars, warehouses, houses, even brothels, and lease them out. A port will bring ships and ships bring money."

227

We followed the stony track down to the Piraeus, which turned out to be a longer walk than I'd expected. Today, with it behind the long walls, we think of it as an extension of the city, but then it was just a fishing village surrounded by farms and allotments where no one really had any reason to go. But a walk in the company of Aeschylus went quickly. I've never heard any man talk so well or know so much and never a word wasted.

By the time we reached the sea I was thirsty and we entered a rough bar recently knocked together out of driftwood. Inside, leaning on a dirty counter with beakers of wine, was a man who looked like an older, rougher and nastier version of Aeschylus and with him, to my surprise, the poet Phrynichus.

"Well, well, it's Miltiades' boy, the one who loves the theatre."

I mumbled an acknowledgement, which he ignored.

"I was telling Cynegeiros that now everything's changed, I'm not only welcomed back but I'm almost a hero because of my play."

But despite his sardonic manner, he was a man to whom the recent months had not been kind, worry lined his face and pulled down the corners of his mouth.

"It's lucky I am welcomed back to the fold. I only just got off Paros a couple of days before the Persian fleet arrived. The rumours from Naxos had spread like the wind from the sea, within hours every available boat had sailed; all riding low in the water with weight of bodies. I was lucky there was an Athenian pentecontor in port, the captain recognised me on the quayside, and lucky too that he loved the drama festivals and my works in particular."

Distressed as he was by retelling the tale, he still directed a self satisfied look at Aeschylus as he said the last piece. He reached for his wine cup and gulped down several mouthfuls before continuing. I noticed his hand shook.

"I managed to get on board whilst the crew beat back others who tried to follow me with clubs and oars. We got off and managed to get out of the harbour without tangling our lines or breaking our oars against the other boats. There was a nasty moment when we nearly foundered turning out of the harbour mouth. I watched the chaos on the dockside as we pulled out. It could have been a scene from my 'Sack of Miletos'. By the way, do people still talk of my great achievement in that ground breaking trilogy that so moved the city?"

He didn't wait for an answer but went straight on as if only talking or drinking would settle his nerves.

"We sailed a straight course, didn't stop at any of the islands and when at last we sighted Cape Sounion sparkling in the light, I fell to my knees, praised the gods and wept. But I think I may have done that too soon because now that I'm back I can see the city is changed. Some cheered as I arrived but others spat, one even threw a stone. I was lucky to bump into Cynegeiros, who brought me here. So, here I am in this bleak fishing village, a guest of my young rival's brother, with no home to return to, only a burnt out wreck."

He stopped talking and I saw that his eyes were wet and a large tear streaked its way through the grime on his left cheek. Exile and fear change a man. I've seen plenty of it since, but even then I'd seen enough to feel pity. Aeschylus put an arm round his shoulder.

"Don't worry, after this is over, people will cheer your plays at the spring Dionysia again. Once we're victorious the 'Sack of Miletos' will get the praise it deserves and you'll be recognised as the only poet to have used an event that happened in his life time for a tragedy. And think, after your travels, wanderings, escapes and exiles, what a play you could write about the fate of Odysseus, and remember a house is soon built. Which is fortunate, because after the Persian visit we'll all have to become builders?"

I think that was probably the cleverest speech I've ever heard Aeschylus make. The two poets began to talk of verse and the relationship between men and gods, and the misfortune they bring in their plays.

We finished the jug of wine and Aeschylus suggested we walk by the sea a while before we went to eat at his brother's house further along the coast. Cynegeiros and I walked ahead with the two poets lagging behind, deep in conversation or rhyme. It was late in the afternoon, the weather fine and there were others like us, walking along the shoreline, killing time and waiting. The whole city was waiting yet there was an atmosphere almost like that of a holiday.

Cynegeiros, like his brother, was good company but with the same serious meaning behind everything he said, even the jokes. I noticed a scar that ran from the corner of his right eye before disappearing under his beard, which was thick black, flecked with grey. Despite the poet's rising status in the play festivals it was his older brother who was at the time regarded as the greater man.

"So will Miltiades lead us out to fight the Persians, Mandrocles?"

"I think he will if he can persuade the others."

"It's not as mad as it sounds. If we stay and defend the city we'll be beaten even if we aren't betrayed first, and it's probable in a long siege that someone will betray. Anyway, we couldn't hold the city, only the Acropolis, and the walls up there are ancient and crumbling. If he can get the army out and choose his ground carefully somewhere where their cavalry can't be deployed, we may have a chance. That's if he survives long enough to persuade the army of course."

This last statement jolted me back to full attention. All anyone talked about in those days was how and when we would fight the Persians. I'd heard so much I'd ceased taking an interest.

"What do you mean, if he survives?"

"If he survives the plots to kill him, lad. Where have you been hiding not to know that? It's the talk of the city, in some of the bars there are bets on who's behind it. You can even get odds on Themistocles."

He noticed my expression and put up his hand to stop me interrupting.

"No, no one really thinks Themistocles is behind it, although he's capable of anything. But his life's in danger and he knows it. He never goes out to the city without armed men, you must have noticed."

I had. Since our return from Themistocles' house he'd not left home without Theodorus, Ariston and a group of the toughest rowers, but I hadn't expected an attempt to kill him in the city, especially since he had been made strategos. Cynegeiros stopped and pointed out to sea as we reached a path that turned inland towards his farm.

"If Phrynichus is right, then just two days' sailing away lying out there is the whole Persian invasion force."

I followed the direction of his arm, the setting sun reddening the sky and the water. For a moment I thought I could see the sails of ships but then they vanished.

"Maybe more than two days, but they're coming and when they arrive you won't have to strain your eyes, Mandrocles. They'll fill the whole bay and stretch beyond eyesight, so many it'll take close to a week for them all to disembark."

231

I remembered the visit to the Bay of Marathon, wider and easier for an invasion fleet to spread out and land. I said to Cynegeiros,

"Then that's why they won't land here, too risky, and where would they deploy their cavalry? The ground's wrong, the landing's too cramped."

He looked at me almost approvingly, the scar puckering up by his eyelid as he smiled.

"You think well, or perhaps you know more of Miltiades' plans than you let on. But, do you know what it's like to fight?"

I told him that he had no need to worry on that account. I had my father's armour and I had already killed Persians.

"There's nothing good about that, when you take a man's life you take all he has and all he ever would have been."

"So, you'd know about that would you, farmer?"

It sounded wrong and I wish I hadn't said it, but he took no offence, only answered softly,

"Yes, I know more about it than I care to."

The poets caught up with us and we walked in silence the rest of the way to the house. We ate a simple meal, drank a jug of decent wine from the estate and Aeschylus and I stayed overnight. The wind blew that night and my troubled sleep was interrupted by dreams of an armada of black ships drifting in off the sea and across the land.

CHAPTER 24

The news from Sparta couldn't have been worse and the fact that it was brought by a familiar face made it no better. Towards dusk on the day after the night at Cynegeiros' estate a weary and travel stained messenger arrived at the house. It was Brasidas and he'd travelled fast. Miltiades dispensed with ceremony, took him straight through to his private quarters, seated him on the most comfortable chair and gave him a cup of hot spiced wine; I followed and was allowed to stay. While Brasidas recovered his breath and drank the brew, Lysias and Stesagoras arrived. Brasidas was different than on previous occasions I'd seen him, less of the impassive Spartan, almost human.

"Give me a space to finish this and get my breath, it was a filthy journey with no rest."

So we waited for what seemed an age until he had finished the wine, his stomach rumbled like that of a hungry man and when he started to speak he belched several times and had to pause. Strange I remember that, true though because if I close my eyes I can still hear that noise, smell the exhalation of sour breath and see him, part in the light of the lamps and part in shadow as we sat round waiting.

"Filthy journey and filthy news; King Cleomenes is dead."

Lysias and Stesagoras gasped, Miltiades gave a low groan and for a brief moment covered his eyes with his right hand. One of the lamps guttered, smoked and went out. Brasidas looked at the General with something like sympathy, and then continued,

"Well, there's much you don't know but then secrecy is our Spartan way isn't it? When he died he wasn't king any more. You must have noticed his mood swings when you came; he was drunk most of the time.

233

But there was something else behind that, a type of madness, like flickering lightening, came out at times and he lost control. His co-ruler, that treacherous arse licker Leotychidas, and his son-in-law Leonidas, had been waiting for their moment. Soon after you left his behaviour became more unstable and his drinking worse. He had taken to walking round the city with a stick like the Ephors carry. If he felt anyone intended to offend him he'd smash the stick into their face. He was as good as mad so, with the agreement of the Ephors, Leonidas had him seized and locked up in the public wooden stocks. The humiliation of being restrained and mocked deprived him of any remaining sanity.

"One night he managed to persuade the helot on guard to give him a knife, and attempted to cut all the flesh from his bones starting with his legs. By the time he got to his stomach he'd cut away most of his thighs and died. At least that's what we were told, he was certainly mad enough. But then to have left him alive would have been both dangerous and inconvenient."

Brasidas paused; a servant entered and passed him another drink. This was one of the only times I saw a Spartan close to tears.

"We'd been friends, as you know."

He pulled himself together and carried on sounding more Spartan.

"Still, all men die and I suppose in a way it's the type of hard death we approve of. So now Leonidas is king in his place and will need time to find his feet. Leotychidas is no leader and so the balance of power swings to the Ephors. You know what that means my friend."

Miltiades said nothing, waited for him to continue and just sat head in hands. So Brasidas continued.

"It means I don't think we'll fight, you can't rely on the Spartans. Now I'm done in, forgive me, I need to rest."

Miltiades, with a surprising tenderness, helped him rise and called the steward to take him to his quarters. As he left he turned.

"But I'll stay so that there'll be at least one Spartan with you when you make your stand."

He left the room and for a time we sat in silence listening to the hiss and splutter of the lamps.

"So, we're alone – on our own against the whole empire, the hypocrites, the cowardly, treacherous, lying hypocrites."

Miltiades hurled his chair across the room narrowly missing his brother's head, and then stood with his hands over his face. Stesagoras picked up the chair, set it back on its legs, he put a hand on Miltiades' shoulder and said softly,

"Shall I send word to Themistocles, Callimachus and the others. We need to consider this news and make plans."

"No."

Miltiades shouted for more wine to be brought then slumped down into his chair.

"No, we need to consider all right, but to consider for ourselves. There's no need to tell anyone else just yet, they'll find out soon enough, no secrets kept in this city. Cleomenes was our best hope, he would have fought with us and together, if the gods favoured us, we just may have won. Now alone, well what do you think?"

He didn't wait for an answer. I sat still hoping not to be noticed and sent to bed, but his eyes fastened on me.

"Well, you didn't bring us much luck in Sparta did you, Mandrocles? What are you doing in here anyway?

He shrugged as if he didn't care.

"But suit yourself, stay if you want; but remember, if we die, you die."

So I stayed and as a consequence learned something of the General that you won't have read in any of the tales of the time or in the book that young Herodotus is rumoured to be writing.

"None of us are safe in this place; I can't leave this house without a guard. The list of those who want me dead is as long as my arm. We have more enemies than friends here and now there's no chance of help: if the Spartans won't fight no one will."

Stesagoras started to speak but Miltiades shouted at him.

"Do you seriously think that without the unbeatable Spartan army behind us our fellow citizens will dare to take the field? Once they believe there's no red cloaked army coming to our aid, they'll turn on the generals, on me."

His brother tried to reassure him.

"No, they have faith; you've fought the Persians for years and lived to tell the tale."

"Well, I must be as good a liar as they say I am if I've fooled you, brother, I've never commanded in the field against a full Persian army. I've never faced the immortals in battle. My victories have been against raiding parties of Scythian tribesmen, small Greek states and a few Persian irregulars. That and a few skirmishes at sea. I'd depended on Spartan discipline and generalship – Cleomenes would have commanded."

I'd seen the General in this mood of brooding darkness before and now I saw its effect on Lysias and Stesagoras. However, he wasn't finished.

"But we do have one throw of dice left. This news would be welcome to the Great King. Aiakes, even my son, both have said I could return to the empire. We could leave in the ships, you would have to quit the city I'm afraid, brother. But without us the city has no hope. So we would have chance to make peace with the Persians and you could return when Hippias is restored as tyrant."

Neither Stesagoras nor Lysias answered him but for my part I would rather have died than go over to the side where Metiochus was. As if he read my thoughts he concluded with:

"For be sure of this, if we stay to fight and lose, we die. The only question is which side would kill us first."

He poured another cup of wine and downed it in one go. Then, for the only time ever, I saw his brother challenge him.

"Miltiades, that Spartan Brasidas set a better example of how an Athenian noble should behave. Think on this, think of the family reputation and the legacy your children will have to carry."

He stood up and left the room followed by Lysias. I stayed because for me, more than anyone in that house, there was nowhere left to go. He finished the wine and called for more.

"Watch this, boy, this is what fortune and the gods reduce us to for their pleasure."

He drank until stupefied when I helped him to his room and bed. I didn't judge him harshly. I knew the strain these last years had placed upon him and that most men would have broken and run or dealt with the Persians earlier.

Next morning it was if that evening had never happened. I think that Brasidas told him he knew from the Persian embassy that they wouldn't have him back; that Metiochus, his son, was prepared to see him dead and that for him too there was nowhere left to go. Or he had worked it out for himself, or perhaps when he woke

237

he decided he'd prefer death to shame. Who knows, but I'd learned even the greatest and bravest men feel despair and live with fear. I think that whether you end a hero or a coward depends more on luck and the whim of the moment than whether one man is brave and noble and another scared and base. The only one who was constantly brave and noble who I ever knew, and I knew most of them, was Cimon.

Such is the way of the world, knowing now there was no choice Miltiades sent messages to Themistocles and Callimachus to visit him to hear matters of great importance. When they arrived they brought news of their own. The day was fine so they sat in the shade of the courtyard amongst the dusty green of summer leaf. Brasidas was present to tell his tale of Sparta but before he got the opportunity Themistocles told us the news we dreaded.

"We've had a report from one of our ships: the fleet's been sighted off the coast of Andros, and it's taken hostages from all the islands en route. So, Miltiades you've been proved right about one thing, they're not going to land near the city."

"No, they'll make landfall in Euboea, no more than a day's sail, and safe waters. That means that they'll anchor at Karystos and they'll have to subdue the whole island; it gives us more time."

"Gives us more time if the Eretrians put up any resistance, you mean, and even supposing they do it won't last long; then they'll come for us."

"I doubt it, they'd have come straight for us, not wasted time on a detour. I think that once Euboea is secure behind their backs they'll cross over the narrow straits and make landfall at Marathon."

"And if you're right how long does that give us?"

Callimachus, who had until this moment sat and listened stroking his greying beard, cleared his throat and said,

"At least a week I think, if Miltiades is right, and I have no reason to doubt it. Remember, they have to defeat the Eretrians, who will fight, they don't know any other way, if there's no one else they fight themselves. In fact that's probably what they will do as they won't be able to agree a strategy of defence against the Persians. But why are you so sure about the Great King choosing Marathon?"

Miltiades got to his feet and wandered across to the statue by the pool and rested his hand on it.

"Because I've seen it and have carried it in my head since the defeat at Lade. It's a good beach for an invasion fleet but, most important, it's long and flat, with plenty of room for his cavalry. Marathon is the perfect place to land his army, all of it, cavalry included. From Marathon he can seize one of the two mountain passes and march across Attica to the city and attack from the landward side. Once over the mountain passes he can control the plains with his cavalry and we're finished. Then his fleet can sail round the coast past Sounion and blockade us from the seaward. A simple but very effective strategy, it's what we'd do in his position."

Themistocles said nothing, leaving the talk to the more experienced Callimachus.

"That will take them at least another three days, maybe four. So we've got up to fourteen days to call all the tribal musters and prepare the defence on the landward side."

Miltiades moved from the statue and took Callimachus by the arm.

"Then sit and wait to be betrayed, have some traitor open a city gate to the enemy one night. No, we get to

Marathon before he can get off the beach, catch him before he's fully deployed and sweep them back into the sea when their numbers won't be an advantage. We force them to the sea's edge and keep them trapped there. I know how to do it."

"Remember, Miltiades, I'm senior general and this decision has to be agreed amongst all ten generals, or at least by a majority. Besides, what you suggest is too risky, better to defend the city, or send away the women, children and old and defend the Acropolis. They'd have no chance of taking that before the Spartans arrive. We need to send to them now. They could be here in days then we could catch the Persians between two forces."

"There won't be any Spartans coming, tell him, Brasidas."

Miltiades face was red with exasperation. He banged the statue with his fist, hurting his knuckles but not showing it. Brasidas had said nothing, just sat listening turned to Callimachus and Themistocles, both of whom looked shaken by the General's outburst.

"Cleomenes is dead, the Ephors hold sway, at present they do not favour a war."

Themistocles then spoke:

"Then there's no chance, once the city hears the news there'll be panic, they won't fight alone. Perhaps there will be an attempt to overthrow the democracy. You've brought this on us Miltiades. I should have let the Alkmaionidai have your head when you arrived."

Callimachus put himself between Themistocles and Miltiades before tempers were completely lost and the first blow went in. But to my surprise it was Brasidas, the taciturn Spartan, who brought the argument to some type of resolution.

"Wait, think on this. Why do the Athenians need to know? The Spartans won't tell; we never do. Keep the secret in this room because if it gets out, Themistocles is right, you'll both lose power and probably your lives."

Callimachus looked relieved and, for the first time, acknowledged the Spartan's presence.

"So, Spartan, what would you do?"

"Me? I'd do what you will when you think about it. Keep this secret in this house, hold your meeting with the generals, decide your strategy and then send a runner to Sparta for help as you would normally have done."

"And what good will that do? You're the one who told us they won't come, remember?"

"Think about it, your Athenians don't know that. It will give your troops the will to fight believing that help is coming, and by the time the runner reaches Sparta things may have changed. The balance of influence between the war party and the peace party is finely balanced. And, if I'm not mistaken, young Leonidas looks like a man with a thirst for glory; he may convince the Ephors."

Callimachus took Brasidas' left hand in both of his.

"I'd never expected such eloquence from a Spartan but your counsel is good, it's the only way, I thank you."

He turned to Miltiades and Themistocles.

"You've heard the Spartan. He has given us a little hope, a little oil in the lamp. Now stop your quarrel, we've only ourselves to rely on."

Themistocles and Miltiades exchanged a kiss of friendship then the three generals sat to plan the next actions. Brasidas, I and the others left them.

That night as I was preparing for sleep, Ariston came to my room.

"Tomorrow the General's taking a party of us across to Brauron to fetch mistress Elpinice back to Athens

241

before the Persians get here. I thought you might want to come but be up before dawn if you do and bring your weapons, we don't know what we might run into."

CHAPTER 25

There was little sleep that night and the General never got to the estate at Brauron because shortly before dawn the house was woken by shouting in the street and banging on the door. A messenger had arrived in Athens from the city of Eretria on the island of Euboea begging for help. The Persian fleet had left Karystos and was sailing for their city. The exhausted messenger was taken by the city watch to the house of Themistocles by the Hanging Gate, where he told his tale: the Eretrians would fight, but only if they got Athenian aid. Themistocles roused the household and sent messages to the other nine Athenian generals to come at once. His summons ended with the words "What we have long feared is now come upon us". In the dark I was told by Miltiades himself as I was hurriedly dressing.

"Mandrocles, your father fought with me when he was no older than you, now it's your turn. I must go to the General's council but the urgency to fetch my daughter has increased, the great fleet is moving. Go now, take the men, Brasidas will accompany you to advise. Bring back Elpinice and my nurse, tell the house steward to bury or hide anything of value, then take the household and slaves and drive the animals up into the hills. Ride quickly; the stable hands are cutting out the best horses. If, when you have them safe, there is a chance to get to Marathon, then make a drawing of what you see that we can use later. Show where they would land and how much space they would have to deploy once their ships are beached. But, most important of all, show the best ground for a small army to make a stand. Do not fail me, the gods go with you."

He turned, shouted to his brother and left the house. I finished dressing and quit my sleeping cell. In the

243

kitchen I found Brasidas sitting down to an early breakfast with Theodorus, Ariston and some men from the Oineis regiment of Miltiades' tribe. Theodorus raised his cup in greeting to me and shouted,

"Hail, o strategos, we are yours to command."

The men laughed, including Brasidas. It was a simple joke but well meant and I experienced a rush of joy. It would be a great adventure with friends. There are times when the gods let you feel that the world is yours for the taking. Of course you don't realise then that it's all a cruel joke. Shortly after, in our riding clothes and armed, we led our horses out from the stables behind the house heading for the city gate.

It was still dark as we left the city going east on the road towards Brauron. We followed a track over the gentler slopes of Mount Hymettus from where we could see the wine dark sea glittering in early sunlight on both sides of the peninsula. Then we followed the track across the plain to Brauron. I was filled with wild happiness on that trip so that the light seemed brighter, the colours more vivid. I listened to the bantering talk of the men, imagined myself a general, leading an army, but most of all thought of Elpinice and of how I might win and bed her. When you are young and foolish nothing seems impossible.

We stopped only to water and rest the horses and by the afternoon rode into the estate yard. There was no sign of Persian raiding parties, no sign of a fleet. There was no sense of danger although once Brasidas thought he saw smoke from a great fire far to the north; otherwise it was a peaceful ride on a summer's day.

The estate stewards greeted us with relief; the area was disturbed by rumours. Tales of farms raided, crops burned, men slaughtered and women raped. But he didn't know of a nearby farm where it had actually happened so for the time being people were staying put.

Elpinice, accompanied by the crone nurse, met Brasidas and me in the house receiving room. I tried to make eye contact with her but as was fitting for a noble woman, she kept her eyes down. We agreed that as there seemed no imminent danger, they would prepare the household to leave while we made a rapid dash to Marathon the next day. Then, with a word of thanks for our journey and an invitation to partake of all that the house offered, they left us. As she reached the door she turned her head, looked directly at me with a smile whose meaning I couldn't read, but which set my brain racing and my loins stirring. Then the nurse shepherded her through the door.

Next day, Ariston, a poor rider, and half the men stayed to prepare the estate for evacuation whilst Brasidas, Theodorus and I, along with the rest, went to scout Marathon. Despite my fatigue I found sleep hard that night, hoping that she'd come to me or send a message. But none came and eventually I fell into a dream of horses riding on the sea which I think must have come from the gods, but of which I could make no sense.

Early in the morning we followed the coastal track to Marathon and reached the Temple of Heracles by midday. We'd brought parchment and charcoal to draw some plans of the land that fringed the beach at the north end of the bay, and the marsh and lake that lay beyond and inland. Brasidas walked the bay to establish the best position for an army to hold and defend the routes inland. Theodorus and two men scouted the road and tracks that descend from Mount Pentele to Marathon and which led to Athens. By mid afternoon we met on the long, sandy reaches of Schoinias beach, where the General had predicted the fleet would land. We measured the space available for cavalry then lounged on the soft sand and ate a frugal meal. Apart from the odd herdsman, the marsh behind us was deserted and the bay empty of ships. Tired after eating, we rested a while; talking died out, replaced by the stillness of the afternoon, the buzzing of insects and the murmur of the sea. We drowsed in the warmth of the afternoon. Time stopped and I fell into a day dream.

I was roused by Brasidas sitting up suddenly.

"Listen."

Somewhere to the north there was a faint sound that might have been someone shouting. We got to our feet. Beyond us the view to the north was blocked by the long thin promontory of Cape Kynosoura, a mass of grey, weather-beaten rock and scrub reaching out into the sea and sheltering the beach.

Theodorus was on his feet looking towards the point where the cape jutted into the water.

"Look, there's smoke, that's not stubble burning, it's something bigger."

Brasidas shouted to gather the horses.

"We'll walk them up to the top of the promontory and see what's happening over there."

It was hard work scrambling up the slope and I was sweating freely. Being lighter on my feet I was ahead of the others and well before we came to the top of the Cape I could smell smoke. A few feet above me there was a small knoll with steep slopes from where I reckoned I'd be able to see everything the other side. I tethered my horse to a small scrub oak and scrambled up the slope to look for the fire. I remember grazing my knee on some sharp thorn as I reached the high point and looked down to brush the jagged points and blood from my skin. When I looked up my blood froze. I wasn't facing inland and the source of the fire but out across Cape Kynosoura at the straits that separate Euboea from the mainland.

The waters were choked with ships, thousands of them stretching farther than I could see into the distance. A mass of sails on dark ships so densely packed you could almost walk across the bay on them. I wiped my eyes thinking it was a trick of light, looked again; fear dried my mouth. I tried to shout to the others to come and look but the words came out as a strangled croak. I couldn't take my eyes off the fleet; it choked the strait, seeming to fill the waters. I was aware of the others blundering and swearing their way up the knoll behind me. I felt that if I moved the ships would see me, come for me, so I stood rooted in a waking nightmare. One by one the others joined me, gasping or muttering when they saw what I saw. Last up, grumbling the loudest was Theodorus.

"Poseidon's balls, you've found them, Mandrocles, the whole fucking fleet, you've found them. I didn't think there were so many of the bastards."

So we stood and watched transfixed as the armada imperceptibly inched away from us towards its prey: the city of Eretria. Brasidas recovered from the shock quicker than the rest of us and took command. He pointed inland at the smoke we'd forgotten. Some ten or so stades away below us was a series of small buildings, a farm estate of some sort, burning but no sign of any people or animals. Brasidas put his arm on the shoulder of one of the troopers.

"Ride directly to Athens, tell Miltiades that the fleet he's been waiting for is here. Get him to send a day runner to Sparta for help. Take my horse, it's the fastest, ride it hard. Don't stop, the men who burned that farm are about somewhere. Not all the fleet's out there, some will have beached to land raiding parties on the other side of the bay."

Then I found my tongue.

247

"Elpinice at Brauron, what if they've landed there too, we must get back."

"No, we'll send a galloper on ahead, we need to take a look, see what size of force has landed."

He directed another trooper to warn the estate at Brauron, telling them to be ready to move tonight.

"Go now. We'll be an hour, maybe two, behind you. If we're later than that then get them moving. You take the girl on a fast horse, the rest can follow."

So our small party of five, Brasidas, Theodorus, two troopers and I, led our horses over the rocky spine into the wilder bay beyond. We took advantage of the scrub and stunted tree growth to use what cover there was. Where the scrub ended and gave way to rock we tethered the horses and inched our way painstakingly over the hot rock and loose shale until we could see directly down to the bay. This side of the cape there was a hot wind blowing down the straits from the north. Below, drawn up on the rocky beach were half a dozen Phoenician troop carriers.

Brasidas asked Theodorus how many troops they could carry.

"At least a hundred but there's not much safe beach space there. It's possible there are other ships that landed troops then moved off to anchor behind the next headland. So, they've split their force, they're hitting us and Eretria at the same time. They must be landing all along this coast.

I could feel my stomach muscles tightening into a knotted ball, my bowels turned to liquid. Brasidas seemed unmoved.

"I doubt it, this is just a group sent to scout out the territory and our preparedness. Maybe they're landing a few exiled traitors, to stir up discord, like the General's son Metiochus. Maybe they've arranged to meet some of your noble Athenians."

I asked why the burning.

"Because they're soldiers, boy, they've been cooped up on their ships too long, they fight for profit as well as the Great King. What they can grab they will. We need to be careful; these will be trained veterans, not boys or new recruits. The quickest way back is past that farm, then on to the track behind the beach at Marathon: it should be safe enough, they'll have moved on by now."

We fetched the horses and led them down to the fields and olive groves that fringed the burning farmstead. At the grove's edge we found two field hands, butchered, and beyond them a woman, now scarcely recognisable, who'd been harshly used. Blood stained the dry earth; black crows were feasting and ignored our presence. By the farms outbuildings we found more bodies and, in the yard, a naked woman, still just alive who had been tied spread-eagled across a cart. Brasidas swiftly slit her throat before I could stop him.

"It's the kindest thing I could do for her. She'll not survive this and if she does, her mind will be broken. You'll see worse in the coming weeks."

We left the horses a distance from the smouldering buildings and walked to what was once the main estate dwelling. Here the flames were still too fierce to go near, but behind it, resting in a stone coral, their backs against the wall, drinking and eating, were four Persian soldiers. They'd been left behind to guard a small pile of loot from the buildings and taken full advantage of the owners' wine store. Even if they'd seen us coming I don't think they'd have been able to do much. Brasidas and the others drew their swords, quietly walked over to the men and butchered them before they knew what was happening. Then they cut bits of them which they threw in the direction of the woman on the cart. They

249

quickly searched the bodies for portable loot and wiped their sword blades clean on the dead men's tunics

I realised then what type of experience war was and what I was in for. The whole act took less than a couple of minutes. I thought I might be sick; but I wasn't, I was fascinated.

Brasidas sent the troops to fetch the horses. We mounted and picked our way along the path that led behind Cape Kynosoura to the Bay of Marathon and the coastal track back to Brauron.

"If we push hard we can be back before the last of the light has gone, if we meet trouble we can't deal with, scatter and make your own way back. If we have to fight we cover Mandrocles so he can get back to take the Lady Elpinice to her father."

The others nodded and we set off. As we reached the bay we could see more smoke to the north, off towards Oione, but we encountered no more Persians. Perhaps they knew all they needed to about Marathon itself.

Later I learned that this was indeed the case, they had been told all they needed to know about the suitability of the bay as a landing place by the traitor Hippias. Brasidas was wrong about one thing though; we didn't get back in daylight. The long shadows from Mount Hymettus had merged into darkness when we rode into the lands of the Brauron estate. Here there was no panic, but there was fear that you could almost taste on the night air. At the entrance to the estate courtyard we were met by Ariston and Elpinice but not, I was pleased to see, the crone nurse. As Ariston supervised the leading off of the horses and listened to Theodorus' account of the day, Elpinice took my hand and led me to a patch of darkness by the wall. I have noticed often since how war, fear and danger loosen the conventions and duties that define our daily lives.

"I thank the gods you're back safe, my love."

She whispered this then kissed my lips. I put my arms around her and ran my hands down her back to her buttocks, feeling the firm flesh beneath the fine wool of her peplos. She didn't move away and said softly and without real anger,

"You're not with one of your whores from the Ceramicus now, Mandrocles."

But what we said or did meant nothing in those brief moments clinging together, we knew what we had and that it was doomed. The next few days we would take paths no one could predict and, in that uncertainty, the gods might allow a period of the happiness of misrule. She pulled away, saying,

"We will have time to talk on the ride over the mountains in the dark. Yaya Dorcus will not be able to keep up with us on her mule."

This was the first time I heard the name of the crone nurse. The estate was swarming like a hive; the animals surprised at being herded at such a late hour were agitated and noisy. Slaves were loading wine jars, food and furniture onto carts. Everything that could be taken from the estate to a place of greater safety was being packed, loaded or herded towards the hills. We could see lights at nearby farms and from noises on the road knew that everyone who could was doing the same.

The news from the north brought by our galloper had precipitated an unplanned evacuation of the area. Ariston collected the freshest horses for our party and a mule for the nurse. This would slow us down so he and Theodorus agreed to bring up the rear with her, while the rest of the party pressed on.

So, that night, lit by moonlight, we picked our way across Mount Hymettus, following the narrow track. Brasidas went ahead with two troopers, followed by Elpinice and me, with the others as a rearguard. In the comparative privacy of the night we rode side by side, sometimes holding hands, talking and whispering to each other depending on the proximity of the other riders. We arrived at the outskirts of Athens as the dawn was breaking. Elpinice, tired, was leaning in her saddle, her head resting against my shoulder as the tired and docile horses shambled along side by side.

As we drew nearer to the city gates we became part of the stream of carts, horses and people leaving the country for safety in the city of the goddess. We pushed our way through the crowds to the house and were greeted by Miltiades and Cimon, who greeted Elpinice with unexpected relief and tenderness. She was theirs now, beyond my reach.

CHAPTER 26

Despite their desperate pleas the Eretrians didn't get any help; we had none to offer but we did send a message to the Athenian colonists on the island encouraging them to help defend Eretria. It seems few, if any, took this encouragement to heart. The Eretrians did fight but left it too late to come up with a strategy that might have saved them. Stupidly they let Datis and Artaphernes land their troops unopposed and opted, as their only remaining choice, to defend the city.

We were able to follow events closely as Datis made no attempt to stop messengers crossing the channel with increasingly frantic demands for help. Perhaps he thought that the flow of bad news would lower morale and spark panic in Athens. This was unnecessary: we all knew that Eretria was doomed, in fact we were surprised they held out as long as they did; five days. On the sixth they were betrayed as the General had predicted they would be and, just as predictably, by men from the aristocratic faction in the town. Some of these opened one of the town gates to the Persians. Once in it didn't take them long to finish off any resistance, identify and protect the traitors of the aristocratic party. Then the soldiers were let off their leash to plunder, loot and rape. The bulk of the population was sold off into slavery and the aristocratic party given what was left of the town. Not much by then. The temples were burned in revenge for the sacking of Sardis. In the later wars I served with a warrior from Eretria who escaped the sack of the city. I could never work out whether he hated us less or more than the Persians.

There was one message from Eretria that did cause a stir in the city though. We first heard about it when a request came asking the General to visit the home of

Kallixenos, son of Aristonymos, where he would hear of matters of great importance for Athens.

I was in the courtyard with the General and Cimon, telling them about our adventures in Marathon. Since we'd been in Athens, the General had begun to spend more time with Cimon. I think he regretted that the boy was too young to fight alongside us, and it was certainly the boy's regret. Cimon, despite his later reputation as uneducated, had a sharp military brain and enjoyed a lively discussion with his father on the best way to deploy our troops at Marathon. So, when the messenger arrived with the invitation, the General had him shown through without sending the boy away. The name Kallixenos meant nothing to me but it clearly did to Cimon: when the man had been dismissed he turned to his father.

"How does that man dare to send such a message, father, surely you will not go?"

The General seemed amused and, noticing my look of ignorance, for I suppose that is how I looked, said,

"Tell Mandrocles who Kallixenos is, Cimon."

Pleased to be given such an adult task by his father, he blurted out,

"He's the worst of the whole Alkmaionid clan, born to be a traitor. He was the one who most wanted my father prosecuted when we arrived. He couldn't be more in favour of the Persians without wearing trousers himself, he's......"

His father stopped him but ruffled his curly hair affectionately.

"It's not that he loves the Persians so much as he hates the new arrangements for the demos. Put next to him, even a man like Aristides appears a radical friend of Themistocles."

This I did understand and dutifully laughed to show it. He continued,

"But this is strange, why should he have news for me?"

He stood up.

"But I'll go and you can come too, Mandrocles, your sharp eyes and ears will spot anything I miss. Whistle up some of the lads, I think it would be wise to be cautious, so take that knife of yours, the one you're always so keen to use."

To my surprise, and more so to Cimon, the summons seemed to stimulate the General's good humour. So we trooped off to visit the home of Kallixenos and a strange visit it was. Most of the ten elected generals were there, including Callimachus and Aristides, but not Themistocles. Evidently Kallixenos considered what he had to impart would be too inflammatory for Themistocles' taste, and he was right about that, if nothing else. I was wondering why he had included the General, who, if anything, was quicker to anger than Themistocles. It wasn't long before I was enlightened.

Leaving our escort outside, the General and I were shown into the receiving room in Kallixenos' elegant old fashioned house. Despite the fact that most of the men present were of the opposing faction and had tried to indict him earlier, there was no apparent feeling of hostility, most nodded. Callimachus crossed the room to take his hand and as he did so, Kallixenos spoke the formal words of greeting before getting to the point.

"We are grateful for your presence, Miltiades, and I'm sure you're wondering why we included you when there are so many here with reasons to wish you harm."

Miltiades inclined his head at this and faced the company with a grim smile as Kallixenos continued. I took an instant dislike to the man, he was too full of himself and this came through more strongly than his good taste and manners. There was something sly and untrustworthy about him.

"You have probably realised that we have not thought to invite our esteemed friend Themistocles, son of Neocles. But it was considered that you, as head of the ancient family of the Philiads, could not be excluded from the discussion of matters of such import. In fact it could be that the greatest decision in the history of the city of the goddess will be taken in this house, and we know that you, by birth..."

Here he paused for effect and looked around the room as if for applause,

"...by birth, if not by inclination..."

There were more smiles at this, particularly from Aristides,

"...are one of us, from one of the families on whom this city depends and that in your heart you have no more love for the demos and their rabble rousers than we have. Therefore here you are."

Although it was clear that Miltiades was not pleased with this speech, he said nothing. I noticed that others in the room were less than sympathetic to Kallixenos' oratory. Callimachus, in particular, and perhaps to prevent Miltiades from making the point he said,

"This is all fine and well but I'm sure you have not brought us all here to discuss the good old days, pleasant though that would of course be, Kallixenos."

Now it was Miltiades' turn to smile but Kallixenos, not wanting to lose his leading role hurried on, but some of the self satisfaction was replaced by a touch of impatience.

"Well then, if there's not to be time for courtesy and friendship, here is what I have to say. I have recently received a message from Hippias, currently with the forces of the Great King in the conquered city of Eretria. He's seen the vengeance of the Persians and, as

256

a true patriot and out of love for our city, he wants to prevent the same fate overtaking us."

Miltiades tried to speak but Callimachus placed a hand on his shoulder to prevent him. Kallixenos noticed this but continued.

"Hippias assures us that the Great King wishes nothing but friendship with our city. He was hurt, understandably, by our participation in the wicked and foolish revolt of the Ionian Greeks. But Hippias has explained that the people of our city, lacking the firm governing hand of the best men from the best families, were misled. Yes, misled by wicked men, men who oppose the natural order of things and the will of the gods."

"And how, precisely, is the Great King proposing to show this great friendship, Kallixenos?"

Miltiades asked sarcastically, but this time Kallixenos was unruffled.

"You of all people ought to be the most grateful, Miltiades, son of Cimon. Hippias has persuaded the Great King that if the evil doers are expelled from the city and the old order restored, then he will smile upon us. Yes, even you, Miltiades. Your father-in-law will forgive you your bigamous relationship with a barbarian queen and your slights on him. He, whose father gave your uncle the territory in the Chersonese, which you have lost: I will say no more on that matter, but the gracious Hippias has persuaded the Great King to forgive you your murderous and foolish attacks on him. In this he has been aided by your true son, Metiochus, whose love for you is perhaps more than you deserve."

As he spoke I saw the light of murder ignite in Miltiades' eyes, but Callimachus kept his hand on his shoulder restraining the outburst he feared.

"So, if we expel those who have ruined this city and given power to those only fit to be ruled; if we create a government of the best men, purge the city of filth and wickedness, restore the rule of natural order; then the golden age of our ancestors will come again and the Great King will smile upon us. And you know, fathers of the city, what the alternative is. It's there to be seen clearly in the smoking ruins of Miletos, the ruins of Naxos, and now the ruins of Eretria. Slavery, rape, dishonour, death and all for a cause we don't believe in and a system of government we despise. All we long for in our hearts will be given to us by the Great King. We would be remembered as the men who not only saved our city but also restored her reputation and virtue."

He paused; his words had subdued the room. He allowed himself the luxury of a small smile of satisfaction then made to continue but was prevented.

"But what of Hippias, Kallixenos, what will he expect?"

To my surprise it was Callimachus, not Miltiades, who had spoken.

"He will expect, and rightly so, to resume his role as father of the city."

"Tyrant of the city, I think you mean."

"Yes and why not? You, the Polemarch, first of the generals, should realise more than any man what the alternative to this is. You, the man whose task it will be to lead our army and city to certain death and destruction at the hands of the invincible might of the Great King."

"That may well prove to be the case but the fact remains, we expelled Hippias from this city for his tyranny. Do you not think it odd that we restore him because he has a Persian army at his back? Tell me where the honour in that is, Kallixenos?"

This coming from the conservative Callimachus seemed to surprise Kallixenos, who continued in the manner of one explaining a simple concept to an unwilling or stupid child.

"Yes, we expelled Hippias. We were wrong to have done so and have been humiliated by the demos ever since. But, you miss the essential point, Callimachus. Hippias is an old man, over eighty; he wants to come home to die. Once he has gratified everyone by so doing we will rule the city; the first families, even Miltiades, will have a place."

Callimachus paused for a moment as if considering then asked,

"And is that all the Great King wants; to enable a poor old man to enjoy his last days in the city he loves? For that he has gone to all this trouble? Raised such a great force of men, just to please dear old Hippias?

No, Kallixenos, that's not the only catch is it? Because if it were then surely the kind hearted Darius could not bring himself to punish us. Strange also that he had no such difficulty in destroying Miletos, Naxos and Eretria. Or perhaps Hippias didn't want to rule those cities."

He stared at Kallixenos then moved towards him and placed a hand on his shoulder.

"Tell me truly, Kallixenos, why should we accept your proposal?"

Kallixenos angrily blurted out,

"Because the alternative is death."

"And is that what Hippias told you? That unless we do his bidding we die, even us, the leading men?"

Kallixenos, I think, realised with that threat, he lost some of the support in the room.

Callimachus continued.

"You are right to name me Polemarch, first of the generals. We have an army. All of us here have fought

259

and taken wounds. Are we to be threatened in our own city?"

I saw them look from Kallixenos to Callimachus. Some now seemed shame-faced; they hadn't expected opposition from such a source. Aristides, the General's enemy, probably the one most in favour of an accommodation with Persia, looked troubled. Then, choosing his time, Miltiades spoke.

"Callimachus, this matter must, by law, be debated by all the ten generals. I notice Themistocles, general of the Leontis regiment, and Stesileos, general of the Aiantis regiment, are not present. Therefore, I insist our course of action be debated as is the law and custom by all the ten generals, guided by you. How can men who are not generals decide the fate and duty of those who are?"

At this point he looked at Kallixenos, who was no general, then turned his gaze to Aristides and spoke directly to him.

"Is that not the right way to proceed? I ask you not as an enemy but as a free Athenian and general of Antiochis regiment."

Aristides didn't answer, just looked away. Kallixenos, less sure and beginning perhaps to worry that he had misjudged the mood of the gathering, began again.

"I don't wish to take away from the generals what is theirs and I would remind you that my family has never shirked battle. But what we are being offered gives us not only peace and honour, but the restoration of isonomy, of the principle of balance that all good men strive for. Soon, if men like Themistocles continue, this balance will be swept away. Soon the rule of the city will be in the hands of the ignorant masses; men whose families do not have tradition, men of mongrel birth like Themistocles. Here you have a chance, one chance, to restore good."

Callimachus raised a hand and silenced him.

"Kallixenos, because this is your house and out of our obligation as guests I allowed you to say this even though the question had been directly asked of me. We thank you for your hospitality. You have made your case most eloquently and we have listened. There may be much in what you say and there may be some here who find your argument attractive. But Miltiades has made a point of law and procedure. This is a matter for the generals, and not all the generals are here. For the city to be advised in times of war the generals must meet, that is their duty. Therefore, I call for a morning session of the ten generals, followed by a meeting of the assembly. That is my decision."

He spoke as if what he said was beyond dispute then looked at each of the other generals in turn, not bothering with Kallixenos. None of them demurred; it was a performance of real authority. He was a man of the old type, he'd listen to different arguments, but once his mind was made up he acted and couldn't be dissuaded until he achieved his goal. It was clear that none of them, even Aristides, thought to argue, although he and Miltiades exchanged a hard stare. Callimachus then instructed the house slaves to bar the door before he spoke further.

"Friends, we owe our gratitude to Kallixenos for bringing this matter to our attention, but I should not need to remind you that there are elements in the city who might not interpret this as an act of civic duty, men who are less subtle than we, who have not the benefits of our host's appreciation of the principles and blessings of isonomy. They might consider, in their simple way, that this is an overture to treachery. Remember, there are many rumours circulating about some of our oldest families, I mention no names. But these rumours allege that they would prefer to deal with the Persians rather than live under the laws that govern the city."

His words were diplomatic but the measured icy delivery betrayed his anger. No one spoke knowing he hadn't finished.

"Perhaps it was unwise to fail to invite two of our number, the two most wedded to the new ways. Perhaps to those who don't appreciate the disinterested statesmanship of the noblest families this may be seen as evidence that we met here to overthrow the state. I therefore insist that what we learned here, what we debated here, stays in this room. I say this not only to prevent a rumour spreading that would panic the city, but also to protect some here whose actions may be..."

Here he paused as if searching for the right word before continuing,

"... misinterpreted by the people."

Then he fixed his gaze on Kallixenos and the generals who belonged to or favoured the Alkmaionid faction. The generals returned his gaze impassively but Kallixenos went white, either through rage or terror, I couldn't tell which.

"Good, so we are all agreed, till tomorrow, gentlemen. Miltiades, our routes lie in the same direction, I will walk with you if you don't mind."

Miltiades agreed, looked round with a smile at the others and we left the room.

Outside it was a beautiful summer's evening. The two generals walked ahead, arm in arm. I walked with the bodyguards, who had obviously got their hands on some wine while they waited. They passed the time on the way home singing obscene songs about our host, his family and certain farm animals. In the days following the war, this song, which spread through the

262

army, became quite popular. Miltiades used it in public debates to raise public anger. You may well have heard it sung by veterans in wine booths. Perhaps it's age, but it still makes me emotional to hear it. Strange that a bawdy song called "The Arse and Ass of Kallixenos" should raise such an emotion, but then those were strange days.

CHAPTER 27

Callimachus and Miltiades moved fast, the board of the ten generals met the next morning, starting early and lasting till midday. I wasn't there of course, only the ten went into the room, there were no witnesses. The door was guarded, no one could overhear or disrupt. But the city wanted to hear, to know; Athens hates a secret and everyone knew that what was being discussed in that small room would decide the future of every living creature within its walls. Everyone from the fullers' slave who collects the waste from the street buckets to the richest and most pampered hetaerae taking a late breakfast of seed cakes and honeyed wine after a night of love.

I was up early that day, restless and unable to settle, I'd agreed to meet Aeschylus and his brother at noon, and go with them to the meeting of the assembly to hear the debate. To fill in the time until then I wandered through the crowded alleyways of the Ceramicus to visit Lyra. But her time of the month was wrong and she was uncomfortable and only wanted to talk. So after a while I left and, feeling impatient and frustrated, hung around the flute girls' academy for a while but could find none to my satisfaction.

Then I walked the streets, listened to the gossip in the taverns and the booths, wandering in a trance while the city seethed. At midday I made my way to a tavern by the Agora where I'd arranged to meet my friends. We'd agreed on this despite the place being expensive and having a reputation for over watered wine passed off as something better, because it was near the Orchestra. The assembly was to meet here as it was the only space big enough to accommodate all the citizens who would want to attend. Aeschylus and Cynegeiros were inside drinking and eating a plate of country sausage when I arrived. They made room and shouted for an extra wine cup. Aeschylus was amused that the space where we would meet to decide whether to fight or not was the same place where Phrynichus' play had so disturbed Athens a couple of years ago.

"That's why he decided not to come along, he's afraid he might be recognised, blamed for our current situation and then strung up."

He broke off as there was a sudden roar from outside which told us that the generals' meeting must have ended and they were making their way through the Agora to the assembly. So we, like everyone else, dashed down our drinks and rushed to the door. Outside the crowd was dense and excited; we joined them. The going was slow, the Agora packed with people pushing, elbowing and shouting. Thousands of feet kicked up dust that stuck to sweat soaked robes and tunics. The day was hot and the heat of the crowd suffocating. Tempers soon frayed and pushes turned to blows. The stench of the mass was foul; thousands of unwashed bodies packed together in the heat. Garlic, sweat, stale wine, such is the raw material of our new democracy.

We joined up with a group of sailors, two of whom were upper bench rowers from the Athene Nike, and with them we pushed our way as far towards the front of the orchestra as we could. Throughout the crowd there were groups of sailors carrying their rope oar loops, which they waved above their heads like banners. Even in those days the seamen were great supporters of the democracy and followed Themistocles and the more radical democrats. It was clear to me that Themistocles had made sure that all his people were there and, although the mood was good, they'd been drinking and it wouldn't take much to provoke them.

There's nothing to match the Athenian crowd. Democracy, theatre and riots are in their blood. In front of us was a fat red faced man with a greasy beard, presumably a butcher as he was waving a link of sausages in the air in mimicry of the sailors and shouting obscene jokes. Most laughed but some threw olives and fruit at him, it could have been a carnival day. One of our group managed to hit him and he turned, laughing, waved his sausages at us, shouting,

"Put your oar loops around this."

We laughed and clapped, Aeschylus shouted in my ear.

"You laugh now, but one day men like that, grotesques from the satyr plays, will have influence."

I didn't take him seriously at the time, yet, as usual, he was right.

By this time the members of the assembly and board of generals had taken their places. The first Archon of the year signalled the crowd to silence with no effect. He then shouted, ordering silence but his voice was weak and failed to carry. The crowd responded as they would at comic plays, they jeered and objects were thrown. Some wit shouted,

"You'll have to speak up, we can't hear."

Then Themistocles stepped forward from his place and bellowed for silence. This was greeted by cheers. Then the noise level fell enough for us to hear Kallixenos loudly rebuke Themistocles for presuming to take upon himself the duties of the first Archon of the year, going on to say with a sneer,

"If anyone should have the right to begin the debate I, by birth, am more fitting than you, son of Neocles."

To which a section of the crowd shouted,

"Oh no, you're not."

Then the jeering and throwing started again. So, in farce and chaos, the fateful debate of the assembly about most important decision the city would ever make was begun as two politicians wrangled over protocol; so typically Athenian.

Eventually they established some type of order and the great debate was able to begin. It started with speeches in the old style, the generals stating their families' line and tradition and members of the assembly replying in kind. But soon impatience set in, both within the assembly and in the crowd. It was obvious that sections of the crowd had been primed to hiss and shout at different speakers.

But the loudest voices in the crowd were the sailors and they were for Themistocles and if they had all brought skins of wine like those from the Athene Nike, it wouldn't be long before they lost all self control. When Themistocles spoke they cheered, when he was contradicted they hissed. Fights broke out, blood was spilled and the mood of the assembly grew angrier. Most of the frustration was because the question of the Persian threat was not debated.

What was debated was whether it was better for the city to be governed by the old families in the traditional way set down by the gods, or by the new men with no pedigree who were little better than the goat fuckers who lived in the hills. Yet, although most of the crowd were for the goat fuckers, the laws and traditions of the city supported the old families. And Athens being a city of paradox, there were gangs of strong arm thugs and wild aristocratic youths ready to fight it out with the sailors.

So for hours as we stood in the heat and watched this procedural standoff we grew tired of shouting and cheering and watching fights. I was surprised that Themistocles had not tried to talk of the Persian invasion fleet and that neither Miltiades nor Callimachus had spoken either. At the appointed time the assembly was adjourned until the next day with no decision and no real debate on the war. The crowd started to grumble when, as if at a prearranged signal, Themistocles shouted over the voice of the herald.

"Countrymen, Athenians, today we have been muzzled. It seems to me Persian gold has already been spent. Tomorrow must be different; someone must speak for the city of the goddess."

Then without waiting to be silenced, he turned and walked off and the crowd began to disperse, muttering, towards the wine booths and taverns. We drifted along with the flow in the company of the sailors and ended up in the tavern of the bald headed man. Theodorus and Ariston were there with a large group from the General's ships, so it looked like a private party. They were in good humour and drinking heavily. Ariston came over and put an arm round my shoulder. I could feel the calluses of his rough hand through my tunic.

"We are honoured that you have come to drink with us here, and even more so that you brought the up and coming poet and his man-slaying brother."

It was rough humour and well meant but I wondered if Aeschylus or Cynegeiros would take offence. Aeschylus gave a slight smile but Cynegeiros was in his element. He grinned broadly and as he did so I noticed the scar pucker up. He placed his hands on Ariston's shoulders and said,

"Well, you'd better get the drinks in, old man, or I'll put you on my list of those to be slain."

Ariston laughed and shouted across the space to the bar for drinks. I didn't want a night drinking with them, I wanted to be near the front for tomorrow's session, which would mean getting up early, and I wanted to get back to the house to see what the General was up to. So I sat for one drink then got up to go. Aeschylus rose too and said he'd walk back part of the way with me.

As we left, his brother said from across the table,

"It's a good decision to go, there'll be trouble tonight, some scores settled. These lads and gangs of democrats across the city will be looking for Persian lovers and traitors so they can shut them up before tomorrow's assembly."

Aeschylus looked at him with a sardonic smile.

"But I notice you're staying at the table, brother."

"Well, someone's got to keep an eye on them, make sure they keep a sense of proportion."

Outside in the night it was still hot with a gentle, warm breeze. We walked back through the city hearing the shouts, singing and laughter from all the wine stalls and bars in the Ceramicus. The sound fading as we walked towards the more respectable districts at the foot of the Acropolis. Before our ways parted and he made his way towards his own house Aeschylus embraced me, saying,

"Make sure you sleep well and rise early, you don't want to miss tomorrow because whatever the decision it'll change our lives; make us different men."

Then he walked off and I watched him go, and listened to the tune he began to whistle until it faded into the hot night.

The General wasn't home and in fact didn't return at all that night, so I learnt nothing. I did, however, run into Elpinice in the house kitchen where she and the cook were preparing a basket of food to send down to the Agora for the General the next day.

Because the General and his brother were absent, she asked me to join her in the courtyard garden so I could tell her about the day's debate; all she had heard had been a message to prepare and send the food. So we sat in the dark of the garden in the hot night and I tried to explain the events of the day. I wanted to talk of other things but her mind was on politics and she became impatient with my account, almost made me feel as if her grasp of the importance of the day's events was sharper than mine, despite her not being there. She would talk of nothing other than her father's chances of leading the army to victory and how hard it must be for Cimon not to be old enough to fight. Then I became impatient out of frustration and she seemed to notice me for myself for the first time. She rose to go, looked at me and I expected some words of love, but she said only,

"How I envy you, Mandrocles, you will be there; you will fight at his side."

Then she went inside leaving me in the dark.

I was up early next day. A strong wind had blown up in the night, the sky over the sea was blue but I remember white cloud piled up behind the mountains and the Acropolis. It looked as if the heavens had split into two camps preparing to fight. The Agora was crowded and there were many organised groups I'd seen the day before, but luckily Lysias and some friends were close to the speaking floor and he called me over to join them. So I had a good view of one of the most remarkable and significant bits of theatre in our times.

It was a set piece to equal any seen in the dramas and it had the mark of Themistocles all over it, even though he, himself, played no part. From the moment that the call to the assembly was cried by the heralds and the opening remarks made by the Archon, it was clear that today's performance would not be a repeat of the first day's ill-tempered shambles. Had I not been so naive I'd have grasped at once that a deal had been brokered by the board of generals and the most influential men in the city. They must have been up all night to hammer out the arrangements and this explained the General's failure to return home.

The first thing that struck me was that all the board of generals wore their hoplite armour. That alone made an impact on the crowd as it shoved its way into the orchestra as it was against tradition and custom. The Archon announced that it had been agreed that Aristides would speak first. This was strange as, owing to his relative youth, he should have come later. The sailors and democrat groups in the audience started to catcall and shout anti-Alkmaionidai slogans but then suddenly stopped in confusion as Aristides, through clenched teeth, said,

"I propose Miltiades, son of Cimon, should open the debate as he has the most experience of fighting...."

He couldn't prevent himself smirking then adding,

"Or rather dealing with, the Persians."

Even the irony of this last bit and the invitation to sarcasm didn't rouse his opponents in the crowd and in the unusual silence that followed the General stepped to the speaking point. In armour with his beard freshly trimmed and thick red hair brushed back he looked like a warrior from the heroic age, like the mature Achilles might have looked had he lived longer.

He stood for a while looking out at the crowd, silent, building anticipation like the main actor will do in the new plays by young Sophocles. Then in a deep voice that carried to those right at the back he spoke.

"You see before you a soldier who has, these past nine years, fought the armies of the Great King and lived to tell the tale. I am as you know, a plain man, not a politician, I speak as I find, so you will hear no fine words from me, just the truth."

Here he paused and slowly moved his head from left to right and it seemed that his gaze fell on every man in the crowd. What he'd said was so implausible that I was surprised he kept a straight face and that no one laughed, but no one did.

271

"You are Athenians, brave men, sons of heroes, warriors since before the days of Theseus. You don't scare easily so I won't treat you like frightened boys. I'll be honest. I will be brutal.

"We face a danger from which we can't run. We sent ships to fight the Persians in the Great Revolt: ten ships. Our fellow Greeks from the city of Eretria sent five ships.

"Where are they now? Where is Eretria that ancient city, just across the waters from Marathon, so close to us?

"It's a great city no more: ruined, wasted; ghosts wail in its streets among the broken buildings. Its men are dead with none to bury or identify them. Its women and children are slaves. They foolishly tried to defend their city and were betrayed."

Again he paused; there was a collective groan of grief in the crowd.

"Yet the vengeance of the Great King for them is as nothing compared with his hatred of us."

He raised the pitch of his voice, spitting out,

"He wishes every one of you dead; well, every true Athenian dead, for although I can hardly find it in me to speak the words, there are some in this city, some vipers accursed by the gods, who would unlock our gates and let in the enemy. Yes, just as Eretria was betrayed. But should this, this city of the goddess Athena, fall then we will envy their fate.

"Listen to me; I know what I am saying only too well. I know the Great King; I know his moods, his cruelty. I have fought with him and for these last years against him. He does not forget a slight; he lusts for vengeance on Athens, so much so that he has a servant whose sole duty is to speak to him three times at every meal that is served, these words:

'Master, remember the Athenians.'

"Then he makes his own prayer,

'Lord Zeus, make it possible for me to punish the Athenians.'"

Here again he paused. There was absolute silence in the crowd; we waited for him to continue. I noticed that even his enemies in the council and on the board of generals, men like Xanthippus, Megacles and Aristides, watched with absolute attention. He waited, spun out the silence, and stretched the tension. Then suddenly, he threw up his arms in the gesture of a supplicant, turned his face to the heavens and raised his voice as he addressed the goddess.

"Oh, Lady Athena hear my words. I, Miltiades, son of Cimon, do swear that even if I go alone, I will go to the plain at Marathon and meet the barbarian invaders who have burnt our cities, desecrated out temples, raped our women and made slaves of our children. I swear that if the army marches with me we will triumph, but that if I must go alone, I will die with honour and in doing so salvage the honour of your city."

He stood maintaining the pose as the echoes of his shouted oath reverberated in men's heads. I was beginning to wonder how he could proceed when Callimachus stepped up to him, placed a hand on his shoulder and, in the manner of a man overcome with emotion, but in a voice loud enough to embrace all the crowd, asked,

"But why, brave Miltiades, would you choose to lead us to Marathon?"

Miltiades made a show of pulling himself together, as a man who had just been speaking with a goddess would need to, and then replied in an equally loud voice,

"Because if we can get there before the Persians manage to get off the beach head, we control the two

273

mountain passes that lead back to the city. We can box them in; contain them at the edge of the sea. Because there, there will be no gates that traitors can open to the enemy. There, there will only be our army, honourable Athenians who would rather die than let down their shield companions. And…"

Here he paused again, placed his hand on Callimachus' shoulder as if this were a private conversation between two old friends, then raised both the volume and emotion of his voice, almost shouting,

"…because there, the rest of the Greeks will see us, a small band of determined Athenians, defending their freedom, and those who have any honour at all will come to join us. The brave Plataeans, the Spartans, and together, we will hold."

He dropped his hand from Callimachus' shoulder, turned his face to us, his audience, again and spoke in a low voice, simulating a whisper but one that still carried.

"For rest assured, friends and countrymen, if I do not come back victorious I will come back carried on my shield."

Again he assumed the position of the supplicant, face turned heavenward as if he were in direct contact with the goddess and the debate of the Athenians could be left to others.

For what seemed an age no one spoke, then Callimachus after a gesture that was supposed to convey the wiping of tears from his eyes shouted,

"Citizens, will we leave brave Miltiades to fight alone?"

There were deafening shouts of "no" or "never". When they tailed off he shouted again,

"So, Athenians, where must we go?"

As one, the other generals shouted,

"To Marathon."

And this was taken up by us all as we stood waving our arms and shouting,

"To Marathon, to Marathon."

So it was decided and just in the nick of time for that night the news that we had so long dreaded was brought by an exhausted and terrified runner.

CHAPTER 28

When I think of that march it's the dust I remember, fine choking dust clouds kicked up by our feet. The day was sunny and hot but with a breeze strong enough to blow the dust into your face, gritting up the mouth and stinging the eyes. I'd never marched with an army before and despite my youth I struggled to keep up, sweating and gasping. It was as well I was among friends. The plan was to march in our tribal regiments in columns six abreast but that didn't happen and no one seemed much surprised.

The regiments got mixed up as each man settled to his own pace. Our regiment, the Leontis, got mixed up with the Aiantis regiment, so I was able to march with a group of men that included Aeschylus, Cynegeiros as well as Lysias and as many of the crew of the Athene Nike who either owned or had been able to borrow armour. So, in this companionable way we trudged through the heat of the day sweating, weighed down with our armour and gear. The columns of six drifted apart until the army was stretched out over miles made up of knots of men who chose to walk together, intermingled with the slaves and donkeys that carried some of our gear. At least that's how it seemed to me. The discipline may have been tighter in other regiments.

By about noon as we were moving up through one of the mountain passes, the order was given to rest and we dropped our gear and stumbled towards whatever shade the rocks, stunted oaks and olives afforded. Skins of water were passed around. Men brushed the sweat soaked dust from faces, arms and legs, and then sprawled out. No one spoke; the only sound was of packs and helmets being dropped and of the men further back in the line from us falling out. I took some water, swilled it round my mouth to clear out the dust, spat, and then drank deeply. My legs ached, my shoulders were rubbed raw from the weight of my pack and my feet were beginning to blister. I made a promise to myself that, if I survived, I'd do the rest of my fighting from the deck of a trireme. I didn't keep the promise and every time I had to march with the army I've regretted it.

Once the seamen got their breath back they began to grumble, swear and moan. Theodorus in particular, a big man, took the march, humping a pack, badly. Cynegeiros, though, was in his element and spent the rest period helping Theodorus and the other sailors adjust the way they carried their gear and showing how they could look after their feet and ankles.

The army had come together with such speed that we were able to move out towards Marathon within a day of the debate in the Agora. The order of march and mobilisation had been planned long before by Miltiades.

Two days earlier when the messenger arrived at the General's house in the early evening he'd been dining with Callimachus, Themistocles and Stesileos, the general of the Aiantis regiment in which Aeschylus and Cynegeiros served. They'd eaten and were sitting in the shade of the courtyard laughing at the way Miltiades had manipulated the audience. Themistocles, who had a talent for mimicry, was recounting the debate, playing both the parts of Callimachus and Miltiades. He'd gone down on one knee as Callimachus, to plead for noble Miltiades, when he was interrupted by a banging and shouting from the outside door. A weary and travel stained messenger was shown in and brought before the General.

"The warning beacon on Mount Pentele has been lit. The Persian fleet's in the bay of Marathon."

277

He stopped to catch his breath, Miltiades carried a wine cup to him and he downed it in one.

"Thank you General, they entered the bay this morning, we watched until we were sure it was the whole army, too many ships to count, they fill the whole bay."

"All right, boy, calm down, you've done well. Go to the kitchen, they'll feed you, stay here tonight. Before dawn I want you to go back, tell your detachment to watch the Persians, record everything they do and send a runner back every few hours to update us. When we get to Marathon report to me and I'll find a use for you."

He turned back to us,

"Well, gentlemen, looks like we got today's play-acting finished just in time."

Callimachus stood up and placed his cup on the table.

"It will take them time to disembark and get their cavalry ready but we need to move quickly. Each general will begin the muster tonight; we can move in two days."

"Two days could be too long."

Miltiades raised his hand to prevent any interruption.

"We send orders to each man to bring his war gear and enough food for a couple of days. We allocate different muster points for each regiment and when they're in place they move off and live on what they can carry. Do that and we can leave in one day and be there before they're ready. We can send a supply train later; it'll be there before we run out of food."

Callimachus bridled at this.

"That's not our way, not how our fathers ordered the hoplite army."

"Our fathers never beat the Persians, nor did our grandfathers, in fact no Greek hoplite army has ever beaten them and if we are going to, we need surprise, because if they get off that headland and deploy their cavalry in open ground, we're all dead men."

He and Callimachus stood face to face, both realising, I think, that whatever decision they took next would decide their own future and that of the city. I saw then how uneasy their relationship was; Callimachus was the embodiment of all that upheld the honour and tradition of the city's nobility. No one knew what the General upheld. And Callimachus was the Polemarch, the commanding general. He was also the noblest of all the generals, certainly a finer man than any today. His thoughts were only of the city, not of factions. He stood for a time thinking of the consequences of his next words. The strain showed in his face, then he cleared his throat and spoke to Miltiades.

"Very well, Miltiades, in one day. But the line of the march will be as follows. All our regiments except the Erechthis will take the main road by the side of Mount Pentelikos. If we are wrong and an advance guard of Persians has already left Marathon, that is the route they will take, the other way won't take cavalry. The Erechthis will follow the track to the North West by Kephisia. I will send a day runner to the city of Plataea and ask them to follow the Erechthis. This way we block any Persian march on the city and as we both know, Miltiades, the Plataeans are the only allies we can count on to fight with us."

So, in that brief conversation the crucial decision was taken. Before the generals dispersed to command their own regiments they sent word to the athlete Philippides to run to Sparta to ask the Spartans to mobilise and move quickly to join us at Marathon.

What they'd do when they got to Marathon they didn't know. So we set off, knowing where we were going but not how we'd fight. Miltiades' words that no Greek army had beaten the Persians on land encouraged and goaded the imp of fear in all our minds.

There was little sleep that night as we began our preparations. Some while before the hour when the lamps are extinguished Elpinices' body slave came to my cubicle and said that her mistress would speak with me in the garden.

She waited on a bench near the statue of the goddess, the night was warm and she wore no cloak. As I arrived she stood and walked to meet me backlit by the moon. I had never seen her so beautiful and I caught the fragrance of the perfume she wore on the light breeze. I moved to take her hand but she motioned me to be still.

"Whatever we might have been to each other matters nothing now, Mandrocles. We are part of something far more important. You must stay near my father and again share your luck with him. He has sworn either to win or to return dead on his shield. You must do the same. But I do not think that'll be your fate and we'll meet again. I have personally overseen the preparation of the food you will take on the march; think of me, condemned to wait here, when you eat it."

She stepped up to me, placed a soft hand on my cheek and gently pulled my face close to hers. I could smell her sweet breath as her lips brushed mine. She whispered,

"Go well, my love."

She turned and walked back towards the women's quarters leaving me standing alone inhaling the ghost of her scent.

I hardly slept and was woken before it grew light to collect my gear and the food she left for me. I walked with the other fighting men of the household to the muster point. The city was crowded with armed men; this wasn't the customary hoplite force that was mustered for a border dispute between city states. All of the men in Attica capable of fighting were there. In addition to the hoplites who were used to military service, there were men who had borrowed weapons which they obviously had never used. In fact it looked to me as if there were as many men with no experience of fighting as there were veterans. There were even slaves carrying arms and I thought that this must break all the laws and customs of the city. Strangely, the presence of the slaves and pressed men gave me confidence. I marched among the armed sailors and hoplites from the General's household. These were men who knew how to fight and I reminded myself that I had killed men in battle.

So, by the time we took our rest in the foothills of the mountain I felt more confident. I was amongst friends in the greatest army the city ever raised. Once we'd eaten and relieved ourselves we moved off again and stirred up the dust devils with our marching. This time I followed the example of the hoplite veterans and tied a strip of wet cloth loosely across my mouth and nose. Because of our numbers and the narrow pass it wasn't possible to move quickly so we ambled rather than marched and the sailors began to sing the rhythmic, obscene songs that they were used to on board ship. Cynegeiros joined in, enjoying himself, as if born for such things. Aeschylus and I slowly pulled ahead of them. I wondered where Miltiades was; somewhere ahead on horseback I imagined.

We passed through a small party of auxiliaries, slingers and bowmen, lightly armed without body armour. These were men from below the hoplite class who would fight from outside the shield wall. Amongst them were slaves. Many today deny that slaves fought with us. They do that for political reasons of their own, not out of a respect for truth. There were some slaves there, trusted men from farms and town houses. The General himself brought some of his own and these men supported us in the battle. Even at the end, amongst the ships where the fighting was worst.

So the great army of near ten thousand was made up not only of the hoplite class as some today claim, but also of others who had less of a share in the wealth of the city, and also, to be fair, of aristocrats of the cavalry who chose to fight on foot with us. In those few great days there was no distinction. We marched out, a citizen army, to fight the greatest empire the world had known; few of us thought we'd survive. Quite apart from the fact that we were outnumbered we had virtually no cavalry and very few archers and would face an army rich in both. If it came to battle we would look to the ability of our hoplite veterans to stand together and hold the shield line.

Some way ahead of us on the path I saw the distinctive red cloak of Brasidas the Spartan and we weaved our way through the men to catch up. He nodded in recognition to me and I introduced him to Aeschylus and asked him why he marched with us.

"I've been asking myself that, lad, why am I marching with this shambles of farmers, merchants and worse towards certain death? The only answer I can come up with is that the gods have made me mad and I have put my loyalty as guest friend to Miltiades above my loyalty to my own city."

Aeschylus bridled at this.

"Well, go home then, no one asked you to fight with us, if it offends you to march besides free men you can go back to your mess hall in Sparta and lord it over the Helots you've enslaved."

"Calm yourself, poet, don't let fear make you tetchy."

This response from Brasidas, containing as it did within a short sentence so many types of offence, roused Aeschylus to rage so, before he could react, I quickly asked Brasidas if he thought we could win, and I think that as I was asking the question the Spartan realised his words had been taken more harshly than he had meant.

"I meant no harm, it's our way of speaking, and I see you are unused to Spartan ways."

This was the nearest thing to an apology you ever get from a Spartan, although at the time it didn't much sound like one. But it was enough to make Aeschylus control himself and walk on in silent anger.

"Can we win? Well, if it were a wager I wouldn't take it. If the Spartan Ephors send an army to support us we may be able to hold them up for a bit I suppose."

"And if they don't?"

I asked, leaving the question hanging in the air.

Brasidas didn't answer directly but he made the longest speech I have ever heard from one of his race so that even Aeschylus stopped sulking and listened.

"Listen, this is how we fight, this is how we are taught from boys, this is the first lesson we learn, passed on from father to son."

Then he recited:

"Let each man stand firm with his feet apart facing the enemy, biting his lips, covering his thighs and shins, his chest and shoulders with the wide expanse of his shield.

"Let him shake his spear bravely with his right hand, his helmet's crest nodding fiercely above his head.

"Let him learn warfare in the heat of battle and not stand back to shield himself from missiles, but let him move in close using his spear to strike his enemy down.

"Place feet against the enemy's feet, press shield against shield, nod helmet against helmet so that the crests are entangled and then fight your man standing chest to chest, your long spear or your sword in your hand.

"These are the words of our poet Tyrtaeus, passed down to us through the ages: and that's what we do. We give no ground, we never turn or run, we stand until the end. If necessary we welcome death. Do you think that your rag-tag army will do that in the face of the Persians at Marathon? Well, do you?"

There was nothing we could say in answer, said as it was with such stark and terrible conviction. Brasidas looked at us with something that in anyone but a Spartan could have been sympathy and said more softly,

"But let's see what we can do when we get to Marathon."

After that we marched in silence, locked in our own doubts and fears. Some hours later we crossed the top of the mountain pass.

Below us glistening in the evening sun was the sea and riding on that sea the largest war fleet the world had ever seen. On the plain next to the sea at the far end of the bay was the extensive camp of the Persian army filling all the space between the mountains and the water.

CHAPTER 29

We filed our ramshackle way down the track through
the lower mountain slopes then across the scrubby
foothills until we reached the south eastern end of the
Bay of Marathon. We'd humped our gear twenty-four
miles across the mountains from Athens, but there was
no time to rest, we had to reform the regiments and
establish a defendable position and, anyway, fear drives
tiredness from the mind. At the other end of the bay
were the Persians, some of their cavalry exercising their
horses in the flat scrub land that divided their position
from ours. They were so confident they rode close
enough to shout taunts and insults.

If they'd been ready they could have had us then,
finished us, finished Athens, and finished free cities
across Greece. They missed their chance: we were dead
beat and strung out across miles. But they didn't.
Maybe they felt they could beat us any time they chose,
or perhaps the gods favoured us.

As we straggled down to the plains officers directed
us towards the grove of Heracles and the precincts of
his shrine. We trudged across the spot where the
General and I had stopped to eat on our visit to this
place and I think I knew then, even through the fear,
that something earth-shattering was to happen. The
grove was bounded by a marsh at its seaward end and
on the other by the mountains. In front the land sloped
down to the Bay of Marathon and across it to the
Persian camp and the beach where some of their ships
had been run aground.

The grove of Heracles was a hive, all activity. A
camp for the army was being laid out whilst a strong
party of men were chopping down the olives and scrub
oaks at the edge of the grove nearest to the Persians.
These trees were then laid down lengthways, the trunks

and roots facing towards our camp, the branches towards the enemy. Under the direction of the generals, supervised by Miltiades we quickly established a defendable position. Why didn't the Persians attack whilst we were doing this? I can only think it was because they knew we would soon be betrayed by traitors in our ranks. Brasidas said it was madness not to and that any Spartan general who failed to exploit such an advantage would be flayed alive.

That night I sat around the camp fire with a group of men that have been my only real friends in life. We shared the food we'd brought and passed the wineskin round. Aeschylus chanted some of his verse and Theodorus played a wooden flute. So we were able to sit under the stars and listen to the greatest poet the world has produced since Homer speaking lines as yet heard by no others. The night was warm, the sky clear and the stars bright. The generals wandered through the camp speaking encouragement to their men. Before we slept, Miltiades, Callimachus and Stesileos paused to share wine with us. Miltiades seemed touched by the gods, his face shone with excitement, possession almost, yet he seemed to radiate confidence and reassurance. Now looking back, I see that this was the moment he had been created for. All his choices and actions had led him here, this was his fate and he welcomed it. As they got up to leave us to sleep, he said,

"How can we lose? I have brought my personal token of luck, isn't that right, Mandrocles?"

They laughed and moved off leaving me glowing with pride. The young today say that we survivors, old Marathoni, men of Marathon, have lost our wits and exaggerate, talk of those times as if they were a golden time, like those of the age of heroes. Well, they're right: we do and it was.

The night wasn't peaceful though there were alarms, our patrols and pickets disturbed their sentries and they disturbed ours. There were also alarms caused by nothing but noises of the night playing on the fears of nervous men on their watch.

In the morning we stood to, very early, expecting an attack but none came, nor the next day. The waiting began to unsettle us. We could see the Persians at the far side of the plain drill, exercise their horses and carry out all the same tasks that went on in our camp but on a much greater scale.

Later that day, we received the only help that any other Greek city dared to offer. Before dusk a contingent of men from the small city of Plataea marched in to join us. Various reckonings of how many Plataeans there were can be found in differing accounts of the battle written by men who weren't there. I know how many because Miltiades took me with him as part of his retinue when he went to greet them. They told us they brought every fit man available for active service in their city; seven hundred and fifty-nine men. They, like us, had left their lands and families unprotected so they could do their duty with us here, far from their homes. Miltiades, Callimachus and the other generals wept when they heard this and now, as I write all these years later, I can feel the tears welling up in my eyes. The only man in our camp who didn't welcome them was Brasidas, who felt this heroism emphasised the inactivity of the Spartans. He took himself off for some time.

Just as well he did for the next morning the great runner Philippides came gasping and foot sore into the camp. He'd covered one hundred and forty miles to Sparta, back again to Athens and then on to us in little over four days and he looked half dead. The news he brought came like a slap in the face to each man.

The Spartans in their usual, self serving, hypocritical way told him they wanted to come and fight, and were mobilised but that unfortunately they were in the middle of the sacred Carneion festival. It was sacred to Apollo and, as all men knew, the god forbade them from putting troops in the field until the full moon. If they did Apollo would curse them and the expedition would fail. Therefore they were sure we'd want them to wait until the full moon.

Typical of them to dress up an act of treachery as pious religious observance. It would be eight to ten days before they could hope to join us. This was the lowest point in the campaign, we were truly alone. Across the plain were over twenty thousand drilled, uniformed, professional soldiers, well supported by archers and cavalry. Here in our camp were less than ten thousand mainly irregulars, in a variety of bits and pieces of inherited and patched up armour. We were men who most days would be behind a plough, tending the fields or looking after a family workshop. We faced certain death, while the best troops in Greece celebrated a religious festival, safe beyond the far Taygetos Mountains: the bastards.

Strangely, the mood didn't last. Miltiades went through the regiments telling them the tale of how on this very plain in the time of the heroes, the Athenian king, Theseus, had overcome the mighty killer bull of Marathon and that, like him, alone except for our Plataean friends, we would destroy the Persians, and the glory, not to mention the rich loot in the Persian camp, would be ours alone.

There was also something far stranger; Philippides said that on a mountainous and wild stretch of the road on the way back from Sparta he heard a voice call his name; a voice unlike any human voice, a voice that struck him with terror. On turning to look, the great god

Pan appeared to him, instructing him to tell the Athenians at Marathon that if they stood firm, the Persians would be defeated and driven from the Greek mainland. The god disappeared in a blaze of light leaving Philippides alone in this bleak, exposed spot as the sun was setting. He was suddenly filled with energy and pushed on through the night. So vivid had his description of the god been, and so clear the message, that most were inclined to believe him. For after all, it echoed the tale of Theseus. Cynegeiros said it was probably the exhausted runner's mind playing tricks, merely a waking dream caused by exhaustion and hunger. But seeing the look on his friends' faces he shut up. The generals, however, held meetings with their regiments where they insisted it had been the god and that he'd appeared to some of them with the same message. Callimachus told us he'd sworn to build a temple to Pan at Marathon after our victory and to sacrifice a goat for every Persian soldier we killed. In the event the first part of the vow was easier to fulfil than the second.

True or not the story and the vow gave us confidence even though the thinking men amongst us saw the hand of Miltiades behind the story. As for myself I don't really know what I believe. But I saw Philippides and he certainly believed what he said or else he was the finest actor ever born. I don't doubt the gods interfere in our lives but I think it's for reasons of their own and in ways that we don't recognise. Perhaps the god merely put the idea into Philippides' mind without going to the bother of manifesting himself in a remote mountain pass. But today, if you visit the shrine of Pan near Marathon and read the inscription, you will find, in that strange place near the mound we raised over our dead, that you believe it. Few visit there without feeling the presence of that terrible god.

But the uncertainty continued and by the third day at Marathon our position began to worsen through indecision and we began to question each other. Of the ten generals of the regiments, five, led by Aristides, were against battle and began to talk of returning to Athens. The others, led by Miltiades and Themistocles, wanted to fight. They argued that if we didn't bring the Persians to battle, they'd split their force and send half by sea to attack undefended Athens. When that happened we'd have to return to the city or risk the city falling and be forced to fight on two fronts. Miltiades said that even if we tried to retreat to the city we'd be pursued and the retreat would become a rout, then a massacre.

I couldn't understand at first why the Persians left us alone but gradually it came to me. They felt they didn't need to bother, we'd destroy ourselves. The camp was thick with rumour that some of the generals had been bought by Persian gold and that at a signal they'd betray their comrades. There was certainly enough contact between the two camps for this to be believed. There was even a rumour in Aristides' regiment that Themistocles was an agent of the Great King. Hippias was in the Persian camp and for all I knew perhaps Metiochus too, and I know for a fact that Miltiades, although he denied it, received messages from across there.

So, as we waited looking for signs of betrayal, nerves frayed and tempers were lost. There were brawls and scuffles and trust between regiments began to bleed away into the dry and thirsty earth. To me the situation was similar to the one we'd faced before the battle of Lade.

Unlike the Persians we had no effective command structure. To keep the balance between the ten tribal regiments each of the generals took their turn day by day to take command of the army. The role of Callimachus, the Polemarch, was to use his authority as a casting vote but he refused. To try to break this deadlock, the four generals in agreement with Miltiades gave up their day of command to him. So, every alternate day Miltiades commanded the army.

On the fourth day one consistent rumour was being spread, talked about over each camp fire. It was that a signal had been agreed between the Persians and the traitors; a shield was to be flashed in the sun to the Persians. Then they would attack and the enemy within our camp would strike from behind.

That night it was my turn to stand sentry, out just beyond our defence of felled trees. Even so close to our camp fires, out there by the dying branches, it was cold and isolated. Any sound made even the bravest man jump. Not long after dark there was movement ahead and a Greek voice with a strange accent shouted across to us,

"Listen, Greeks, the Persians are embarking most of their cavalry under darkness, they will sail for Athens tomorrow."

All along the lines similar messages were being passed, probably by the Greek captives forced to work in the Persian camp. We didn't know if this was a trick but the man on duty with me told me to find Miltiades and tell him. The General was talking to Brasidas over a cup of wine when I found him and as I passed on the message he smiled.

"So it begins. Go to Callimachus and tell him to summon the generals."

I had no problem finding him because, as usual, he was talking with Stesileos, whose regiment was camped next to ours. He sent runners to summon the other generals, and then got slowly to his feet, brushing away the dust. His face was drawn and I think he realised that now he would have to make the decision that, like his fate, had been waiting for him all his life and he'd tried so hard to avoid.

One by one they arrived, Aristides, Themistocles and the rest until all eleven stood on the flame lit space in front of Callimachus' tent. They divided into two groups of five with Callimachus between them. Around them, watching and listening like the rapt audience at the festival plays, stood the soldiers of our divided army.

We were lost; it had come upon us so quickly, what were we doing here? I think this was also what Callimachus thought as he stood waiting and wondering what he could say to give some direction. Eventually, after a long tense silence, he spoke.

"Tonight we must make the choice; we can no longer wait here doing nothing."

The words weren't helpful, conjuring an image of decay from within, of a leaderless beleaguered army. He paused for a moment not really knowing what to say next, brushing back his thick greying hair with both hands. The movement of his arms casting elongated shadows thrown by the light from the fires. We could sense the weight he felt pressing him. At last he spoke.

"We are split as to what to do. I must make the choice but time is not with us so I call upon Aristides and Miltiades to speak briefly for both arguments. While you talk I pray that the gods will advise me."

Aristides went first, but he too seemed troubled. I can't remember his exact words but he spoke briefly: spoke for those who didn't want to fight. He said that we couldn't fight the much larger Persian army; we had to reach the city before the enemy fleet got there. We should slip away tonight, leave a rearguard where the pass narrowed to hold them up and buy time. He promised he'd fight with the rearguard.

Despite being the wrong advice it was a sincere speech and for the first time I saw nobility in the man. When he finished, some murmured agreement.

Then Miltiades moved into the firelight and standing directly in front of Callimachus spoke to his face, but loud enough for his voice to carry outside the circle of light into the dark groves where the army gathered. This speech, we who were there remember as well as if the words were burned into our souls.

"Callimachus, I appeal to you. Right now you will have to make the choice that will either enslave or make free the Athenians and thereby leave a memorial of yourself that will be greater than any other man's. Right now Athens is in the most desperate moment in her history, everything depends on your choice of what you would have us do. Hippias and the Great King have shown what our city will suffer if it falls into their hands. But..."

He paused for a moment.

"But if we win and our city survives she will become the greatest city in Greece. This can only be possible if you make the choice, as we ten generals are split. If we don't fight the split will run across the city and half will go over to the Persians and then our story ends in disgrace and slavery.

"But if we fight and fight now before those cracks show, we can survive. How can we not fight when, as we know, the great god Pan demands that we do? My friend, I speak to you like this because only you can save the city. It comes down to you, it depends on you, and all hangs on your decision. Now if you vote with me, the city of your fathers will be free and admired in all Greece. You must decide right now. You, Callimachus, must decide the future."

He finished speaking, placed both hands on Callimachus' shoulders then stepped back, leaving

293

Callimachus the only shadow left flickering in the firelight. For a moment he stood there silent, his shadow stretching out across the patch of open ground into the darkness of the grove. The whole world stopped. He raised his arms to the heavens for a moment.

When he let them drop he turned his gaze onto the army, looked to the generals on his right and then on his left. With the confidence of a man whose road has suddenly become clear, he spoke.

"We fight."

The two groups of generals moved towards each other, clasped arms and then embraced. From the army spread out amongst the groves and the Herakleinon precinct there came a roar, starting at the edge of the firelight and spreading out into the darkness like some terrible earth tremor.

CHAPTER 30

Men say the night before a battle is worse than the battle itself and there's some truth in this. How to describe that night? First, the indecision that had crippled us since we arrived disappeared as quickly as the darkness does the instant an oil lamp is lit in a small room. It was replaced by a frenzy of organisation amongst the generals and senior officers who gathered outside the tent of Callimachus. The rest of us were ordered to return to the exact spot where we had slept for the last four nights. The generals would, therefore, know the position of their individual troops. We were told to prepare our armour and weapons and be ready two hours before dawn so we could be led to our battle stations and briefed about our tactics before the sun appeared from below the horizon beyond the sea. So the soldiers dispersed knowing only that next day they would take up their battle positions on the other side of the barricade of trees in front of the place where they slept.

We knew roughly where the fighting stations of the various regiments were and this gave us some idea of tomorrow's formation. We, along with the Aiantis regiment, led by Stesileos, were to be two of four on the right wing, the place of greatest honour, and Callimachus, being of that regiment, would fight with us. This not only made us proud but gave us confidence as those two, along with our general, Miltiades, were the three best and most experienced in the army. I know that on the left the Plataeans were given the place of honour and supported by four of the city's regiments. This distribution of the regiments was not understood by the veterans of infantry battles.

It meant that the centre, normally where the strength of an army was deployed, would comprise only two

295

regiments, those led by Themistocles and Aristides. Veterans such as Cynegeiros and Brasidas opposed this. It meant that the centre regiments would be spread too thinly to cover the ground they held and wouldn't be able to fight six rows deep like we were trained.

Cynegeiros in particular was wary of this, it was the first time I had seen him confused.

"I can understand them putting Aristides and Themistocles together; it's so they can keep an eye on each other and it forces them to work and fight together. But they'll only be able to fight three deep and widely spaced, it's asking for trouble."

The sailors who had never fought in a hoplite army didn't seem bothered. They just told him to shut up and have faith in the General. Theodorus put a heavy arm round Cynegeiros' shoulder.

"Listen, friend, I've sailed and fought with Miltiades for years, he never does nothing without a reason, he's a cunning bugger, that's why he always comes down butter side up see, so stop moaning, you'll upset the lads."

It was good advice and Cynegeiros turned to his brother and started a different conversation, but I could see from his face and that of Brasidas they were unsettled.

That night was like being trapped in a nightmare that seems to last forever: frightening and tedious at the same time. I tested my armour, its straps and ties. I tried my greaves with padding to prevent them rubbing, and then without. Neither felt right. The armour seemed to chafe along the upper chest and shoulders and it seemed too small. I realised I'd grown bigger than my father: I wondered what he was doing and almost missed him. The shield grip and helmet seemed about right as did the leather battle cuirass, but it would be too hot under the armour, weigh heavy and restrict movement.

Everyone else seemed happy with their gear, even the sailors who'd been given or lent their stuff. Their advice was use what's comfortable and leave the rest, but I couldn't decide.

I've always hated waiting, it's when you lose the freedom to act, when you wait you're powerless, have no control and the longer you wait the worse it gets. I sharpened my sword, dagger and spear point on the stone until I was told I'd wear the points to nothing and the stone was taken by someone else. So I sat staring at my father's old fashioned plate armour and wondered how I'd be able to last through the day in it and how I'd be able to sleep that night.

When men began to roll out their bedrolls I did the same but sleep wouldn't come. My heart hammered and at times blind terror overtook me and I had to open my eyes and sit up gasping. Around me were the noises of the camp, some groans and snores and the murmurs of an army: anxious men, tossing, turning, coughing and waking suddenly from dream.

After lying for what seemed hours I got up and wandered across to the nearest camp fire. Sitting by it, deep in a whispered conversation, were Aeschylus and Cynegeiros. The brothers ceased talking on seeing me and made space for me to sit between them. But my arrival had broken the gist of their conversation so we sat in silence staring at the embers until two officers walked by, returning from Callimachus' tent. They came into the firelight and I saw that it was Lysias and Brasidas. They greeted us and then told us to grab a few hours' sleep; we'd need it to get through tomorrow. As I got up Brasidas took my arm.

"It's always like this before a battle, lad, it never gets much better. Is all your gear ready?"

"My father's you mean."

I didn't want to tell him about my failure to wear it properly but I think he guessed.

"Then wear what fits, it's best to go light, it'll be a long day, shield and helmet over the leather cuirass will probably do. Come on, let's see what you've got."

I showed him my father's panoply.

"Old fashioned plate, leave it here. Look, I've got a spare set of shoulder pieces, leather with metal discs; they're light and flexible. Put your cuirass on, I'll get them."

I pulled it on, he came back and fitted the shoulder pieces; they felt good.

"There, that'll do."

He was about to walk on but suddenly stopped and spoke again,

"Remember that piece by the poet Archilochus that you Athenians find so funny but we Spartans have quite rightly banned."

And then to my surprise he quoted from memory,

"Well, some Thracian is enjoying the shield that I left. I didn't want to, it was a good one, besides a bush. But I saved myself. What do I care about that shield? To hell with it, I'll get another just as good."

Then he smiled,

"There you see, there's always a choice. But I don't think that you'll let your father's reputation or his war gear down tomorrow, you won't throw your shield and run, your father will be proud of the way you use it, Mandrocles. Now get some sleep."

Not what you expect from a Spartan, it was kindly meant and helpful. Strangely enough I must have got some sleep without realising it as the next thing I remember was being shaken awake even though it was still dark. Men were getting to their feet quietly, gathering their armour and weapons. What the General

298

had plotted was here at last and like all the main events in life it took us by surprise. My mouth was dry, my limbs unsteady and my bowels churned. Are you surprised at this, reader? Is this not how you expected the heroes of Marathon to feel? Well, that's how it was and we all felt it to some degree.

Looking back now I wonder how it must have felt for the leaders, Callimachus, Themistocles and most of all Miltiades, who had worked to this end and whose politicking had brought us here to this bloody plain. I don't suppose anyone asked them how they felt and if they had, what would have been the reply? Not a true one I would wager. They were leaders and were expected to be strangers to fear and indecision. Not that we would ever know, and besides, within a year two of them would be dead.

Once we had our gear we moved towards the felled trees that marked the edge of our camp. Officers ordered their men to keep silence, not to let their armour clink, then led us in single file to the ground where we would form ranks. I found my friends and picked my way behind Theodorus and Cynegeiros, Aeschylus followed behind. I remember that as I passed between the dying branches of the trees they brushed against me scraping my legs as if trying to hold me back. I tried to keep calm by telling myself that I fought beside experienced men and that the officers of our section, Lysias and Brasidas, would keep me safe.

I couldn't stop yawning, I couldn't control my face and I think I disturbed some muscle or bone in my jaw, something that I still feel pain from to this day when I chew tough meat. This walk towards battle stations seemed to last for hours, we could only move in single file through the gaps in the tree trunk defences that our sappers had cleared in the night.

Then it took ages to get us into line in the dark. I was glad as the regiments that made up the right wing got mixed up so I was able to stand in line with my friends from both my regiment and the Stesileos. By the time we'd blundered and fumbled ourselves into some sort of order greyish blue light began to tinge the horizon.

We stood waiting for dawn and those who could face it ate what food we'd left and the wineskins were passed along the ranks. Everyone drank as much as they could of the lightly watered wine. As the skin was passed to me Theodorus said,

"Get as much down as you can, boy, it may be the last drink you get this side of Hades and it'll ease the passage."

As we stood drinking, shaking with nerves in the cold of dawn, the officers of each section told us how we'd fight that day. For our file, the briefing was from Lysias, which encouraged me as I was used to being commanded by him on the Athene Nike.

"Listen carefully to this, boys, your lives depend on it. We won't be hanging around here for them to decide the day, at first light we attack. We get to their left wing and smash it. Once it runs we halt, reform the lines, then turn to our left and attack the centre. Their best troops are in the centre and we've left our centre weak to strengthen the wings. We destroy their wings then we fall on the centre.

"We have to be quick because while we fight their irregulars, those poor buggers under Aristides and Themistocles have to hold their centre until we arrive.

If there's somewhere you don't want to be today it's there in our centre. They're only three deep and double spaced, each man for himself. We lucky lads are six deep and closed up. Remember, when we engage you

300

kill the man in front; your mates on either side will protect your flanks.

"Now we march the first two miles but when we get within bow shot listen for the signal to charge. We run the last two hundred yards so decide now how much weight you carry. Once we break the wings you listen for the order to reform and fall on their centre, and when we've broken that you can go off and loot their camp. But whatever you do you listen for orders to reform. Everything clear?"

Someone down the ranks asked why the centre was fighting three deep instead of the usual six.

"Simple, there's more than twice as many of them as us. If we fought six deep all along the line would be too short, they'd outflank us, roll us back on ourselves then slaughter us. Clear enough for you?"

The man shouted back.

"So, we're a short thin one, not a long thick one."

We laughed and the wineskins were passed back along the line. Visibility was growing; somewhere at the limit of the sea there was a haze of pale, golden light. Lysias looked towards it, and then turned to us.

"Almost time, boys. If you need to piss, this is your last chance."

Men emptied their bladders and bowels and I noticed many shed their armour. So, in the end, most of us fought light and I no longer felt out of place and vulnerable. I decided to take off my father's greaves to free my legs.

The sun rose out of the sea and the darkness was lifted from the surface of the plain like a cloth pulled away from a statue. Now ahead of us, across the bay, we could see them, the Persian horde. At this distance they seemed no bigger than insects but it was clear that they'd been warned and were hastily drawing their army into battle order. But there was something else;

we saw that some of their ships were pulling off the beach. So, it was true, they had been disembarking. Miltiades was right, we had to fight today. You could feel and hear the realisation of this ripple along our ranks. We had called the dice right, we were ahead of the game.

A loud voice roared.

"Athenians, salute your generals."

From out of the ranks along the line Callimachus and the ten generals moved to the front, then turned to face their army. We roared our cheers, clashed our spears against our shields, the sound like thunder. Now it could begin. The generals had agreed what to say as each shouted the same brief message to his regiment.

"Today we kill the barbarians and drive them from our lands. If we don't, tomorrow they'll be in Athens, raping your wives and killing your children. But if we beat them then our bloodied hands will loot the riches of their camp.

"You are the saviours of all Greece. We few Athenians and Plataeans will make Greece free. Well, do you want to live the rest of your lives as heroes?"

We threw back our heads and roared the names of the generals. For our regiment it was, "Callimachus, Miltiades."

The generals signalled for silence, then spoke a last time.

"Greeks, today the goddess fights with us. Today, the field general is Miltiades; wait for his signal. Officers to the front, dress ranks."

The generals walked along the line checking the order. I was in the second rank behind a man I didn't know. I remember glancing to my left and thinking how thin the ranks in the centre looked and silently gave thanks that I didn't stand with them. Miltiades reviewed us, god-like, his armour burnished, his beard war-like, and I remember what Brasidas had told me of how a warrior should look and fight. The General stopped in front of me.

"Mandrocles, luck bringer, why aren't you in the front rank? If you stay there your father will never forgive me."

He spoke softly to the man in front of me,

"Forgive me, Athenian, but the man behind you brings me luck, he must fight at the front."

The man changed places. Miltiades smiled at me.

"Your father would be proud if he could see you today, Mandrocles – bring us luck."

He reached out and touched my right shoulder and walked on. Then the sailors from the Athene Nike left the ranks and touched me, then all the soldiers, even the man whose place I took. It seems that when it comes to it, on the day of battle soldiers are just as superstitious as seamen.

Lysias shouted,

"Helmets."

All along the ranks we pulled our helmets down over our faces and entered a darker, narrower world. If you've ever fought in a helmet you'll know what I mean. When you wear one vision's limited to what's right in front and your hearing's muffled. You rely on the men at your sides and if you fall out of formation you're lost. Each man embraced the man on either side of him, promised he'd hold the line and protect his comrade's flank. On my right was Aeschylus and I swore to myself I wouldn't disgrace him.

Along our lines the sun was flashing on helmets and spear points. In front, down the slope in the distance, we could see cavalry that the Persians had not embarked riding out to strengthen their wings. Some thirty yards in front of the army was a ruined mound said to be a memorial to some ancient hero. Miltiades walked forwards alone beyond the ranks and climbed it. Then, turning his back on the enemy, faced his army. For a time he stood there motionless, locked in thought, the rising sun caught him and he became enveloped in flame.

Then, holding his spear he raised his arm aloft so the sun glistened on its point and waved us forward. He turned and began to walk towards the massed Persian ranks. The generals in front of their regiments lifted their spears in salute, urging us on. There was a blast of a horn from our lines as we moved and so it begins.

CHAPTER 31

Unless you fought there, you're surprised by what you read. All the stuff about us not making up our minds until the last moment then making a charge at a fast run. Since Marathon I've become sick of hearing talk from idiots who claim that we ran all the way and then fought till sundown. Think about it, could you run two miles in full armour, at a fresh enemy.

But we did have to beat them quickly and then get back to Athens before the troops they'd embarked on those ships already moving in the bay got there. It would take their ships around twelve hours before they could reach Athens. It would take battle weary men about eight hours the inland, direct route back. So, in the first part of that impossible day we had to defeat an elite force twice the size of ours. Then, having beaten them, the survivors who could still march would have to leg it the twenty-four miles back to Athens and perhaps have to fight again. But we were free men, fighting to preserve that unique freedom on home ground. Understand that before you read on, my friend.

Once he'd given his signal, Miltiades turned towards the enemy and with the echoes of our battle paean ringing in his ears set off down the slope. He led from the front that day. The officers and the other generals walked behind and we followed them. There were no more war chants or paeans; we'd need our breath when we closed with them. We marched in silence.

Soon, we began to feel the strength of the sun as it began to flex its muscles. By the time we'd covered half the distance we were hot and had sweated out most of the effects of the wine. It's a lonely experience, fighting in the front line and I've never got used to it. You can see all of their ranks and almost none of your own. I tried to blank out my mind and just stared at the red cloak of Brasidas as he walked ahead of me. It gave me confidence that he commanded this part of our line. I watched how that cloak shifted with each step, how one corner of it briefly trailed in the dust on his down step. Just below his right shoulder there was some type of rough patching where the colour was different, something I'd not noticed before. But as we got nearer, other things occupied my mind. Along the line men were fidgeting, making adjustments to their gear, grunting, muttering prayers or curses and then the strange mixture of odours, sweat, fear and worse, as men's emotions overcame bodily control. Yes, we marched in fear, anyone who doesn't feel like that must be mad or a liar, even amongst the Spartans it's the same. I never looked at the enemy ranks, I daren't in case what I saw would freeze my mind, make me mess myself or, worse, break ranks and run. So I walked on, isolated inside my helmet, trembling in my own world of uncertainty. And that's why what happened next took me by surprise.

The first I knew was sound, like a rainstorm, of something hard bouncing off armour or shield and the odd, soft thwacking sound accompanied by a grunt or curse. I heard, felt, a whistling sound flashing past my helmet, I couldn't tell which side even.

Then a loud shout and we all stopped; this brought me out of my trance and back into the world and I looked about me. Our ranks were uneven; there were gaps in the line. We were just within range and taking hits from arrows and stones, though most of them had spent their force when they reached us.

In front of us now, so close every detail was clear, were the Persians, almost close enough to smell. There was a command of

"Close ranks, shields up."

I became aware of the weight of my father's shield trying to drag my left arm down. Then the officers fell back into line in the front rank. The General backed into the position on my left. So I fought that day with Athens' greatest hero on one side and her greatest poet on the other, but didn't have time to register the wonder of it. We closed ranks, shields keeping off the spent arrows. Then, from Miltiades, on my left side there was a tremendous shout,

"Charge them."

That's when it happened; when we ran, that's when the world changed, when we shouted our paean and ran full pelt across that space: the killing floor of the Persian archers. The ground was uneven; our lines got ragged so we didn't hit them with a solid shield wall.

That's how we lost the advantage of our heavily armed troops hitting them at speed and they didn't break as planned. Instead the first of us to close were hard pressed to stay alive behind our shields until the rest arrived. But in moments the six deep lines were reformed and we began the hoplite tactic of pushing. The man in the front fought behind his shield, the man behind him placed his shield against the fighters' back and so on. If you went down you were dead, skewered by a Persian or trampled by your mates. I just concentrated on protecting my body with my shield, head down, trying to stay on my feet. For what seemed an age I faced a bearded Persian, his wicker shield against my heavy hoplite one. Nothing else existed, my whole world was that I pushed and he pushed back. I heard Miltiades next to me shouting, mad with rage,

"Break them, break the bastards; break them now."

I felt him start to shift forward; the man facing him slipped and unbalanced my bearded Persian, who stumbled back. I felt a body go down under my feet and stepped over it, we were moving. The wicker shield in front gave way; I felt it move as his balance went. I saw the expression on the bearded face: surprise, fear; saw him wanting to turn and run. On either side my comrades pushed forwards with me and then my spear had space to move. As he panicked and turned to save his life, which was all he had, he exposed the back of his neck where it meets the shoulders, a patch of strangely vulnerable and pale flesh. Lifting my spear above the shield rim I brought it down into the back of that neck, felt the point I had honed so finely the night before pass through and out of the front, easy as a knife through cheese. A grunt of surprise and he was dead before he hit the ground.

Lurching forwards into the gap he made, pushed from behind, I lost my father's spear as it was twisted out of my hand by the weight of his falling body. I jerked my shield back up and into the shield of the next Persian; felt a sword blow glance off the shoulder protectors Brasidas had given me. I took my sword and, as our line suddenly lurched forward, thrust it round the shield and up through its owner's belly, then out as he fell.

Now they broke. I saw Miltiades leap forward; felt Aeschylus move with him and then the whole of our line was surging and they were running or trying to. Those at the front in most danger were held back by the men behind them while those further back, not realising the line had broken, were still pushing forward.

This chaos as the line breaks is the most dangerous time for the defeated, and we didn't waste it. We killed most in their front few ranks as they got entangled with the men behind. Step forward as they try to turn, push in the sword, pull it out, finish the man, step over him, and again into the exposed back of the next man or through the face or neck of the man on his knees begging for his suddenly very precious young life. I was drunk on it, extreme sensation, a kind of madness. I don't know how long I stepped forward and killed but suddenly I was pulled to a stop and saw someone shouting into my face.

I couldn't make out the words but saw in front of me there was no one left to fight. I pushed my helmet up, the Persians we hadn't killed were running, trying to escape across the marsh back to their ships. They left behind a strip of land about thirty yards wide covered with their dead, broken and bloody. My head stopped spinning, my breathing came back. Aeschylus was trying to tell me something. I saw my sword red with blood and it covered my hand and most of my right arm. We were pushed back into line by our officers. Miltiades, blood splattered, was pacing along our ranks shouting orders.

"Reform the lines, get ready to turn about, now do what you're told, damn you."

Our line gradually turned towards the centre and I saw for the first time, as my head slowly cleared, what was happening along the rest of the battle front. Towards the mountains our left wing of Plataeans and Athenians had broken the Persians. It looked as if, like us, they were reforming their ranks and turning towards the centre. The enemy on both wings was routed and running for the camp. In the centre it was very different.

Each man fighting on the right wing had worked out for himself that once we had closed with the Persians their main weapon, their archers, could play no part, similarly the few cavalry they employed at the wing couldn't charge a phalanx of armoured hoplites. Their tactic was to ride close to the enemy, loose a volley of arrows, and then withdraw. By closing with the enemy so quickly we'd taken any advantage they had out of the fight. In close combat the generals had said we were better armed and protected and so it proved.

But when we saw the fight in the centre we realised the difficulty we faced. Our army was broken into three parts; the two wings had pushed the enemy back towards their camp. But while we had done this our centre had itself been pushed back. Our weak centre, deliberately left weak, was isolated and outflanked with its edges harried by Persian horsemen trying to get in behind. For a time it held its line and slowly retreated but that's a hard thing to do under constant pressure and killing blows. Each casualty disrupted the line and fighting only three deep and double spaced the line had neither weight nor reserves. Gradually the edges were bent back and the centre encircled. From our position we could see the heavily armed Persian officers moving among their men. They were on horseback and able to see the pattern of the battle and direct their troops accordingly. Our generals had hoped that our wings would be able to rejoin the centre, reform the original battle line and push their centre back. Now we couldn't and so, like every other engagement I've fought in, the plans disintegrated into chaos. It became a rolling fight where different clusters of men either win or lose their own personal battles and where those who give ground die.

Our reformed line was different from the original one, the regiments were mixed up with the one closest to our left flank, the Hippothontis I think, the most broken up. Their survivors took longer to reorganise and formed up behind the rest of us, so in a formation eight deep we marched towards the fighting and caught the Persians on their left flank.

I fought this part of the battle amongst my friends in the centre of our line. Just before we closed, the Persian officers managed to turn some of their troops to face us but had no time to effectively deploy their archers. So we marched to within about twenty paces, then Callimachus at the front with Miltiades and Stesileos shouted the charge and for the second time we ran at them. It was a short run so this time so we hit them more or less in formation and they gave directly..Ahead of me Callimachus engaged one of the mounted officers and managed to push his spear into the man's side just below the armour above the hip as he was trying to turn to protect himself. The man hacked the spear away with his sword but Callimachus seized him by his belt and pulled him from his horse to crash the ground on his back, then stamped him down with his left foot and pushed his sword through the gap in his helmet into his mouth which was open. He shouted in surprise and then gurgled in death. We fought here by smashing our metal and wood shields into their wicker ones until their shield arms lost strength then we stabbed them with the point of our swords, forcing them back into their comrades. We had space moving forwards, they were pushed together crushing and cramping each other, trapping their sword arms and jamming their shields.

I saw Miltiades fighting mad, shouting and cursing, pass his sword through the body of one man then into the neck of the one behind who was trapped between his dead comrade in front and the live one in the rank behind. He had no room to fall and stood there, the blood rushing in gouts from his neck into Miltiades' face. Cynegeiros and Aeschylus stood shoulder to shoulder stabbing and cutting, then moving over slippery bodies of the dead and killing those behind. Cynegeiros fought shouting and grunting, his brother made no noise but crouched behind his shield dealing death with his spear. Brasidas, Lysias, Theodorus and I fought as a group round the body of Ariston, whose left

311

hamstring had been cut by a Persian he had wounded but failed to kill. As he had passed over the man he pulled out a knife and slashed the back of Ariston's thigh bringing him to the ground and allowing the enemy he faced to slash his face open with a scimitar. But this was the Persian's last living act for as he withdrew from the blow he lifted his head and provided a glimpse of his neck which Brasidas almost cut in two with one sword blow. He pushed the half decapitated man back to impede the two behind him, and as they struggled to untangle themselves killed both of them with sword thrusts. So we cleared a space round Ariston and fought from there, Theodorus like a madman wielding an axe he had picked up somewhere, lopping off arms and hewing into the gap between men's shoulders and necks. And that's all I am clear of, I crouched behind my shield, my blood rage gone; I wanted to live. I may have killed: my sword thrusts sometimes seemed to hit something soft and yielding. I felt Lysias gasp as he fell against me, blood spouting from a wound in his thigh. I shifted to let him fall into a space behind then closed rank, my shield locked against that of Brasidas and there we stood and hacked and stabbed in the dust heat and noise. How long we stood I don't know, it could have been any time from five minutes to five days to me. But then the pressure in front eased, our rough lines reformed and we began to move forward again as they began to give ground.

I learned later that they'd almost broken our centre when we hit their flank. That it was a display of heroism by Themistocles and Aristides that held them up long enough for our charge to begin. The two of them stood for a while, back to back, ahead of our shattered centre and cut down any Persian who came near enough. Both men took wounds but kept their position as the number of bodies at their feet grew.

Their bravery inspired some in the Athenian centre to push forward to join them and it was while they were attempting this that we and the Plataeans fell on the Persians' unsuspecting, unprotected flanks. The seasoned troops that we faced held their ground for a time but their position was impossible and they gradually began to fragment as they were pushed back. So, step by bitter step, we forced them to retreat towards their camp.

Ask anyone who has fought in a phalanx, he'll tell you a fighting retreat is the most difficult manoeuvre. You step backwards over rough ground fighting at a disadvantage. Your fearful mind tells you that the rest of your comrades are slipping away from the fight and you're alone. You begin to see your death in the face of the man cutting at you. Then at some point, either through uncertainty or realisation that the line is crumbling, you break. And once you break there's no protection, no order, no thought, no control, just panic. And they broke.

To have been there when the Persian veterans, undefeated conquerors of the empire, broke is the honour that only a veteran of Marathon can claim. We were the first to ever make them run. As for you, reader, you may well have fought at Mycale, Eurymedon, even Plataea but you'll never have the greatest honour. That's ours and ours alone for eternity and we deserve it; for we broke the empire, not you; we were the ones who did it, the ones who forced the world to change.

Then, even better; once they broke to be pursued and hunted down like dogs in the marsh we saw what they had fought to protect. Not far ahead was the beach from where their loot laden ships were being dragged towards the sea.

CHAPTER 32

It was still early in the morning but time and place meant nothing, the old order was cracking. Our left wing pursued their centre as it shifted from retreat to rout. They would harry, kill and drive them into the marsh then return to loot what was left of their camp. Our centre was spent, there were few men there not carrying wounds. But we on the right wing, nearest to the water, were closest to their ships and they were too rich a prize to ignore. So we charged them killing anyone in our way.

By the time we reached the beach all order was gone and we were strung out over a wide front. The quickest runners at the front well ahead of those in the rear. On the beach it was chaos. The Persians got some ships into the water, which were pulling out to sea. The ones still beached were surrounded by desperate soldiers trying to push them into the sea or simply trying to scramble on board and save their own lives. I think we felt like Hector storming the ships in the fight at Troy, but those of us at the front were in danger of overstretching ourselves just like Hector.

Led by Callimachus our section made for the ships at the near end of the beach. A Persian beach master organised such troops as would obey him to form a line to meet us. However, even strung out as we were momentum was with us and we burst through them. Callimachus cut the beach master down then ran his sword into the ribs of the Persian behind him before he could defend himself. The man went down; the sword stuck fast in his ribs and was twisted out of Callimachus' bloody and slippery hand.

We were close to the nearest ship now; it was guarded by a screen of archers and spear men commanded by a heavily armed officer, carrying a throwing spear. Callimachus knelt to draw his sword from the dead man's belly but as he rose to rush the ships an arrow hit him in the thigh. He tried to pull it out and failed but got to his feet and charged anyway. I was closest to him. Despite his age he was out in front. Perhaps in that moment he saw himself as one of the old heroes engaging the Persian officer in single combat. When he was about twenty yards off, the Persian officer poised to throw. I saw, even as I ran, the man had good balance and skill. He released the spear, which hit Callimachus below the left shoulder just above the shield. He stopped in his tracks: surprised; surely this wasn't what the gods intended for him. The Persians cheered, Callimachus staggered to his feet and lurched forwards but his shield was down and within a couple of paces eight or nine spears sliced into him piercing him right through.

He stood, swaying on his feet, staring in disbelief at the spears and arrows puncturing his body and the streams of blood swamping his chest and legs. Then with a low moan of anguish he slowly pitched forwards and that's the true account of how the noblest of the Greeks at Marathon was killed.

But even in death he served us well for as he began to fall the hilts of the spears that killed him jammed in the ground. So he hung there half standing like some fallen statue of the war god held up by the spears that took his life while his blood soaked the sand. With our general's corpse still standing, encouraging us even in death we fell on them, thirsting for revenge. Theodorus and Cynegeiros hit them first, side by side. Theodorus with his bloodied axe and Cynegeiros with his great spear, both were terrible and grim to behold and any Persians who stood in their way were quickly beaten down to dusty death. No one chose to face them, taken over as they were by blood lust, but of those Persians within reach few saved their short young lives.

Beyond them were the ships. This part of the fight was the most desperate; there was no order or control. Some of us took flaming branches from the enemy camp fires to burn the ships, others just fought to try to board them. No one tried to restore discipline, though of the generals, both Miltiades and Stesileos fought with us.

Here the resistance was fiercest, the Persian sailors and marines fought with desperate fury in fear and despair. Theodorus reached the first ship, cutting down two fleeing Persian marines to reach it. A sailor attacked him with a long, metal-spiked boat hook. Theodorus neatly, for such a big man, side stepped the lunge and split the man's head apart with a savage axe blow. He then grabbed a trailing ship's rope to try to pull the boat back onto the beach. Cynegeiros pushed his sword through the groin of a sailor standing above him on the boat's deck and grabbed hold of the bow with his other hand to help Theodorus. For a time the boat moved back and forward with them trying to pull it out to sea and us trying to pull it onto the beach.

The water in the shallows was stained red and no longer seemed like the sea. I had picked up a long spear lying by the side of a dead Persian and Aeschylus and I jabbed at the men on deck to keep them back while our comrades tried to pull the boat up onto the beach. From the deck Persian archers fired a stream of arrows forcing us to crouch behind our shields. But gradually we began to pull the boat out of the sea. Cynegeiros was our inspiration; he pulled at the boat with one hand, keeping the sailors back with his spear. All the time he roared us on.

Then a massive bare chested Persian sailor wearing only ragged trousers, pushed between his own archers.

He was consumed with battle madness, swinging a great axe. Cynegeiros had turned to shout to us to rush the boat so couldn't see the man who bent forwards and with a fierce downward cut caught his wrist between the wood of the boat's prow and the sharp blade of the axe. The severed hand remained clinging to the prow like something with a life of its own, but the arm jerked upwards drenching the axe man with blood, temporarily blinding him.

Screaming in anger, Aeschylus, rushed forward, pushed the point of his spear into the axe man's belly and out through his back, then levered the impaled man over the side and into the water where he thrashed about like a stuck fish. Cynegeiros was lurching about in the shallows staring as if in wonder at the rapid flow of blood from his open wrist. His brother dropped his shield and dragged him to the shore trying to stem the bleeding with his tunic. The boat's prow crunched into the beach and the boat stuck fast jolting the men on board off balance. We swarmed over the side.

The surviving men on board knew that it was over for them now, there would be no escape, no prisoners. Some fought as we fell on them spreading death like contagion, a few jumped overboard to swim or run for their lives, others covered their faces and waited for the end. They didn't have to wait long.

I'm proud to have been among the men of Marathon but not of everything I did that day. There is one act I would change if I could. In those days I was not as capable of dealing death like Theodorus or Brasidas; in fact I never became a killing machine like Brasidas. On board the ship I followed in their wake and pursued one Persian to the end of the boat as he tried to escape.

He reached the prow and for a moment I thought he would jump into the water and swim for one of the other boats. He was a boy on the point of manhood, younger than me. I wouldn't have followed; I'd have let him go as I'd begun to feel sick and wanted to be away from that place of death.

But he didn't jump. Perhaps he couldn't swim. He turned to face me and I saw from his eyes what he saw: a murderous, blood splattered enemy with a bloody spear. One glance was enough for both of us, he dropped his gaze and covered his face with his hands as if he could block out reality, avoid his fate. I pushed the spear through his belly below the ribs and felt its point tear free at the back. He dropped his hands from his face to scrabble at the messy spear shaft that was now like a strange and terrible part of his body. He looked down at the spear as if in wonder, then lifted his gaze to me and I saw the expression in his eyes as life left them. I see them still some nights when I can't sleep.

We looted the dead, and then jumped down from the boat to help our comrades fighting over the other ships. Sitting in the shallows, cradling the white, dying face of his brother, sat Aeschylus. When you see or read his great play, "The Persians" and you weep at the grief it contains, or hear the line

"Hell to ships, hell to men, hell to cities"

from his "Agamemnon", then understand that's where the sadness came from. No one who fought there will fail to remember to his dying day how high the price of freedom was.

All along the beach the battle raged and was fought without mercy on either side. Almost all the ships that would escape were now pulling away from the shore, some were on fire, and the rest were beached: swarming with hacking, stabbing and looting Greeks.

Miltiades and Stesileos were trying to regain order and pull the men back from looting and killing. The day was advancing and at the edge of the bay, out to sea, were the ships full of troops that the Persians had embarked in the night heading for Athens; worse, their sails were full swelled by the following wind that blows each morning along this shore. We could see from the ships' wakes that they moved at a good speed and we were still fighting on the beach.

There remained only one beached ship untaken, it was held by an experienced group of archers who had shot down every man who tried to board it. Our officers were shouting us back to the ranks, beating our backs with the flat of their swords if we didn't respond.

Slowly we came to our senses and the madness of bloodletting lost its grip. While Miltiades tried to organise the regiments, Stesileos supervised the taking of this last Persian boat still fighting. He was ordering men behind their shields to make a concerted charge in force and pushed his helmet back so his voice would carry. He was lifting his hand to pull it back down when one of the last arrows from the ship took him in the throat and turned the shout to a gargle. He fell to the ground and his armour rang about him as his soul fled, wailing, to Hades. I think he was the last of us to be struck down that day, killed as our men rushed the boat, crouching behind their shields and finished them off.

We took nine ships and burnt others, but most escaped and the fighting on the beach lasted almost as long as the battle on the plain. For us: the right wing, the beach was the worst; it was where we took our heaviest losses.

Once the army had been brought to order, Miltiades formed us up and marched us past the grim figure of Callimachus, still half upright in death, so we could salute him. As we filed past I thought how different a dead face looks from a living one. Miltiades touched one of the bloodied wounds on Callimachus' body and wiped the blood onto his own forehead. Then he had the bodies of Callimachus and Stesileos laid out in state side by side, friends in death as they had been in life.

We were given an hour to take drink, and food for those who could manage it. Whatever you may have been told battle doesn't give you an appetite. Later hunger returns with vengeance but not just after fighting, the stomach is either too tight or too loose depending on your constitution. It was while we were resting, lost in our own thoughts, that the rumour of the flashing shield started. As we sat, some asleep, others weeping or in some cases laughing at being alive, someone shouted he could see light being flashed from a shield towards the enemy fleet as it sailed towards Athens. The flashing came from the olive groves that surrounded the shrine of Heracles, where we slept the night before. We began to shout we were betrayed and traitors in our city would open the gates to the enemy if we didn't get back before their fleet .Suddenly the tiredness had gone and we were eager to begin to march the twenty-four miles back to Athens.

We left Aristides and his regiment behind; they were too badly mauled to be of any use. Aristides himself was weak from blood lost through at least half a dozen wounds. Before we left, Themistocles, who himself carried several gashes, embraced Aristides in a show of unity which at the time I believe he felt. After all, for a few minutes, the two had stood alone against the whole of the Persian centre. It was left to Aristides to look after and honour our dead and wounded.

The world knows that we lost less than two hundred killed in the field while we killed over six thousand enemy. But what is not told is that most of us were wounded that day, some badly and a great deal more than two hundred subsequently died of their wounds. The route back to Athens was littered with the bodies of those who couldn't make it.

We waved goodbye to our comrades and the Plataeans, who would look to their own dead, and started marching, the fear of treachery driving us on.

Looking back I'm not sure what to believe about the flashing shield but I'm certain not one amongst us that day was a traitor. There were many Alkmaionidai who died and most of them fought in the centre. Anyway, what good would a flashing shield have done? If it had been flashed before the battle, maybe, but we deployed in the dark.

Perhaps it happened. If it did I suspect it was a trick of Miltiades. No better way to get the men on their feet and marching. If you've fought in the line, even in a lesser battle, you know that once the fighting's over and you sit down to rest, you're dead beat, marching is the last thing you want to do. So having someone flash a shield in the distance is exactly the type of ruse that Miltiades would dream up to get you moving. And, whilst I'm thinking this way, let me clear up another myth.

That ridiculous story of Philippides running back to Athens with the news and then dying of exhaustion. You think about it. He'd already run more than two hundred miles in three days, then fought a battle, and he did fight, and well. He'd be the last person anyone would send as a runner, he didn't even march back with us; he stayed with Aristides and the burial detachment. Anyway he's still alive. Well, he was at the spring festival two years back, I saw him, he was with his son in law and we had a drink together.

So we set off back, carrying our wounds and our weapons, each man at his own pace but every man pushing himself to the limit to keep his feet moving. To get back to save his city, we hadn't turned the world upside down to fail now.

I can't remember much about the march; I was asleep on my feet for most of it. But we were weighed down by more than just tiredness; anxiety and the fear of being too late were worse. Though we marched back the same way that we got there, in groups, the fittest at the front, the oldest and most heavily wounded at the rear, the groups were different. Lysias, Cynegeiros and Ariston weren't with us; neither were Callimachus or Stesileos. Miltiades led the line, Brasidas, Theodorus, Aeschylus and I walked behind him. Themistocles was at the back, not through lack of courage but because of his wounds. We marched through the heat of the afternoon and into early evening. When we came to the top of the pass and saw the city with its temples standing on the Acropolis, each man in turn cheered and many wept. It still stood.

By dusk we stumbled through the city boundaries. There was no smoke, no noise of battle. Some citizens came to greet us and the city council had water brought out in carts. We needed it; we'd finished our last water hours earlier. We pushed on through them to the Bay of Phaleron and halted at the Herakleinon at Kynosarges just above the bay.

Miltiades was the first man there and he ran the last steps to see the sea. Riding just off the bay was the advance party of the Persian fleet with the others strung out behind. We'd got there first. They wouldn't land and face us again. We'd saved Athens. Miltiades had saved Athens; he had saved free Greece.

AFTERWARDS

It took many hours for us all to arrive at Phaleron, the last arriving barely alive. We were exhausted mentally and physically. We supported each other, tended each others' wounds as evening became night. Then we slept, but tired as we were, it was fitful sleep, men cried out in nightmares and jerked awake. That's the strange thing about battle; your mind heals more slowly than your body, if it ever really heals.

In the first light of morning the Persian fleet was still riding in the bay but as the day wore on they began to pull away and begin the long and bitter trip home. It is said that Hippias, the man who'd have been restored as tyrant if we'd lost, died of a broken heart on the way back. I wish Metiochus died with him, and later had cause to regret that he hadn't.

Miltiades walked down onto the beach at Phaleron with Themistocles that morning. I think both generals found it hard to believe they'd won, that all the scheming had actually worked. I don't think that any man there could quite believe what we'd done. I followed them to the beach like a loyal dog, close enough to hear a conversation which at the time I didn't fully understand. Themistocles was standing next to Miltiades and had his arm round his shoulders, with his other arm he pointed to a wrecked fishing boat lying in the shallows.

"One day, Miltiades, when I was little, my dad, Neocles, brought me for a walk on this beach. As we walked he pointed out a wrecked boat, like that one and said,

'That, my boy, is how the Athenian people treat their leaders when they have no use for them so beware.'"

Then noticing me he stopped, they turned and we walked back to the army.

Later that day the Persians disappeared over the horizon and we trudged back to the city. It wasn't really a triumph. We marched in through the crowds; they cheered, threw flowers, and pressed food on us. At one point I thought I saw Lyra waving. But we were tired and wanted our beds. So without ceremony we dispersed, went back to being whatever we'd been before. Men embraced their comrades and went their own ways. I followed Miltiades thinking how many more of us there'd been when we set out for Marathon, which seemed a lifetime ago.

The household and family were waiting for us in the courtyard of Stesagoras' house. Cimon ran to his father in joy, he was dressed in play armour with a sword. Behind him, slim and beautiful, was Elpinice. She saluted him as a dutiful daughter but her eyes were fixed on me in an expression I couldn't understand. But that, as my friend the poet Aeschylus would say, belongs to another play.

Glossary

Agora: Greek for market place. In Athens it was the main square and centre of city life

Andron: Room for entertaining in the male section of a Greek house

Areopagus: Ancient criminal court with powers to supervise entire public administration. Regarded as too conservative by democrats and had its power reduced in 462 BC.

Archon: Group of aristocrats with authority for power over the state. At the time of Marathon open only to the wealthiest class and serving for one year with a president called the named Archon

Boule: Council for Athens representing the Athenian tribes

Ceramicus: District of Athens originally of potters workshops. At the time of Marathon seedy drinking, red light district

Choregus: Wealthy citizen who finances a play

Chorus: Performers of the plays at religious festivals

Chou: Measure of liquid used for ordering wine

Deme: Administrative district

Demos: Greek word meaning the people. Democracy means sovereignty of the people

Dionysia: Spring drama festival in honour of the god Dionysus

Ephors: A board of five elders elected to supervise all activities in Sparta including the actions of the two kings.

Heraion: A temple in honour of the goddess Hera

Hetaerae: Courtesan or up market sex worker

Hoplite: Heavily armed foot soldier

Krater: Jug for mixing wine

Kottabos: Drinking game involving flicking dregs and wine from a wine cup.

Nike: Greek goddess of victory

Panonium: Sacred place for Ionian Greeks at Mycale

Polis: City state

Pornoi: Sex worker

Strategos: A General. In Athens there was a board of ten generals who were elected.

Symposium: Greek drinking party

Thalamioi: Bottom tier of rowers on a trireme

Thranitai: Top tier of rowers on a trireme who rowed through an outrigger and were the rowing élite

Trierarch: Captain of a Trireme

Trireme: A fighting ship with three banks of oars

Tyrant: A ruler with full power of a city state or territory. The term did not have quite the modern day pejorative implications and some tyrants were regarded as benign

Zugioi: Middle tier rowers on a trireme

Lightning Source UK Ltd.
Milton Keynes UK
UKOW05f2208221113

221673UK00002B/74/P